Dawn's New Day

A Love Story

Book Two of the Dawn Trilogy

B.J. Young

"But the greatest of these is Love"
I Cor 13:13
BJYoung

Cover Design by B.J.Young

ISBN-13:978-1495423086
ISBN-10:1495423085

2nd Edition
Printed in the United States of America
Publishing Date:2/14

For my son,

Jason E. Young

with love and fond memories.

Acknowledgements

There are many who have traveled with me on this journey to publication. My dear family and friends, you know who you are, so if I fail to mention you we will blame it on the number of years I have lived.

I must first thank my Lord and Savior, Jesus Christ. My desire is that any words I write will point others to Him. May they see Him as their Redeemer, their constant companion, and the source of all joy.

Thank you to my family. To my husband, Ed: thank you for your patience, love and support. For giving me space and time to write, and for making my coffee every morning, I am grateful. To my daughters who are not only my first readers, but my inspiration and greatest supporters, I love all of you with an endless love.
Thank you to my dear friends: Cathy, Beth, Dolly and Linda. You have believed in me, encouraged me, and been like sisters to me. I love you all.

I will forever be grateful for my mother, She is gone from our presence, but her light still shines. And for my dad, you have been my guide and my anchor when I needed one. I love you both.
To my sister and my brothers: Thank you for sharing the first steps of my life journey with me. The memories of those days make me smile. All of you are such an important part of who I am today, and I continue to feel your influence in my life.

Almost done…thanks to my volunteer copy and content editors, Kathy and brother, Sam. You do your jobs well and I always feel better when you have critiqued, edited and reassured me.

And last, a big thank you to the readers of my debut novel, *A Portrait of Dawn.*
Your words of encouragement, your enthusiasm, and your request for more have inspired me to continue the journey.

We woke at dawn and watched in awe

as God used the sky for His canvas.

He began to paint for us a picture of our coming day;

it was a parade of resplendent color that took our breath away.

Then the clouds came,

and our only hope was that the memory of dawn

would brighten our way,

as we struggled through the darkness that enveloped us.

.

PROLOGUE

I'm one of the lucky ones. I grew up the child of parents who treasured me.

My biological mother has often told me the story of the moment she knew she loved and wanted me. She was sitting alone in an abortion clinic, waiting for those who would end my life when she recognized God had a plan for me. In that instant, she followed her heart and chose to give life to me.

Six months later, with tears in her eyes and a heart that was broken, she placed me in the loving arms of my adoptive parents, a couple who desperately wanted a child to love and care for.

I grew up happy and thinking I was in need of nothing. Then I met Ben.

I didn't know it until I met him, but there was a Ben-shaped void in my heart and in my life, and he was the only one who could fill it. His love made me feel adored and cherished.

Ours is the kind of love my parents have for each other. It includes respect and kindness. It's sometimes difficult to find that kind of love in our world, but I witnessed it in all four of my parents, and I wanted it for myself. Yes, I have four parents. I'm part of a blended family, and it was a great way to grow up.

I grew up knowing I was blessed. Not every one is that fortunate. Some people grow up never feeling loved by any parent. My birth mother grew up in a home with an abusive father; that's why she had to choose adoption for me, even though she didn't want to. She was terrified of him. It wasn't until he went to prison that she was able, with God's help, to build her own life, a life free of intimidation and fear.

I didn't know about fear until I was sixteen years old. I had those normal anxieties about snakes and spiders. But real fear, the kind that makes you weak in the knees, and makes you feel like the wind has been completely knocked out of you, was foreign to me.

When I was introduced to fear, I remember thinking I might die before all my dreams came true. Even at sixteen, I could imagine a day when a special man would hold me in his arms and make me feel cherished. I had to wait ten years for that dream to come true.

The first time Ben told me he loved me, I looked at him and saw the tears glisten in his eyes. I knew then that he was the guy I had been dreaming about, the guy I wondered if I'd meet before I died.

With Ben's love came the dawning of a new day, in a new season of my life.

Chapter 1

The trauma unit's head nurse rushed into the break room with her ever-present clipboard in hand.

"Katy, her you are. The medical helicopter will be here in ten minutes, Can you and Denny be ready to meet them?"

"No problem. I just sent my patient up to ICU. Ten minutes will give me enough time to eat the lunch I warmed up an hour ago."

I put my fork down and swallowed hard. I know talking with your mouth full is rude, but microwaved frozen meals aren't fine dining in the first place. The lunch I'd warmed an hour earlier had become barely edible. As a trauma nurse, I survive on cold lunches, missed dinners, and ultra-fast bathroom breaks, but I love my job.

I've wanted to be a nurse since I was a little girl. When I was sixteen, I planned for a career in nursing—if I survived. A personal experience in a hospital confirmed my life plan for me

I was just swallowing the last bite of my lunch when Denny came through the break room door. "There you are! You finally got lunch, that's good. I need your help for a minute, in room three. And I hear we have a chopper patient coming in."

"Okay, let's go. Did you find time to eat?"

"I grabbed a candy bar an hour ago. That should hold me." He grinned at me "I know, not healthy. But it gave me the boost of energy I needed."

I was six hours into my twelve hour shift in the trauma unit when the air ambulance team brought Mrs. Johnson into room four. The report I received said she was seventy six, had fallen at home, and hit her head on a table. When her neighbor found her she was responsive, but confused.

The first responders to her home called the medical helicopter because of the head trauma. After they did their assessment, they suspected she had a probable subdural hematoma, a collection of blood on the surface of the brain. It can be fatal, especially in the elderly. The air ambulance team then called us. Our neuro team was on standby.

When we slid her from the gurney to the examination table, I thought I heard a soft moan, and I saw her forehead furrow. Denny hooked her up to the machine that would monitor her vital signs while I checked her for pupil response, listened to her lungs, and palpated her belly. The nurses on the flight team had already put an IV in her right arm, and she appeared to be stable.

The neurologist rushed in, his white coat billowing around him and his pager beeping for his attention. "What do we have?"

"Mrs. Johnson, age seventy-six, blunt head trauma. Confused, mumbling, vital signs stable." Denny parroted the report we'd been given.

"We need a CT scan of her head, chest x-ray and a CBC. Get her lytes while you're at it. Is there a family I need to talk to?" He spoke rapidly as he wrote his orders on the appropriate forms, pausing only to give Denny an expectant stare.

He knew, as I did, Denny isn't a people person.

"Katy, can you go check on the family? I'll get the lab called." Denny wanted to do the technical things and leave the interpersonal things to me. That was fine; working with people was one of the reasons I went into nursing. I'm a caretaker by nature.

I went to the trauma reception desk and asked if Mrs. Johnson's family had arrived yet.

"She doesn't have any family. When we picked her up the neighbor was with her. She said there was no one to call."

I turned from the desk and looked up into the darkest blue eyes I've ever seen. They were unforgettable blue eyes, midnight blue, and they matched the color of his uniform perfectly. I had already seen the uniform in our trauma unit, but I'd never seen those eyes.

"How can someone have no family? There has to be someone who cares about this lady!"

"We got the name of a lawyer. The neighbor said he's her Durable Power of Attorney. It's on the transfer record."

"That's all you have? Are you sure she doesn't have anyone else?"

Mr. Blue eyes lifted his eyebrows and shook his head no.

"Did you get the name of the neighbor lady? I'll call her and see if someone can come in and be with the patient. People shouldn't be alone at times like this. Where did she come from?" I took my pen and note pad out of my scrubs pocket.

"Brooksville. It's about fifty miles north of here."

"I know where Brooksville is. What I need…is the name of someone who cares about this lady."

"Well, you don't have to be so grouchy!"

"I'm not being grouchy." I sucked in a deep breath then blew it out.

"Yes, you are. You just about bit my head off! It's not my fault she has no family."

Another deep breath. Frustration brings out the worst in me. "I'm sorry. It's been a long day…Ben." His name tag said he was the helicopter pilot. "I always feel bad for patients who don't have anyone."

"Yeah, it's sad. Unfortunately, there are lots of people just like her in the world." His eyes left mine, and narrowed for a second. A shadow seemed to move over them, turning them from blue to a cloudy gray.

"I know, but that doesn't make it any easier for this lady."

"No it doesn't…Katy, R.N." I saw him look at my name tag. "Are you new here? I haven't seen you before."

"I've been down here for two weeks."

"And where were you before?"

"Neuro ICU." I really didn't have time for a "get acquainted session," I had work to do.

"So are you about done with your shift?"

"Hardly! Six down, six to go."

"So you're off at seven? Twelve hour shifts are rough."

"Yeah, they are. Sometimes, they make me snippy. I'm sorry." I put the notepad back in my pocket and turned to go.

"You already said that. Tell you what… I'll forgive you for being snippy if you meet me after work at the deli across the street. I'll buy your supper."

I stopped, turned, and looked at him again. "Why should I do that? I don't even know you."

"I'm Ben. It says so right here on my name tag. And your name tag says Katy, R.N. We've been formally introduced. What more do you need to know?" The blue eyes were having fun.

"Well, Ben. A name tells me nothing and I need to get back to work."

"Ask around. I'm sure Denny can vouch for me. He can probably tell you anything you want to know. I'm in here a lot."

He didn't seem to be getting the hint. I didn't have time to talk to him; I had a patient to take care of.

"Bye, Ben. It was nice meeting you."

"See you at seven."

"In your dreams."

*****

I've worked at Tampa General for three years, first on surgical unit then in neuro ICU. When they told me on the first of December I could transfer to trauma, I felt like I'd been given an early Christmas gift.

There were several reasons why I wanted to do trauma nursing. I wanted to be where the adrenaline kicked in every time the doors slid open, and I wanted to be there because I knew what it felt like to be the patient. I had experienced the fear of not knowing what was happening to me. I wanted to be there to give support and reassurance to patients and their families in their times of crisis.

We work in teams in trauma. It seems to work best that way. So many of our patients and their families come in hysterical or in shock. A second pair of hands always comes in handy.

Denny, my teammate, and I clicked from day one. I like him as a person, and he's a great nurse. He's been in the unit for three years and is well respected. It's his job to teach me the ropes in trauma. It's my job to learn and assist him until I feel confident enough to work with someone less experienced. It's a great system.

It was after three o'clock before the two of us were able to sit down together for a break. Mrs. Johnson had been sent to surgery. There was no one else in the break room at the time so I decided to ask him about Ben. I had thought about those blue eyes a few times since I'd met him. And it wasn't just because he was good looking; something had connected between us in the brief minutes we talked.

"So…how often does the medical flight team bring someone in?" The yogurt I'd brought in two days earlier was still in the refrigerator, so I dug it out and was eating it. Denny was eating a sandwich from a paper bag. I wondered if he brought it in himself or had just found it in the refrigerator. He has a reputation for eating whatever he finds if it doesn't have a name on it. He says most of the stuff in the refrigerator goes to waste anyways.

"It depends. Some weeks we see them every day, especially during the winter and spring months when there are so many tourists here."

"They don't stay long when they come in, do they?"

"No. They get out of our way. But we know most of them pretty well. Some of them party with us after hours."

"I've never seen the pilot that brought Mrs. Johnson in."

"Yeah, I think he's been gone for a couple weeks. Don't know where he's been, maybe vacation."

"Has he been on the team very long?"

He looked up from the sandwich.

"He's been around for a few years. I hear he's a great pilot, but I think he's kind of arrogant. Most of the single nurses, and some of the married ones, fall all over themselves when he walks in. I noticed he was talking to you." He raised his eyebrows and smirked at me.

"So he hits on all the women?"

"They wish. That's the strange thing about him. I don't think he's ever gone out with any of the girls from here. I'm wondering if he's gay."

"So you don't know anything personal about him?" I was trying to sound like I was just making conversation.

"Nope. He doesn't party with us…someone said he has another job. Why the interest? You don't seem man hungry like the rest of the girls around here."

"Just curious. But he did ask me to meet him at the deli at the end of my shift. So it's uncharacteristic for him to do that?"

"As far as I know. Were you flirting with him?" He grinned at me, as he tossed the empty bag at the trash can, missing it by a foot.

"Flirting? Me? Not hardly! In fact, I didn't even notice him until he started to tell me about Mrs. Johnson."

"So are you going to meet him?"

"Goodness, no! I don't make a habit of meeting strange men after work."

"Then you really are different from the other girls around here. Do you date at all?"

"I've been a little busy the past few years. I actually have to study when I go to school."

"I heard you're working on your masters. But even intellectuals need a love life, girl. You want me to set you up with someone? There's a single guy I play softball with. You and he could double with me and my wife. She's been bugging me about going out some night."

I got up to retrieve his trash from the floor. I didn't want him to see the flush I felt crawling up my neck.

"That's nice of you to offer, but I'm thinking your wife probably doesn't want another couple tagging along on a date with her husband."

"Okay, but if you change your mind, let me know."

I knew I wouldn't change my mind. Sure, I sometimes wanted that special someone to share my life with, but my future still seemed so uncertain. I just couldn't risk loving and being loved by someone. Not now, not yet.

Chapter 2

I couldn't go home until I knew how Mrs. Johnson was doing. The CT scan we did in trauma had confirmed the subdural hematoma and she was taken straight to surgery. The neurosurgeon asked me to call her neighbor to see if we could get any more information about her medical and family history. What we learned was not in her favor. She was a sick lady before her fall, and she didn't have any family.

She was in neuro ICU when I found her. She had just returned from recovery and was alone.

I sat down beside her bed, and took her frail hand in mine. It was small and pale, and her veins lay like blue cobwebs under her skin. There was a thin gold band on her left ring finger. The tape they put around it in surgery was still holding it in place.

The whooshing and clicking of the ventilator coincided with her chest moving up and down. The tubes going into her body provided her with nutrients that kept her body hydrated, and medications to keep her brain from swelling. Her condition looked like it was stable.

To some at the hospital that day, she was "the subdural hematoma." To others she was "Number 205." I like to think of my patients as people; a wife to a husband, a mother to a child, or maybe a long time, beloved friend. I wanted to believe that this lady, in the middle of all the medical paraphernalia, was important to someone.

She was frail looking with her wrinkled skin. Her hair was pure white and as fine as cotton. It was also disheveled, so I tried to smooth it down for her.

As I sat and watched her chest go up and down with the the precision that can only be maintained by a machine, I wondered who Mrs. Johnson was. All I knew was her name, her diagnosis, and that she was from Brooksville. I also knew she had a neighbor who found her when she had fallen, and a lawyer who would more than likely make the final decisions for her life.

Looking at the thin wedding band, I had to believe that she had, at one time, been loved by someone. What had their life together been like? Was she childless? Or had she experienced the joy of children, then the sadness of being left behind by them?

The tears began to build behind my eyes. I couldn't help it. They come easily for me, especially when I'm tired and troubled. This wasn't just a patient I had spent a few minutes with today, this was a person with feelings. And I wondered if anyone loved her, besides the God who had created her. I could only hope and pray she had faith in Him and could sense His presence in what appeared to be her personal valley of the shadow of death.

I haven't been a nurse very long, but I firmly believe people in deep comas can sense another person's presence and can sometimes hear their voices.

"Mrs. Johnson? My name is Katy. I was in the emergency room when you came to the hospital today. You've been in surgery, and we're waiting for you to wake up. I'm going to sit with you for a little while, and pray for you. Try not to be afraid. God loves you, and He's with you." I got no response from her, not even the flutter of an eyelash.

"Katy?" The voice came from behind me. It startled me. Turning around, I saw the blue eyes I had seen earlier in the day.

"Ben! What are you doing here?"

"When you didn't show up at the deli, I decided to come over and see how Mrs. Johnson was doing. For some reason, I'm not surprised to find you here."

"Do you always follow up on the patients you transport?"

"Not always. But I knew this one was alone in the world, and I wanted her to know someone cared. How is she?"

"I think it's too early to know. I can leave if you want to stay with her."

"You don't have to leave. Maybe the sound of our voices will make her feel not so alone."

Arrogance? Sorry, Denny my friend, I just don't see it.

What I did see was a very good looking man who seemed to have a heart that was focused on someone beside himself.

"You're probably right. Pull up a chair; I was just getting ready to read to her. I like to think she knows someone's here with her. If I were her, I would want to hear something besides the sound of all this medical equipment."

I always bring a little book of inspirational stories with me when I come to work. The thought is that I might have a minute, sometime during my day, to read to someone who's lonely. That has never happened when I'm clocked in, but sometimes I find a patient I can give it to. I kept it today, thinking it might be something Mrs. Johnson could benefit from.

I could feel Ben's eyes on me while I was reading. I looked up once and he smiled at me. It was a nice smile, and it made my heart thump a little faster and harder against my chest. I faltered and lost my place.

I heard him chuckle, like he knew his presence was making me feel a little self conscious. Mostly though, I was just impressed he was here, in the room of an old woman he didn't even know.

In the half hour we spent with her, Mrs. Johnson gave us no indication she knew we were there. Except once, when I was reading the twenty-third psalm and her heart rate went up. Ben saw it on the monitor, reached over, and took her hand.

*****

We stopped at the nurses' station on our way out, and I asked if anyone had called to inquire about her. Her nurse couldn't give us any information due to the need for confidentiality, but she did take my phone number. She told me she'd call if Mrs. Johnson woke up agitated or in need of someone to sit with her.

"I'm assuming you haven't eaten, since you didn't keep our date?" The eyes were having fun again. When he grinned this time, I noticed a dimple digging a hole into his right cheek.

"I don't remember making a date with you."

"You said you'd see me in my dreams, and I've been dreaming about you all day. So I'm thinking, if we go to the deli now, it will actually be our second date."

How could I say no? A man who would visit a lonely old woman on his own time probably wasn't a serial killer I needed to fear.

The deli across the street from the hospital was open twenty four hours a day, and was usually busy with medical staff who grew tired of institution food. At nine o'clock at night, it wasn't busy at all. We found a booth, and within minutes a waitress brought us water and a menu.

I was starving. I decided since Ben had initiated this so-called date, I would let him pay the bill. So I ordered a whole meal. He said he ate earlier when I hadn't shown up. All he ordered was a milk shake.

When the waitress put the double burger with fries in front of me, his eyes got big.

"Are you actually going to eat all of that?"

"That's why I ordered it. I haven't eaten in hours and I'm starved." I took a long sip of the milk that came with my meal.

"A girl with a healthy appetite; that's something I don't see often. Most girls tend to eat like rabbits. Hard to believe you're a nurse though; don't you know about saturated fats?"

Dipping a fry in some catsup, I decided to play with him a little bit. He didn't have to know I was being honest. "I only eat like this when I'm on a date, and someone else is paying the bill. The last time that happened was about six months ago."

Laughter spilled from him, and I saw mischief written all over his face.

"If you ate like this you probably scared the poor guy away, or left him penniless. So you aren't afraid to eat in front of a guy, and you aren't embarrassed to admit you haven't had a date in six months. You are a very unusual girl, my dear!"

My heart fluttered at the endearment, and I felt heat rise to my face.

"Hey, life's too short to play games."

"It is, isn't it? And just so you don't consume too many saturated fats that will shorten your life, I think I'll help you with those fries."

"That's so thoughtful of you. But I really think you have your share of fat grams in that milkshake."

"I'll work them off at the gym tomorrow." He helped himself to a few fries from my plate.

"You have time to fly helicopters and go to the gym?"

"I make time for the gym. You want to go with me tomorrow, so you can work off the burger and fries?"

Now it was my turn to laugh, making me almost choke on my burger. I just can't understand why people who live so close to a beautiful beach they can walk on, pay money to go to a gym.

"What's so funny?"

"I don't do gyms."

"So how do you stay so skinny when you eat like this?"

"I told you, I don't eat like this all the time. And I get all the exercise I need working twelve hour shifts! Do you know how many times I actually sat down today?" I held up three fingers.

"Okay, I admit it. Nurses work hard. What do you do on your days off? You work three twelves a week, right?"

"Usually, but sometimes I pick up an extra shift for one of the girls who has a lot of family stuff going on."

"So you have three or four days off every week? That's kind of nice, isn't it? I do three twelves, too. So why haven't I seen you in trauma before?" He helped himself to a handful of fries this time.

"I just started working there a couple of weeks ago. But I've actually been at the hospital since I got out of school."

"And how long ago was that?"

"Three years." I saw him doing the math in his head.

"So you're what? Twenty-four or five?"

"You're close. Twenty-six…I did a BSN program. How long have you been a helicopter pilot?"

"I've done it here in Tampa for two years."

"Where were you before?"

"Afghanistan."

Thoughtful of old ladies who are all alone in the world, and a man who has served his country. Once again Denny, I don't see the arrogance. Perhaps you're just jealous of him because he has fun blue eyes and a dimpled smile. And now that I've had time to examine him, a very nice build! Men, you're all so competitive!

"That's a story I'd like to hear."

"And you will. But only if you go on another date with me."

"You call this a date?" I couldn't help but smile.

"Yep, our second. The first one was in my dreams today. So when and where do you want to go on our third date?"

I had to laugh at him.

"It's about time you let me decide when and where to go on a date! Can you take me to a ball game this Saturday? My Yankees are in spring training at Steinbrenner field, you know."

"Your Yankees? Tell me it isn't so!"

"Yep. I go watch 'em every chance I get."

"You're kidding me, right?"

"No, I'm not kidding you. My brothers and I have loved the Yankees for as long as I can remember."

"Why?" He sat back in his seat and just looked at me. I guess he'd finally eaten enough of my food.

"Because they're the best baseball team in America! We grew up in Philly, and our Dad grew up in New York. He always took us to the games."

"Who are they playing this week?"

"The Astros."

He threw his head back and hooted. I really didn't see anything funny about being a Yankee fan. When he finally pulled himself together, I asked him to share the joke.

"I'm from Texas. The Astros are my team."

I thought I heard an accent in that voice!

"Oh, this is going to be great. My Yankees are going to beat the pants off your Astros!"

"You are one strange girl, Katy! By the way, what's your last name?"

"Clinton."

"Katy Clinton. I like that name."

"And your last name? Just so I know who's gonna be crying in his beer at the game this weekend."

"Browning. Ben Browning. You want to meet me at the field on Saturday or can I pick you up?"

"I'll probably be too heavy to pick up after I finish these fries."

"I doubt that."

"If I let you take me to the game…are you going to make me walk home when my team beats your team?"

"No, I'll take you home. But you have to pay for our fourth date if my team loses."

"It's a deal."

"What's your phone number? I'll call you when I get the details of this civil war date all set up." He opened his cell phone and punched in the numbers as I gave them to him.

"You working tomorrow?"

"No, I have the day off. You?" I finished off the milk and put my napkin on my plate. I had worked as a waitress in high school and always appreciated the customers who cleaned up after themselves.

"Yep, extra shifts this week. Pilots are in huge demand right now. I'm working every day till Saturday."

"Maybe I'll see you on Thursday or Friday then."

"That's a possibility. You ready to go?" He took a money clip out of his pocket and dropped a twenty on the table as he got up. *Generous. Nothing worse than a stingy tipper.*

"I am. And thanks for dinner."

He walked me all the way to my car. It was still parked in the hospital parking garage.

"You be careful on your way home. There are some crazy drivers out there!"

"You too. And thanks for the second date."

"And thank you for the first one. It was lovely, even though you weren't physically there." I saw him grin when he closed my car door for me.

Trying to fall asleep after the evening with Ben was near to impossible. Even though I was worried about the risk of falling in love, I knew he was bringing to life, a part of me that had been dormant since the day I was born. You know how the buds on a tree burst into beautiful green leaves in the spring? That's how I felt when Ben came into my life.

Chapter 3

When my phone rang on Wednesday morning, I knew it would be my sister, Abby.

"Hey, are you still coming over today?"

"Of course. I'm in need of some serious play time with my nephews. How are they today?"

"They're into everything already." I heard her sigh into the phone.

Abby and her husband, Brett, have two little boys. Kyle is three, and Konnor is eighteen months. They are adorable, but very high energy, like their mom.

"Do you need me to stay with them for awhile, so you can have a break?"

"No. Carly didn't have school today, so she's here. She's a big help. I just need you to come over and provide me with some adult conversation."

"You got it, but it might be another hour. I have to stop at the hospital for a few minutes."

"Okay, see you then." I heard some squealing going on in the background before the phone went dead. Abby's life was always noisy, compared to my quiet solitary one.

*****

I had thought about Mrs. Johnson as soon as I woke up. I knew the hospital wouldn't give me any information on her if I called, so I had no choice but to stop, and see if she made it through the night.

There had been some light frost on my low-lying plants when I got up early, and the forecast was for a cool day in Tampa; so I pulled on my favorite pair of jeans. After growing up in Philadelphia, I love Florida's warm climate. But sometimes I do miss wearing jeans and sweatshirts. January was just about the only month I got the chance to do it.

It was nine by the time I got to the hospital. I didn't see any nurses at the station so I went straight to the room where I left Mrs. Johnson the night before. She was still there. I picked up her hand and called her name. There was no response from her.

According to the monitor, her vital signs still looked stable. I sat down and was telling her about the cool weather when a man walked into the room.

"Hi. Are you here to see Mrs. Johnson?"

"I am. And who would you be?"

"I'm Katy. I was working in trauma when she came in yesterday. I just dropped in to see how she's doing."

"That's nice of you. I'm her lawyer. I got a call from a social worker yesterday afternoon. She told me my client was here. Do you happen to know who I can talk to about her care?"

"I can find her nurse for you. You'll probably want to talk to her doctor too, won't you?"

"That would be good. Can you let them know I'm a little short on time?"

"Of course...it was nice to meet you."

When I left her room, I wondered what kind of decisions would be made for Mrs. Johnson in the coming hours. And I wondered if she'd still be here when I returned to work the next day.

*****

I usually spend every Wednesday with my sister. We have a lot of lost time to make up. We didn't meet until we were sixteen.

We were born on the same day, and we look alike, but we aren't twins. We don't even have common blood. I know it doesn't make sense, but we're still sisters. We're sisters because her biological dad is married to my biological mom and we share Carly, our ten year old half sister. My family is definitely not a traditional one, whatever traditional means.

In addition to family, Abby and I have a lot of other things in common. But we're a world apart in personality. I've always been a little reserved and serious. She, on the other hand, is vivacious and more fun than any one I know. Maybe that's why we get along so well and have been best friends since the day we met.

We met ten years ago at my biological grandmother's house in Indiana. I had just met my birth mom a few months prior to that. My adoptive parents contacted her when I was first diagnosed with the leukemia. My doctors said I might need a bone marrow transplant and the marrow of a sibling would provide the best match. We were hoping my biological mom had other children.

I had known I was adopted since I was a little girl, but because I was so happy and content, I never had a desire to meet my birth mom. My parents had told me about the day she gave me to them, and how sad she was. They said she loved me and really didn't want to give me away, but she knew it would be best for me. At sixteen, she couldn't take care of me.

As a child, it was enough for me just to know she gave me away out of love, rather than because she didn't want me.

Meeting my birth mom was one of the best things that ever happened to me. It was the good that came out my leukemia. When she and her husband, Alex, arrived at Philadelphia Children's Hospital, I felt an instant connection to her. Maybe because she had prayed for me, and loved me from the day she gave birth to me. She immediately became my Mama Beth.

My adoptive mother loves her too. In the past ten years, I've often heard her say, "Why wouldn't I love her? She gave me the best gift a childless woman could get. She gave me the gift of you."

When Mama Beth and Alex got to the hospital in Philadelphia, I was pretty sick. I had been on chemo for a couple of months and had an infection. My doctors told all four of my parents I had an excellent chance of going into remission and staying there, but they were going to put my name on the bone marrow transplant list "just in case" I'd need it.

Soon after Mama Beth arrived at the hospital, they tested her to see if she could be a potential marrow donor, but she didn't match. I wonder sometimes if my biological dad would have matched. But he was never tested; he didn't want to be involved. After he paid for the abortion my Mama never got, he disappeared from my life.

Mama Beth was devastated when she couldn't donate marrow for me. And she was sad because she had no other biological children who could be tested. After me, she hadn't been able to have any more of her own. I had no biological siblings who could donate the marrow I might need.

It was then, Mama Beth told me about "my sister," Abby. Abby was seven when her dad married Mama Beth. They have an adopted son, Jon, too. He's the same age as my adopted twin brothers. I still think it's fascinating how similar my birth family and my adoptive family are.

We all decided, since my leukemia brought us together, we would continue to see each other. The first time we all got together as one big family was at my grandmother's house in Indiana. It was a central place, since the Phillips family had to travel from Tampa and our Clinton family had to travel from our home in Philadelphia.

It was an amazing Christmas. Abby and I became instant sisters and friends, and our little brothers had so much fun together. It was like two families meshed into one that Christmas. It was a miraculous Christmas too. Mama Beth and Alex told us they were pregnant with my half sister, Carly.

After Mama Beth and Alex left me at the hospital in Philadelphia, they went home and made an appointment to see a fertility specialist. They had always wanted a baby and after they read that cord blood from a sibling would be a better match for me than regular marrow, they had an even greater reason to have a baby of their own. The baby would have the same biological mother as me, and its cord blood would have the potential to save my life.

When they arrived at the fertility clinic, they discovered they were too late to be helped. Mama Beth was already pregnant. I guess that's proof that God's plans are better than our plans, and His timing is always perfect. They told all of us about the baby that Christmas, and I became a believer in Christmas miracles.

Chapter 4

When I pulled into the driveway at Abby's house, I noticed three small heads at the window. By the time I got to the front door, it was open and three kids immediately attached themselves to my legs. There is no better feeling in the world than being loved.

"Katy, where have you been? The boys and I have been waiting forever for you to get here!"

"Hey, little sis! I got here as soon as I could. I heard you're skipping school today."

"I'm not skipping. The teachers had a meeting and mom and dad said I could stay all night with Abby. When can I come and stay all night with you again?"

Ten year old Carly is the half sister Abby and I share. It's a toss up who loves her most. Abby was around her constantly for the two years after she was born. Then she left for the Chicago Art Institute. I got to be around her for the next four years when I decided to go to nurses training in Tampa. Actually, it took me five years to get through a four year program because my leukemia came back. I had to take a year off for the bone marrow transplant.

I know Abby loves our little sister as much as I do, but I feel especially close to her. When she was born, her cord blood was harvested and they used it for my transplant. I feel like I have a part of her coursing through my veins, and I will always be grateful for her.

"Let's see. I have this weekend off. You could come Friday or Saturday night, if Mama Beth and your Daddy say its okay."

"That would be great! I'll call them right now!"

"Me too? Me too?"

Three year old Kyle loved his Aunty Carly and seemed to think he should be able to do every thing she did.

"No Kyle, you can't come this time. Katy and I are going to do girl things."

So of course he began to wail, and when he wails, so does Konnor.

"What on earth is going on?" Abby came through the kitchen door, wiping her hands on her pants. I had to laugh. Sometimes her house is so chaotic, and today she looked like she hadn't even taken time to brush her hair. And she's the high maintenance one. Well, she used to be.

"Carly wants to come to my house this weekend, and she told Kyle he couldn't come too."

Abby picked up the still sobbing Konnor, and I picked up Kyle who was still yelling "me too!" I heard Carly arguing on the phone with Mama Beth. There just wasn't any other word to describe the room, except chaotic. And I loved it.

"Katy, Mom wants to talk to you."

"Can you tell her I'll call her back when the boys stop crying?"

"Okaaaay."

"Gee, Abby, why don't you have a few more kids so it can be a real three ring circus around here!"

"Oh, shut up! You and your nice, quiet, single life!"

We were both laughing by the time we got to the kitchen. We put both boys in high chairs and she dumped some cheerios on their trays before she collapsed in a chair.

"Take a deep breath. I'll get the tea."

"What would I do without you? You always seem to know when I need reinforcements."

"Hey, what are sisters for? How long is Carly going to be here?"

"Mama's coming to get her at lunch time. She's bringing pizza, I told her to bring some for you too."

"Good, I haven't seen her since Christmas."

"That's what she said. So your mom and dad went back to Philly this past weekend?"

"Yeah, I miss them already. But the boys are coming back for spring break. I told them they could stay with me, but I think they're going to get a place at the beach with some friends."

My adoptive parents are what you would call well-to-do. They have always been generous with my brothers and me, but they didn't spoil us. We had to work for the extra things in life we wanted. But I have to admit, we probably did have more opportunities to work than most kids.

"Oh, to be young again! Jon just went back to school this week too. It's hard to believe our little brothers are almost adults isn't it?"

"Almost? Before you know it, they'll be getting married and having kids."

"No way. They don't get to do that until we get you married off. I'm going to have to tell Brett to set you up with someone again. Even if you didn't like the last two he got for you."

"For your information, dear sister, I can get my own dates."

"Yeah, right. I just can't figure it out. You're twenty six years old, smart, beautiful and kind…and still not married. Mr. Right has to be out there somewhere."

"I've already told you why I'm not in a hurry to find Mr. Right. It would take someone really special to deal with the baggage I come with."

"And I've told you…that's crazy talk. Just because you had leukemia ten years ago doesn't mean it's going to come back."

"But it did come back."

"Yes. But that was before the transplant, and it's been six years since you had that. Your chances of survival are going up every year!"

"But how horrible would it be to fall in love with someone, and then die on him?"

"That isn't going to happen. I think it's time for you to put that fear out of your mind and focus on how happy you'd be with the right guy."

"I wish I was as sure as you are."

My mind flashed to Ben. I was just about ready to tell her about him when Carly burst into the kitchen to tell us Mama had finally agreed to let her stay with me on the weekend.

"Is Saturday night okay? Then I can go to church with you. You know Dad will be furious if I miss church!"

Abby and Carly's dad, my stepdad, is the pastor of the church we all go to. A kinder man can not be found. When he and Mama Beth came to see me at the hospital in Philadelphia that first time, I felt his love for me instantly. He told me later he and Mama prayed for me everyday after they got married, even though he didn't even know me.

"Okay, Carly, we'll do Saturday night."

As soon as the words were out of my mouth, I remembered I had a date on Saturday. But it was an afternoon game, and I would be home by the evening.

"Can I come over early so we can go to the beach?"

"Can we do the beach on Sunday afternoon instead? I'll pick you up Saturday evening and we'll go shopping and out for pizza."

"I thought you didn't have to work this weekend?"

"I don't, but I'm going to the ballgame with a friend on Saturday afternoon."

"Can I go with you too?"

I heard Abby clear her throat.

"Carly! Katy told you Saturday evening. Now, can you take the boys back into the living room and help them build something with their blocks?" Abby knew I caved-in to whatever the my little sister wanted.

She sighed deeply, the way ten-year-olds do when they don't get their way. When the three of them were gone, Abby grinned at me. "It must be nice to be the fun sister. All she gets to do here is take care of little boys."

"She loves it, and you know it. She inherited Mama Beth's nurturing gene."

Abby calls my birth mom "Mama Beth" too. Her own biological mother died from ovarian cancer when Abby was six.

"So who are you going to the game with on Saturday?"

"A friend from work. That reminds me, the saddest thing happened at work yesterday."

I don't know why, but I just wasn't ready to share Ben with Abby yet. I was afraid she would make a big deal about it, and there really wasn't anything to make a big deal about. So I told her about lonely Mrs. Johnson instead.

Chapter 5

I stayed at Abby's house and visited with her and Mama Beth all afternoon. We always have a good time together. Mama is only sixteen years older than the two of us, and there were times when she felt more like a big sister than a parent.

When I finally left Abby's house, I went to the beach to take a walk. It was a good time to walk since it was close to sunset, and I never tire of watching the sun sink into the waters of the Gulf of Mexico. Walking at the beach is my favorite thing to do, even in January when it's sometimes cold and windy.

The air was cool, but I was glad I had a pair of shorts to walk in. The hot Florida sun beating down on the white sand can make you feel like you're in an oven.

My love for the beach began when I moved to Florida after graduation from high school. It may have something to do with growing up in Philadelphia where it can be brutally cold in the winter months. But I think it has more to do with my first experience at the beach. My parents let me travel alone to see Mama Beth during spring break of my senior year. She took me to the Caladesi State Park beach, and we got to know each other there. I'll never forget that first day with her. The Gulf waters reflected the color of the cloudless skies and I felt in tune, not only with the majesty of the world around me, but with the mother who gave life to me.

It's hard to believe ten years have passed since that day. As I walked, I thought about what Abby had said about putting aside my fears and planning for a happy future. It's a difficult thing to do when so many of the people you meet in cancer treatment end up dying. I know my chances of survival are getting better every day, but there is still that chance…I could lose the battle.

But didn't I deserve to be happy after all I had been through? I'm not one to feel sorry for myself, but occasionally I let myself wallow in the "it's just not fair" mud. But that was becoming less frequent. I had made it through school and now I had a career I loved. My life was a good one.

Maybe it was time to start thinking about sharing it with someone else. Maybe that person could be Ben. It was still a little unsettling how he had appeared so suddenly in my life. And now, just twenty four hours later, I found myself thinking about him so frequently.

I had told God years ago that I would depend on Him to bring the right person into my life at the right time. Had He finally done it when He allowed Ben to walk into my life yesterday?

*****

I woke up early for work. Again, my first thoughts were of Mrs. Johnson. Then Ben. The two had come into my life together, so I guess it was natural I would think of both of them, when I thought of one. I decided to go into work early, so I could check on her. It was doubtful I would get away from the trauma unit during the day.

When I got to her room, she was still there and the night nurse was with her. It was a nurse I had worked with before.

"Hey, Katy. What are you doing here? Trauma unit not working out and you want your old job back?" She grinned. She knew how much I had wanted that transfer.

"Trauma has been great. I just came in to check on Mrs. Johnson. I met her when she came in. How is she?"

"Walk with me."

I gave Mrs. Johnson's hand a squeeze, told her I'd be back later and left the room.

"So you met her when she came in on the helicopter? I guess that means you're as close to family as she has, just like the rest of us are. Poor thing, it must be horrible to have no one at the end of your life."

"I know. I think that's why I can't get her off my mind. Have they made any decisions about her care?"

"Her lawyer was in yesterday. We're going to start weaning her off the ventilator today. He said her Living Will states she doesn't want any extraordinary measures taken to keep her alive."

"Has her doctor said what her chances are?"

"Not good. If she survives off the vent, we're going to send her to hospice tomorrow."

"Poor lady. Wouldn't it be horrible to die all alone?"

"She'll have the hospice nurses. They're good out there at the inpatient unit."

"I know. And we do have to follow her wishes, don't we?"

"It's in the job description. Hey, you have a good day. I need to get ready for report. We miss you up here, but I'm glad you like your new assignment."

*****

The day was a busy one. Every once in a while, I wondered if the medical helicopter would bring anyone in, but it never did. I feel awful admitting it, since they usually bring in the worst traumas and that means lives are changed, but I was a little disappointed they never brought us a patient. To be honest, it wasn't the patients I wanted to see; it was the chopper pilot.

It had been two days since I'd met Ben and given him my number. I was beginning to think he had changed his mind about going to the game with me. He said he would get back with me about the time and other details.

I clocked out at seven and went back up to see how Mrs. Johnson was doing with her vent weaning. Many people in her condition die as soon as the vent settings are reduced. Others do okay with it. Mrs. Johnson appeared to be one who was tolerating it well.

I sat down beside her and took my book out of my pocket. I had been reading for a few minutes when I looked up to see her lawyer coming in the door.

"You're here again? Do you have some special interest in my client?"

Well, hello to you too!

"Good evening. I had a few minutes before I go home and thought I'd drop in and sit with her for awhile. I like to do that for patients who have no families."

"Why?"

"I don't think people should be alone at times like this. Is it a problem?"

"No. I just don't understand it. Just so you know, she won't be here tomorrow. If she survives the night, she's going to hospice. That was her wishes."

"They'll take good care of her there. Would you mind if I check in on her while she's there?"

"No, I don't care…I just don't understand why you want to. But that's your business."

"Thank you. Are you at liberty to tell me anything about her personal life? I like to talk to her when I'm with her. Did she have any special people or interests in her life?"

"I usually don't get involved in the personal lives of my clients. Even if I did, I wouldn't be at liberty to tell you anything. You understand client confidentiality."

"Of course. But thank you again for allowing me to visit with her."

"Sure. I guess I better go talk to someone about her transfer. My assistant will be handling her case from here on."

I left Mrs. Johnson, hoping her lawyer's assistant was a little warmer than he was.

I was still thinking about her later that night as I was drifting off to sleep, when the phone rang.

"Katy? It's Ben. You weren't asleep already, were you?"

"Almost. Some of us work hard during the day, and we're tired at bedtime."

"Sorry. I was hoping I'd get to see you today at work, but all our flights went to other hospitals. I just got home but I wanted to call so you wouldn't forget me. And I wanted you to know I hadn't forgotten you."

"I was beginning to wonder if I had imagined you."

"You have other imaginary friends?" I could hear the laughter in his voice.

"Wouldn't you like to know."

"Yes. I want to know everything about you. But not now, you sound tired. The game starts at two on Saturday. I'll pick you up at one, okay?" I felt almost breathless, he still wanted to see me!

"Sounds good. Do you need my address?"

"I guess that would help, wouldn't it?"

"I'm on Tampa Road not far from the airport."

"Really? You aren't too far from me. If I don't see you at work tomorrow, I'll see you on Saturday."

"Okay. See you then."

"Katy?"

"Yes?" I felt breathless again.

"Sorry I woke you up. Sleep well."

"It's okay, and thanks." *And feel free to call anytime.*

I'm sure I was smiling when I went to sleep.

Chapter 6

I did get to see Ben before Saturday. He brought a patient in about nine the next morning, but there was no time to talk before his beeper went off and he had to rush away to another accident.

He did call though as soon as I got home that evening.

"Hey, how's my favorite trauma nurse?"

Having heart palpitations at the sound of your voice?

"I'm good. Did your day slow down at all?"

"Not really. The snow birds from up north are keeping us busy, and we had a horrible accident out on the interstate. I'm looking forward to the weekend off."

"I bet you are. But your job sounds so exciting to me. Maybe I'll look into being a flight nurse someday."

"That would be great. We would be a great team!"

"I didn't say anything about being on your team."

"You're already on my team, Katy. You just don't realize it yet."

Okay, there may have been a little bit of arrogance in that statement, but I kind of liked it.

"The jury is still out on that one. I have to find out if you're a good loser first, and I'll know after the game on Saturday."

He was still laughing about that one when I closed my phone a half hour later. Ben Browning was definitely a fun person, and I couldn't wait to get to know him better.

*****

When I got off work on Friday, I drove to hospice to check on Mrs. Johnson. It was out of my way, but I'd never had a patient who moved me emotionally like she did. And I couldn't understand what it was about her that was doing it to me.

I had never been to the hospice house, but I had heard good things about it. Alex told me it was a wonderful place with a caring staff. He would visit one of his church members there on occasion. What I heard didn't do justice to what I found. The setting was so beautiful and peaceful, and when I walked in the door there was a sense of serenity. It was so unlike the ICU at the hospital where the bells and whistles of life-saving machinery never ended.

She was in a room that looked out onto a beautifully landscaped tropical terrain. It was a shame she couldn't see it, and I wondered why they put a comatose patient in a room with a view. Then I noticed the building was built so all the rooms had the same view. Besides, if Mrs. Johnson would have had family, the view would have been comforting to them.

She looked more frail than when I had seen her at the hospital. But there, the IVs had kept her hydrated. Here, everything was stopped, so nature could take its course. I noticed her breathing was regular, and when I took her hand, my fingers went automatically to her wrist where I felt a pulse that was rapid, but regular, and still strong.

"Mrs. Johnson? It's Katy from the hospital. Your lawyer told me they were bringing you here to hospice. It's a beautiful place…I wish you could open your eyes and see it. You have a beautiful view outside your room and there's a swan swimming in a pond. I brought my book with me, and I'd like to read to you again. I hope its okay with you that I read to you. For some reason, I think it's something you're enjoying."

I read to her for about twenty minutes again. As before, there was still no response.

*****

I woke up nervous on Saturday morning. It had been a long time since I'd been on a real date, and I started to fret about what I was going to wear. This was something new for me. Jeans and a sweatshirt or t-shirt always seemed appropriate for a ball game. But not today.

I wished then I had told Abby about going with Ben. She would have loaned me something nice to wear and told me what make up to put on. But it was too late now. I would just have to wing it.

I found a white v-neck top in the back of my closet. It had some lace at the neckline, and I remembered wearing it to Abby's bridal shower a few years ago. It didn't look too bad but I threw it in the dryer with a dryer sheet to freshen it up. With a pair of khakis and my light jean jacket on top of it, I looked not too dressed down or dressed up.

Then I remembered the multi colored scarf Abby had given me for Christmas. It had a little bit of Yankee blue in it so I wrapped it loosely around my neck. It was still cool out, but if it got too warm I could shed the jacket and the scarf.

I dug an old tube of mascara out of my make up bag. Abby says mascara makes my eyes look like dark chocolate instead of milk chocolate, so I gave my lashes a couple of swipes. I've always been pretty low maintenance. Then, after my hair fell out from the chemo when I was sixteen, I realized there really are more important things in life than wasting time on appearances.

Looking in the mirror one last time, I noticed I still had some pink in my cheeks from the walk on the beach a couple days earlier. I was ready.

Except for shoes! I had forgotten about shoes. I have my nurses' shoes, my walking shoes, a half dozen pairs of flip-flops, and two pairs of what I call my church shoes. I usually wear flip flops or my sneakers with my jeans, and the one pair of dress flats with the khakis. Neither one seemed appropriate for today.

It was noon and I had one hour to find shoes or completely change my outfit to something more casual. There was a discount shoe store about a mile from my home. That seemed to be my best option. Slipping on my old flip flops, I grabbed my car keys and headed out the door. By the time I got there I was angry with myself. The sneakers would have been fine. But I was here now, so I might as well look around for a few minutes. It would be better than going home and sitting around for an hour just waiting and fretting.

I tried on leftover sandals from the summer before, wedged ankle booties (not worn often in Florida), and a pair of Converse tennis shoes. Nothing seemed to work, and I was getting ready to give up when the attendant finally approached me.

"Can I help you?"

She was young and looked like she was fashion savvy, so I threw caution to the wind and asked her what she would wear with the outfit I had on.

"I have just the thing. What size do you wear?"

Five minutes later I walked out wearing a pair of cute woven canvas flats. They were comfortable too. Abby was going to be so proud of me when I told her about this day.

Ben was waiting in a chair on my deck when I got there. It was just a few minutes after one.

"There you are! I was beginning to think you ditched me."

"Just had a last minute errand to run. You ready to go?"

"I've been ready for five whole days. I thought this day would never get here. You look nice, but I really expected you to be wearing a Yankees sweat shirt."

"I have one. I can put it on if you'd like me to. And I have an extra one my dad left here. You could wear it. We could be Twinkie Yankee fans."

"Come on, you crazy Yankee. I hear my Astros have won four in a row."

"Their winning streak is over today, Cowboy. Where's your car?" I hadn't seen an unfamiliar one when I drove down my street. "Or are you going to fly me there in the chopper? Where did you land it?"

He very formally held out his crooked arm for me.

"For a lady as fair as you, my best chariot awaits you."

It was a big black Dodge truck. What did I expect? The man was from Texas.

Chapter 7

It was an amazing day and an equally exciting game. The score was tied at the end of the eighth inning. The Astros were up to bat first and brought in two runners. Ben wanted to leave right then.

"There's no way they're going to catch us now. The Yankees are known to be horrible under pressure. Your only consolation is that if my team wins, you don't have to pay for the next date."

"We aren't leaving this game until it's over, Cowboy! My team still has a chance, and I'm all about chances. I've overcome all kinds of odds in my life, and I know it can be done."

"What odds have you overcome?"

"Maybe I'll tell you someday. Right now my Yankees need my full attention."

The Yankees had two on base and two outs when their power hitter came up to bat. If anyone could bring the Yankees home it would be him.

He had one strike and two balls when my phone rang.

I was tempted to let it ring, but it was Carly. I knew she would just keep calling if I didn't answer.

"Katy, are you still coming to pick me up tonight?"

"Yes…but I'm at the ballgame right now. I'll be there by seven like I promised you."

"Okay." I heard her sigh. "I just thought maybe you could come earlier. I'm bored."

"I need to go sweetie; see you soon."

It was when I snapped the phone shut that I heard the bat make contact with the ball. I was on my feet. It was going left and long. As the guy on second rounded third and headed home, I heard the ball hit leather. The power hitter flew out!

The Astro fans, few as there were, went crazy.

"I can't believe this! It was almost to the fence!"

Ben was right next to me and I heard him whisper in my ear.

"The key word is "almost". Sorry, pretty girl. Your team loses! But if it's any consolation I'll take you to the best restaurant in town right after this."

I tried not to pout. And I was grateful he wasn't one of those guys who gloats. Well, not too much.

"I still like you, even if you do have a loser team."

"They aren't a loser team, they just had a bad day."

"I'm sorry. Really, I am. But I'm still puzzled about how a girl can be such a passionate baseball fan. Are you sure you don't have a boyfriend on the team? I saw you watching that pitcher an awful lot."

"I just appreciate a good pitching arm."

"Okay…if you say so. Do you want to go somewhere for dinner? I'll even let you pick the place since you're feeling so bad about your team."

"I'm sorry. I can't go to dinner with you Ben."

"Why? You aren't that upset are you?" He was so serious, I had to laugh.

"No, I'm not upset. But I promised my little sister I would pick her up at seven. She wants to go shopping and out for pizza."

When the game was over we had sat back down on the bleachers, and were letting people walk around us as they left the stadium. I was in no hurry to leave and Ben didn't seem to be either.

"Can't your little sister go out with her own friends?"

"She's only ten. Her friends don't drive yet."

"Ten? You actually have a ten year old sister?"

"Yes. And she gets snippy if I don't follow through on the promises I make to her."

"Snippy, huh? That must run in the family."

"Hey, I apologized for that, and you said you'd forgive me if I went on a date with you."

"But this date isn't over, and you're telling me I have to take you home already. You know I'm going to expect you to finish it. How about tomorrow afternoon?"

"I can't. I promised Carly I'd take her to the beach."

"Is Carly the little sister who takes precedence over me?"

"She is and does. Sorry, but she's a very important person in my life."

"Okay, so we're down to tomorrow evening. Are you and Carly doing something then too?"

"Don't you think we should leave before they lock us in here?"

"That would be fun." But he took my hand and put it in the crook of his arm as we left the stadium. "So what about tomorrow evening?"

"I was going to see Mrs. Johnson tomorrow evening. Did I tell you they sent her to hospice?"

"I went up to neuro yesterday to see her. One of the nurses told me she'd been discharged."

By the time we reached my house, I had filled him in on our mutual patient, and we decided to go see her the next evening. Then we'd finish today's date by going out to eat. Ben walked me to my door and unlocked it for me.

"I'm sorry I couldn't go out to dinner with you tonight, but I do have time if you want to come in for a soda."

"I thought you'd never ask. Do you have a picture of that little sister who's so important to you? Little sisters must be very special people."

"This one is very important to me. I always wanted one when I was little. This one came into my life at just the right time."

"How so?"

"That's a long story. I'll have to tell you about it some time. Do you want a glass for this soda?"

"No, I'm good. I had a really good time today."

"It was fun, even if I did have to spend it with a cowboy who cheered for the other team."

"Maybe by the end of summer you can convince me you have the better team."

"You can count on that."

"That means I can count on still seeing you this summer?" We were standing in my living room, looking at the pictures of my family when he turned around and looked at me. I felt a little flustered and backed away.

"Don't move away. Stay right where you are, so I can look at you for a minute."

He put his soda down on the end table, took mine out of my hand, and put it down too.

"Come here."

We both moved a step toward each other. Taking me in his arms, he studied my face for a few seconds. "You are really pretty, do you know that?"

"Thank you…you aren't bad looking either, for a Texas cowboy."

"I can't wait till tomorrow evening. I'll be thinking about you every minute till then."

"Every minute?"

"I have no doubt." He pulled me closer and held me with his arms around my waist for a few seconds. He studied my face with those blue eyes that looked like deep pools of water then let me go. I could have stayed longer.

"I really have to go?"

"I wish you didn't, but I need to go too. I can't disappoint my little sister."

"O-kaaay." He drew it out like a sad little boy would do. I walked him to the door, still holding his hand.

"Thanks for today, Ben. It was fun. I'll see you tomorrow."

"Tomorrow is a long time from now." I had to smile.

When I closed the door, I decided the perfect life would be like one long first date; a life that contained a spark of promise, a connection that felt electrical, and just enough desire to make a girl feel like she was glowing.

Chapter 8

Carly was waiting for me when I got to Mama Beth and Alex's house. They asked me to come in and visit for awhile, but I could tell Carly was anxious to get going.

Their home had been my home during my first two years of college and for the year I was recuperating from the bone marrow transplant. Mom and Dad wanted me to stay in Philadelphia with them after the transplant, but were understanding when I told them I wanted to stay in Florida. They and my brothers flew down for a weekend every month to see me, and my two families became like one big one during that time. I recognize how rare that is and am so grateful for it.

Carly and I went to the International Mall first. There was one store there that she just couldn't get enough of. She'd been taught not to beg for things, but when I saw her looking longingly at a little charm bracelet, I couldn't help myself.

She was only two when they used her harvested cord blood for my transplant. A few years later when she got older, I asked everyone not to tell her about it. I was afraid if I ever relapsed, she would think the gift she gave me wasn't "good enough." No kid should have to deal with something that heavy.

We stopped and got the pizza and a movie on the way home. She had a bedtime, and even though I always tried to follow the rules with her, enforcing them was one of the areas where I was a little weak. It didn't really matter, she usually fell asleep before the movie was over anyways.

After I tucked her into my bed, I sat and looked at her for a few minutes. She's a beautiful little girl with blond curls and blue eyes. She looks like her dad. She and Alex are the only blonds in the family. Abby and I are both brunettes, like our respective birth mothers, and our brothers are all from different ethnic backgrounds. Jon is biracial and my brothers came from an orphanage in Haiti. I find it remarkable that it isn't common blood that makes a family, it's love that does it.

I thought about Ben and realized I didn't know anything about his family. He told me, when we were talking on the phone, that he grew up in Texas, but had left when he graduated from high school to join the Air Force. He said he did four years of active duty and they paid for his education to become a pilot. But he hadn't mentioned family.

I decided to call him. I wanted to get to know him better.

The phone rang several times (and I was beginning to wonder if he had found someone else to finish our date) before he answered. He sounded sleepy. I didn't even say hello.

"I'm so sorry. I woke you, didn't I?"

"Is this payback for me waking you the other night?"

Funny, even when he's tired. I really like this guy.

"Of course! Why should you be asleep when I'm not?"

"Where's the kid sister?"

"In my bed, sound asleep."

"I wish.......oh never mind what I wish."

I think I knew what he was wishing.

We might have to talk about what I consider appropriate dating behavior.

"I'm calling to tell you I wish we could have spent more time together today, and I wanted to thank you for taking me to the game. It was fun."

"I had fun too. We're still going to see Mrs. Johnson tomorrow, right?"

"I'm planning on it. I'm wondering, do you think it's kind of weird for us to be going on a date to a hospice to see a lady we don't even know?"

"No, I'm actually looking forward to it. I have something I want to tell her."

"What?"

"I want to thank her for bringing us together."

I felt the tears spring to my eyes. Ben Browning was definitely an unusual man.

"Katy? You still there?"

"Yes. I was just thinking about what a sweet, sensitive man you are. How did you get that way?"

"Sweet and sensitive? Don't tell the other guys, okay? It could ruin my macho reputation."

"I like sweet and sensitive."

"You don't like macho?"

"I like the way you wear it."

I heard the smile in his voice and knew it was in his eyes.

"I like you too, Katy."

"Good night, Ben."

"Sleep well."

I danced all the way to bed.

*****

Carly and I slept late, but made it to church, just in time. She went to children's church, and I found a seat beside Abby and Brett.

I love our church. And it isn't just because my stepdad is the pastor. It's a huge congregation, and Alex has been the pastor for over twenty years. It's an independent church, and their main goal has always been to reach out to the community around it. Recently, we have also begun to support small congregations in other countries.

When our church started to do the foreign missions ministry, many of the members began to go on mission trips to help out. They came home with amazing stories about how God was working overseas in ways we sometimes don't see in America. Several of the families had even adopted children from the countries they had visited.

I have always wanted to go on one of the trips, but my doctors encouraged me to stay away from that. I guess they think my immune system will be impaired forever. When I argued with them, they told me that leukemia is never cured, but it can be kept in remission. I still want to go on a mission trip some day. And I know…if I can't have kids, I will adopt.

After church, we all went out for lunch. Jon still lives at home, even though he's a freshman at UT, so there were nine of us, including Kyle and Konnor. We crowded around two tables we pushed together. Since I've lived in Tampa, our Sunday dinners have always been the favorite part of my week. I don't get to go every week, because of work, but I always look forward to it. Sometimes we even have extended family who join us. It's the one time of the week when we can share with the rest of the family what's going on in our respective lives.

After we ate, we all decided to go to Caladesi to look for shells for Konnor and Kyle's sandbox at home. Carly rode with me since the beach had originally been our plan, but I told her she would have to ride home with her mom and dad.

"Why?"

"I might have to leave early."

"Why?"

"I'm going to go visit a lady who is sick."

"Can I go with you?"

I think the child would live with me if she could!

"Not this time, peanut. Mama said you don't have your homework done for tomorrow."

"But it's boring."

"You still have to do it. Sometimes I have to do boring things I don't want to do too."

"Like what?"

"Clean my house."

"I'll help you clean your house, if you help me do my homework!"

"Oh Carly-girl, you have an answer to all of life's problems, don't you?"

If we hadn't arrived at the beach, she would have had time to solve all of mine.

Chapter 9

Ben was waiting for me again when I got home. I felt bad and apologized. I didn't want him to think I was a chronically late person.

I asked him to come in while I changed my clothes. I bought my townhouse soon after I got a job at the hospital. My parents had given me a down payment for it when I graduated from college. Unfortunately, it was a mess. Carly and I had left in a hurry before church.

"Excuse my clutter. Carly and I partied pretty hard last night, as you can tell. Ten year olds can get really wild; then we overslept and were almost late for church."

"Well at least you went to church. I don't know many party girls who are able to do that after a night of having fun."

"You know a lot of party girls?"

"I've known a few. Not my favorite kind of girls."

"Sounds like an interesting story. There are some sodas in the 'frig if you want one. I'll just be a minute."

"Okay."

Now I had to figure out what to wear again. If this kept up, I might have to break down and take Abby on a shopping trip with me. I pulled on a pair of brown dress pants and a light weight tan sweater, a leftover from my college years. I really need to get some more color in my wardrobe. But the fun red necklace and earrings my mom bought me for Christmas brightened up the outfit.

When I returned to my living room, Ben was looking at my family pictures again. I have them hanging on almost every wall in my house. I'm about as original with home décor as I am with my wardrobe.

"Who are all of these people?"

"Mostly family."

"You have a huge family!"

"Yep, it's great. Did you figure out which one is Carly?"

"She has to be the blond princess who manages to get herself into almost all the pictures."

I had to laugh. He had described her perfectly.

"That would be her!"

"So come tell me who everyone else is."

"This could take awhile."

"Mrs. Johnson won't care if we're late."

So I told him who everyone was. It took awhile and there were a couple of times when he looked confused.

"So what ya'll *(there was that Texan twang*) did was take two separate families and make one big family out of them?"

"Yea, I guess that's how you could describe it."

"And you are the common factor in both families?"

"Lucky girl, am I not?"

"You are. So how and when did this all happen?"

"Now that's an even longer story!"

"Can you tell me on the way?"

"It would take longer than that."

I just wasn't ready to tell him the whole story. I don't know if I was afraid I would scare him away or afraid I wouldn't. As much as I liked him, there was still that nagging feeling that I shouldn't be falling in love with anyone. I felt like my life was too uncertain, and I wasn't convinced it's better to love and lose, than to never love at all.

*****

When we got to the hospice house, Ben was as impressed as I had been. The lights were dim, and there was soft comforting music being played over the intercom. The aroma was even soothing, I think it was lavender.

We stopped at the nurse's station and asked to speak to Mrs. Johnson's nurse. We explained to her who we were and asked if anybody else had been in to see her.

"Actually, there was an older lady here last night. She said she was a neighbor. She came with a younger man who introduced himself as the visitation minister at her church."

"Oh, I'm so glad someone else is coming to see her. That's why we're here. We felt bad because she didn't have anyone else to be with her. Has her condition changed at all?"

"We can tell her body is beginning to shut down. It's natural for that to happen at this stage."

"Do you think she's in any pain?"

"She doesn't appear to be uncomfortable when we care for her. We're giving her medications that would relieve any pain or pressure she might have from the head injury."

"That's good. Do you have any idea how much longer she can last? We're both in the medical field, but hospice is a specialty we don't know much about."

"It could be anytime now, or she could last for a few more days."

"Isn't it difficult for you, as a nurse, to be around death all the time?"

"No, not really. I like to think I'm giving comfort at a time in life when it's needed most. It can actually be very rewarding work."

"Well, thank you for helping her and taking care of her. I'm sure if she could tell you, she'd say the same thing. Is it okay if we go see her?"

"Of course, we have unrestricted visiting hours."

Ben took my hand and squeezed it as we walked down the hall to Mrs. Johnson. I really could not think of another man I had ever met who would take me on a date to a hospice facility.

What was it about this lady that had touched both our hearts?

When we reached her room, I went ahead to the side of her bed and took her hand.

"Mrs. Johnson, it's Katy again. I brought someone with me to see you. It's Ben, the helicopter pilot who picked you up at your house."

Ben went to the other side of the bed and picked up her other hand.

"Hello, Mrs. Johnson. I went to see you at the hospital on Friday so I could tell you something, but you were already gone. When Katy told me she was coming tonight, I wanted to come see you too. I need to tell you something." He took a deep breath and glanced at me.

"You probably don't realize it, but you're responsible for something really wonderful. When I flew you to the hospital this past week, I was able to meet Katy for the first time. I think the two of us are going to be really good friends. It's like you introduced us to each other, and I want to thank you for that."

I watched him as he talked to her. I felt almost mesmerized by the kindness and gentleness I heard in his voice. I could feel the tears streaming down my cheeks, and I didn't even care. My mom told me once that crying easily was evidence that I felt deeply, and it was a rare and beautiful gift.

Ben's words held the answer to the question that had plagued me all week. Now I understood why this lady was so special. God had used her, even in death, to do something wonderful.

I have believed my whole life that God created us for Himself because He longed to have a relationship with us. But I also believe we were created to do something good for the people whose lives we touch. Mrs. Johnson had fulfilled that purpose at least once. It was the day she brought Ben and me together. I could only hope she somehow knew it.

We sat down beside her bed for awhile, and I read to her. The last thing I read was a verse from Isaiah. It's one of my favorite verses because it reminds us to fear nothing; because no matter what we go through in life, God will be at our side.

Mrs. Johnson died later that night.

Chapter 10

When Ben and I left the hospice, it had grown almost cold, and it was dark outside. Cold is so rare in Florida, so when we do get it, I usually bundle up and take a walk in it. But I don't think either one of us was in the mood to walk. I felt emotionally drained. Mrs. Johnson's nurse had said it was an honor to help a patient make the transition from this life to the next one as peaceful as possible. But I still did not understand how hospice nurses could care for the dying, day after day.

We ended up at a bookstore with a coffee shop in it. Neither one of us felt much like eating either, so we ordered hot chocolate and found a small couch in a corner. We spent the rest of our evening talking. We never did look at any books.

We spent the evening getting to know each other. I told him what I knew about my birth. Mama Beth had grown up with a physically and emotionally abusive alcoholic father. So when she got pregnant by a high school boyfriend, she felt like her only option was to give me up for adoption. She was so fearful of her dad and had good reason. He went to prison for attempted murder.

I shared with Ben the joy of growing up as a much loved adopted child in Philadelphia. I had a wonderful childhood. My adopted twin brothers, David and Doug, and I are still close. I didn't talk about being diagnosed with leukemia though. I still wasn't ready to share that part of the story with him. It seems to weigh people down, and they usually don't know what to say. I didn't want to do that to him, not yet.

"Okay, your turn. Tell me about Texas and your family."

He grew up on a small horse ranch in West Texas. He said his parents were "earth people", growing all their own food and living off the land.

"I guess you could say they were modern day hippies. I have a sister, Sage, who's ten years older than me. We grew up without a lot of discipline, but a whole lotta love. "

"That doesn't sound like a bad way to grow up."

"It wasn't. As far back as I can remember, I have good memories of the years we lived on our little farm. I think my parents were as close to soul mates as two people can get. There were a lot of evenings when my Daddy would take Mama's hand and say, "Come on darlin', let's go for a ride." Sage and I would sit on the front porch and watch them ride off into the sunset, on their horses. Sometimes they didn't come back until I was asleep."

"That's a beautiful memory for a kid to have. Actually I think the best gift parents can give their children is to love each other. I always knew my adoptive parents loved each other, even though they weren't openly affectionate. What other memories do have as a kid?"

"I remember having a lot of freedom, and I got to be on a horse every second I wasn't at school or asleep. I even road my horse to school sometimes. Little country schools like the one I went to were open to almost anything, as long as you came.

"You rode your horse to school? Where did it stay while you were in class all day?"

"It was an old school and still had a well. I would tie him to a tree and go out at recess and lunch to give him a drink."

"That's like something out of *Little House on the Prairie*."

"Yeah… it was a different world. My parents taught me to love nature and we probably spent more time outside looking at the stars and the moon than other kids watched television. We lived simply, but we were happy. Only problem with parents who are so laid back is that there wasn't a lot of money."

"Money doesn't buy happiness."

"I know that. But it does put food on the table."

"So is your family still in Texas?"

He paused for a few minutes and got that faraway look in his eyes again. I had seen it one other time.

"No. My parents died in an auto accident when I was ten, and I went to live with my maternal grandmother. Sage had already left home and moved to California."

"Oh, no. How horrible for you."

"It was a long time ago, and I had a wonderful Gramma."

"Had?"

"She died when I was in Afghanistan."

"Oh no! I am so sorry. Was her death sudden?"

"To me it was, but not to her. When I graduated from high school she encouraged me to join the air force so I could get an education. My parents died penniless, and she raised me on her Social Security check and by cleaning houses. But she raised me right. She made me go to church and study hard, and she wanted me to go to college."

"She must have been a wonderful lady."

"Mrs. Johnson reminded me of her."

I reached over, took his hand, and held it while he finished his story.

"When I came home from basic training, she sat me down and told me she'd been diagnosed with stomach cancer. She knew it when she encouraged me to join the air force. I wanted to find a way out of my commitment, but she said she didn't want me to do that. She wanted me to have something to keep me busy after she was gone, and she really wanted me to remember her like she was when she was healthy. Even when she was dying, she was thinking only about me. It was because of her that I have such a deep respect for elderly people. They are so wise."

"I wish I could have met her."

"I wish she could have met you, too."

"So was anyone with her when she died? Was your sister there? Did you get to come home from Afghanistan for her funeral?"

"We had a wonderful church family. It was a small congregation, but they all helped each other through everything in life. There were several people who took care of her in the end, and they postponed her memorial service for six months, until I got home. She did want me to have that closure."

"I'm glad you got to go to her funeral, and that you had something to keep your mind busy after she was gone. She *was* a wise lady wasn't she? So you spent four years in the Air Force?

"I'm still in. I did my four years of active duty, and have been in the reserves for eight years. I go to a training weekend once a month and to two weeks of field training exercises once a year. The Air Force paid for me to learn to fly. I've been called back into active duty twice in the past six years. The first time was for eighteen months; the second time was for six months. The Air Force has been good for me. It taught me a lot."

"And your sister?"

"I haven't seen her since my parents died. That was twenty years ago. She was always kind of headstrong, and all she ever wanted was to get away from Texas and the ranch. Before she left, she was insolent and cynical about everything. After my parents died, she would call Gramma a couple times a year. Then when I was about fifteen, the phone calls stopped."

"Oh, Ben. I'm sorry. That's so sad. Do you ever think about finding her?"

"Every once in a while, but I really doubt if she wants to be found. The last time she called, she told Gramma she was in Vegas working as a dancer at a club. It about broke Gamma's heart. Maybe someday I'll try to find her again."

"So you don't have any family?"

"I have a couple aunts and uncles and some cousins in Texas, but I haven't seen them for years either."

"So, how old are you? Thirty?"

"Yep. Had the big 3-0 in November."

"You've been through a lot in thirty years. Why did you choose flying as a career?"

"One day when I was about seven, my sister and I were out riding and I saw a crop duster on the big ranch next to our little farm. I was fascinated with it. I remember telling my sister it looked like the pilot was having fun. He would fly in real low then at the end of the field he would take the plane almost straight up. I told her I wanted to do that someday." He got that far-away look in his eyes again. "I remember her saying she was going to get on a plane someday too, and fly far away. I guess both of us had dreams that came true."

"So you've been so busy flying for the past twelve years that you haven't had time to get married?"

He grinned. "You girls are funny, you always want the dating history! I came close to getting married once, but things just didn't work out. Guess that was good or I wouldn't be here with you right now, would I?"

"Guess not. Can I ask you something else?"

"I think I already told you everything. I don't share this stuff very often."

"Denny told me you're kind of private. He also told me that a lot of the nurses find you attractive and would love to go out with you, but you don't ask them. Why me? You knew absolutely nothing about me when you asked me to go to the diner with you."

"I watched you with Mrs. Johnson. You were so gentle and kind with her, and so upset when you found out she was alone. You weren't just doing your job. You cared, and it showed. I knew there was something different about you…a depth of feeling that most people don't have."

I still had his hand in mine. I looked at it. It was a strong hand, yet gentle enough to give comfort to a dying old lady. I wanted to hold it forever.

"I think you are the one with depth. Most of the guys I know are so…superficial. But then most guys haven't had to deal with the losses in life like you have."

"Gramma told me that difficult times can make you a better person or a bitter one. She also told me she expected me to be a better man than most. I loved her so much. She's the one who taught me that touching and loving are the very essence of life. I think her love for me made me who I am today."

"I think you're probably right."

"And I also think I need to get you home. Don't you have to work tomorrow?"

"I do. You too?

"No, I got a three day weekend, because I worked so much last week."

"Aren't you the lucky you! You going to do anything special?

"Probably just day dream about the prettiest girl I've ever met."

I don't blush often, but he seemed to enjoy it when I did.

We were quiet on the way home. It was a comfortable silence, though. We had both learned a lot about the other in one evening, and I had a feeling that he was processing it all, as I was.

He walked me to my door and unlocked it for me. When I turned to tell him good night, he pulled me into his arms and held me close for a few seconds. Then he took my face in his hands and looked at me…before he kissed my forehead and both my cheeks. I didn't want him to stop, but he did.

"Katy?"

"Hmm?"

"My Gramma told me once that we don't choose love, it chooses us. And once it grabs hold, it doesn't let go. I think it has chosen us,"

"How can we know it's love that has grabbed hold of us Ben?"

"I know because I don't want to let go of you."

I couldn't stop myself, I reached out and touched his cheek. I wanted to pull him towards me and hold him forever. But he simply took my hand, opened it up and kissed my palm.

"Good night, Katy. Sleep well.

Later, after I was in bed, I opened my hand and could still feel his lips where he had planted that kiss. I'm not sure I slept at all; I felt like I was in a dream state. Like I was being captivated by Ben Browning. My head was full of him, and I knew if I allowed it, my heart would be too.

Chapter 11

He sent flowers to me at work the next day. The card said, "Still dreaming about you. Talk to you tonight."

It was a long day.

I expected a phone call from him at bedtime, since that's when he usually called, but he was sitting on my deck again when I got home from work. His feet were up on the rail and he looked quite at home. He had a bag of take out Chinese on his lap.

"Excuse me, sir, but I believe this is the third time in the last three days I've found you loitering at my front door."

"Can't help it. The girl who lives here has invaded my dreams. I'm hoping she's hungry and likes Chinese."

"The girl who lives here loves Chinese, and she's starving."

"You're always starving! Good thing I brought double of everything."

"Sounds wonderful."

I pushed my door open, and hung my work bag on the hook behind the door.

"Come on in and make yourself comfortable. As you can tell, I still haven't cleaned up the party mess from the weekend. Can you get us something to drink while I change?"

"I can, but first I need you to stop and come over here so I can show you something." He was standing with his back against the door we had just come through. When I walked toward him he placed the sacks of take out on the counter. When I got close to him, he took my hands and put them on his chest. He pulled me close to him and just looked at me.

"You're so pretty…do you know that?"

My throat had grown dry. "Thank you." It came out in a whisper.

He took my face in his hands again, like he had done the night before, and I watched as he lowered his head to mine. I felt his lips brush mine. He lifted his head slightly and looked at me again. There was a question in his eyes. I didn't move away so I think he had the answer he wanted. It was a tender kiss, soft and sweet, and one I'm sure I'll never forget.

It was better than I imagined it would be, and I had to push him gently away, or I would have stayed there, in his arms, all night.

"Wait. Don't leave me yet. You have to know, I've wanted to do that from the minute I first saw you. You have very inviting lips. Can I kiss them one more time?

"I'm not sure we can do just one more."

"You're probably right." He let go of me. "Go change, and we'll eat."

I shut my bedroom door after I went in. I needed to catch my breath. I needed to be alone and think for a few minutes. I needed to figure out, in my own mind, where my limits would be with Ben—at least for tonight. I had only known him for one week, but I was already having feelings for him I had never had with anyone before. I felt a strong emotional connection with him from the beginning, and the week had only deepened that. Now I was sensing physical needs I had never had to deal with. I had dated my share of guys, but none of them did to my heart and body what Ben was doing to it.

"Katy, you okay in there?"

"Yeah. I'll be right out." I knew I was going to have to talk to him about what I was feeling. I had to be honest with him. I had decided a long time ago I wanted to be a virgin when I got married. Ben had to know that, and probably tonight.

I slipped into my jeans and a long sleeved cotton shirt, and returned to the kitchen.

He was standing with his back to the sink, sipping on a soda. I stopped for a minute and really looked at him. Not just his eyes, all of him. In his jeans and a t-shirt that hugged his chest,it was obvious he had a very good build, probably honed by hours of training for the reserves. His blond hair was thick, and even though it was cut short, I could tell it probably had some curl in it. His tanned face made his eyes look bluer than I remembered. I wondered if he had been to the beach today.

His lips were full, and I already knew how they felt on mine. His shoulders were wide, and I knew what it felt like to be pulled tightly against his chest.

He seemed to be studying me as I was studying him. I had to pull my eyes away from his. I could see the intensity in them, and they were inviting me to come closer. They were like a magnetic force that pulled at me, wanting to hypnotize me. And I wanted to be pulled, to be put under his spell, more than I had ever wanted anything else in my life.

He pushed away from the counter, and I knew if I didn't move away from him, I would be back in his arms. I had to break the spell that had both of us in need.

"I see you found my dishes and the utensils. Thank for bringing supper. I didn't have a clue what I was going to eat when I got home, probably a bowl of cereal."

"I noticed you don't have much to eat in the 'frig. No wonder you're so thin."

"I'm not thin."

"Let me look at you again." He stopped where he was and looked at me.

"You're right. In some spots you're a little rounded. But it looks good on you."

"Do guys get lessons on how to make a girl blush?"

"I think maybe it just takes the right guy to make you blush."

"Whatever. (Carly's favorite word) Let's eat before I starve to death here. You want to watch TV while we eat?"

"No, I want to watch you."

I really needed to get him talking about something else besides me.

"So what did you do all day? Your face looks a little sunburned. Did you go to the beach?"

"I did, but I think its more windburn. The wind out there was brutal today. Am glad I wasn't flying in it."

Since he already had the table set, we sat down and opened up the boxes of food he brought.

"Have you ever had any close calls while you were flying?"

"There've been a couple of scary moments, but usually we don't go up if it looks too dangerous."

"You love your job, don't you?

"I really do. I like knowing we're making a difference in life and death situations. You know that feeling. You do it in your job too. But you haven't told me why you wanted to be a nurse. I'm surprised your parents didn't want you to do something more…lucrative, financially rewarding."

"Why would you think that?"

"I don't know. It just seems like the children of wealthy people usually follow in the footsteps of their parents. Didn't you say your dad was in business?"

"You need to meet my parents. I think they would be the same people *without* money that they are *with* money. They realize they've been blessed, simply so they can help others. Watching them help others with their money made me want to help people by going into nursing. And they wanted me to do something with my life that would bring me joy."

"I'd love to meet your parents…all of them. I'm still amazed you have so many people in your life. Do you ever wonder why things turn out the way they do? Like, why do you think God gave you four parents and took away the only two I had?"

"I wish I knew the answer to that. But I don't think God makes bad things happen…and I'm positive He's around to help us pick up the pieces when they do happen." I was picking at my food. Unlike my first date with Ben, I was more interested in the man than the food.

"So do you go to church, Ben?"

"I got away from it when I was in the military and going to school. Since I've been in Tampa I haven't taken the time to find a good one. Growing up in the small one Gramma took me to, kind of spoiled me. They were real, authentic Christians."

"There are authentic Christians in big churches too."

"I know. I've gone to a couple and I could tell they were good places with good people. But I felt really lonely going to church by myself."

"I've heard other people say that too. I need to talk to Alex about changing that. Church should be the best place for single people to find other single people."

"I personally think trauma units are good places to find other single people." He grinned at me and I felt my heart speed up again.

"You done with your food? I'll pack up the leftovers and you can take them to work with you tomorrow. Looks like there's enough to share with Denny."

"Denny loves good food. He'll be thrilled."

"I think Denny likes you too. The two of you seem to work well together."

"We do. He's taught me a lot about trauma nursing already."

"So, he's just a teammate to you?"

"Well, of course. Wait a minute! You aren't the jealous type, are you? He's married, you know."

"I know he's married. I'm just jealous because he gets to spend more time with you than I do."

"That's silly." I began to put the dishes in the dishwasher and could feel his eyes on me. "Why don't you go put some music on while I do these dishes…unless you want to do them? I have one of Gramma's old aprons around here you could wear."

"Oh no; I cooked, you clean."

After the kitchen was put back in order, we made our way to the living room and Ben once again went to my "picture wall." He seemed in awe of it, and I wondered if there was a lonely little boy inside him that longed for a family of his own again.

"So would you like to come to church with me sometime and meet my family? We get together every Sunday afternoon for lunch."

"I think maybe I'll hold off on that for awhile. Right now, I just wanna get to know you. I think making-out would be a great way to get to know each other, don't you?"

"I think we need to talk about that first."

"Doing it is a lot more fun than talking about it."

"I'm sure it is, but we still need to talk."

"What? You don't like the way I kiss?"

"I love the way you kiss. I might even like it too much."

"I didn't think it was possible to like good kissing too much."

"Come over here and sit down beside me, okay?"

He could have sat on the other end of the sofa, but he didn't. He had to sit down, right next to me. I could feel the heat from him and the smell of his aftershave mixed with the scent of Chinese food. I could feel where his leg was touching mine, and I desperately wanted to skip the talking and just spend some time kissing.

"Ben, how long have we known each other?"

"It will be one week tomorrow. And a lovely week it has been." He reached out and brushed the hair away from my eyes.

"I think so too. We've shared a lot of emotions and unusual experiences in one short week, haven't we? We had fun at the ball game, and we've cried with Mrs. Johnson.

"It has been a little unusual, hasn't it?"

"Yes, it has. And I think, because it's been so intense, we've grown close, very fast. And to be honest, it kind of scares me."

"Do I scare you?"

"No, you don't scare me. It's just…well, you seem, intense. That intensity scares me a little bit because it has drawn me to you so quickly. And I'm having feelings for you I don't know how to handle."

"Don't fight your feelings if they're good ones, Katy. Just go with them. I have them too, and I love what I'm feeling. Going with them will help us get to know each other better. Like right now. I want to kiss you, and if you'd let me do it, we would probably learn some new and wonderful things about each other."

"Oh, you are a smooth talker, Cowboy."

"Just sayin' what's on my mind."

"I want to kiss you too, Ben. But I'm afraid we won't be able to stop with the kissing and it will lead to things I don't want to do."

"Things like what?"

"You aren't making this easy for me. Let me explain it this way. I read a book once about something called the dance of intimacy."

"That sounds like fun." I could see the smile playing at the corners of his mouth.

"Stop it. I'm trying to be serious here."

"Sorry. Go ahead."

"Anyway, the book said there are several steps in the dance of intimacy, and if you go through those steps too quickly or skip over one of them, you miss out on the full enjoyment of the dance. When you miss a step, you can never get back the magic of those moments. They're gone forever so you've lost something very precious. Is this making any sense to you?"

"So far, I think I'm following you. What I hear you saying is that we have started our dance of intimacy and you want it to be a slow dance?"

"Yes. I want to take things slow and savor every minute with you. I don't want instant gratification. For that to happen, we're going to have to keep ourselves out of compromising situations, like the one I feel we're in right now."

"Okay…I hear what you're saying. But you're 26 and I'm 30. We're both adults with feelings and needs."

Oh, no. He's going to tell me I'm being silly and naïve. Am I? Am I going to lose him if I don't give in to his needs?

I felt like I was going to cry, and my face must have reflected it because he reached out and took my hand.

"It's okay, Katy. I understand. And because we're both adults, I think we can control our actions. I'll do my best to keep my needs under control because I already admire you, and want to please you. Okay?"

"Thank you, Ben. And I'll do my best too, even though you are the sexiest cowboy I've ever met."

"Me? Sexy? Well now, ma'am, that's just about the nicest thing any girl has ever said to me." The excessive Texan twang was a little much and I couldn't help but laugh at him.

"Can I ask you something personal, Katy?"

"Sure."

"You don't have to tell me, but I'd like to know for future reference. Have you ever completed a dance of intimacy with anyone else?"

"No, Ben, I haven't. I decided a long time ago I wanted to be a virgin when I got married. So, there's a place where the dance stops…until I'm married."

"Wow. You are even more amazing than I have been imagining. Come here."

He pulled me close to him and kissed my forehead.

"Katy Clinton, I think you are an incredible woman, and because of that, I promise I will never do anything with you that makes you feel uncomfortable."

I lifted my head off his shoulder and looked up at him.

"Thank you, Ben. Now, can you give me another one of those kisses I already love?" And he did. And the second one was even more tender and sweet than the first one.

He got up and pulled me to my feet.

"I believe our dance of intimacy has begun, my dear, and I hope it never ends."

"I think it's going to be a wonderful dance."

"I'm gonna leave now… so I can think about this. But I need to know when I can see you again." He slipped his arms around me again. I was glad I'd been honest with him, I already loved being in his arms.

"When is your next day off?"

"Thursday and Friday. Yours?

"Wednesday and Thursday."

"So Thursday, it is?"

"But that's so far away!"

"I know, but you can call me every night until then."

"Deal! If it's nice on Thursday, do you want to go flying with me?"

"In the chopper?"

"No, silly. In my plane."

"You own your own plane?"

"Well…flying *is* my passion. At least it was until you came along. How about I show you the Gulf of Mexico from a twin engine?

"It sounds amazing. Oh Ben…this is going to be so much fun."

"Flying or falling in love?"

"Both!"

Chapter 12

I called Abby Tuesday night, as soon as I got off work. I knew Ben would call later on, and I didn't want anything to interfere with that.

"Hey Abby, you busy?"

"Just finishing up the dishes. Brett's playing with the boys. What's going on?"

"You doing anything tomorrow afternoon and evening?"

"Just the usual, why?"

"I was wondering if you could get away and go shopping with me?"

"You want to go shopping? Are you sick?"

"No, I'm not sick! But I've been going through my closet, and I don't have anything nice to wear anymore. It's all old stuff, and I'm just in the mood to buy some new clothes."

"Now I know you're sick. When's the last time you bought anything new? Excluding scrubs for work."

"I know. That's why I need to go shopping. But I need your expertise."

"Honey, for you, I'll make time. What time do you want to go?"

"I'm free all day, but I know you have the boys. What's best for you?"

"Let me call Mama and see if she can watch the boys tomorrow afternoon. Brett could pick them up at her house after work, if he's free. I'll call you back later."

"Sounds good! And thanks."

"No, thank you! I've had a bad case of cabin fever this week and need to get out."

Fifteen minutes later the phone rang.

"Okay, everything's all set up. But I'm still in shock. I don't ever remember you asking me to go shopping with you. You taking a trip or something?"

"No, I told you, I just need some new clothes. Do you want me to pick you and the boys up and take you to Mama's? Then I can just drop you off at your house when we're done."

"That sounds good. One o'clock okay?"

"See you then."

I had just hung up the phone, when caller ID told me Ben was calling. I wondered if my heart was going to speed up every time he called.

"Hey, how's my little dancer doing tonight?"

"Are you making fun of me?"

"I would never do that. In fact, I've been thinking about our dance of intimacy all day today. I think I'm going to love doing it with you." I could hear the smile in his voice.

"Mmmm, it's going to be fun, isn't it? So how was your day?

"A little boring. Maybe that's why I had so much time to think about the dance."

"Okay Ben, you've made your point. I'm going to love dancing with you too."

"So what are you going to do tomorrow while I'm working hard?"

"Abby and I are going shopping. She was so excited when I called her…I think the two little boys drive her stir crazy sometimes. But they are so cute. I can't wait for you to meet them."

"I've never been around little kids very much."

"You'll love them. You know the other day when you were telling me how older people are so wise?"

"Yeah."

"Well, I think little kids are wise too. I love seeing the world through their eyes. The smallest things hold so much wonder for them. I love going to the beach with them. It's such a huge adventure for them, every time. Maybe we can take them sometime so you can see the pure pleasure on their little faces."

"I'd like that. But you'll have to teach me what to do with them."

"Honestly, Ben! If you can fly an airplane, you can play with kids. They aren't that difficult. So tell me about this plane of yours. You really own it?"

"Yes, I really own it. I bought it four years ago with thoughts that I would turn it into a business." I could hear the excitement in his voice when he talked about flying.

"What kind of business?"

"You know, flying business people around."

"How big is this plane?"

"It's a Cessna 340. I can fly four passengers at a time. That's actually what we're doing on Thursday. We're going to fly two business guys up to Tallahassee in the morning and bring them back in the evening."

"Wait a minute. On your days off at the hospital, you have another job?"

"I suppose you could call it a second job. It's more like a hobby that pays, and I do pretty well with it. I have some regulars who call me."

"Actually, you have three jobs, if you count the Reserves…why didn't you tell me this?"

"The subject didn't come up. Why? Does it matter that I have three jobs?"

"No. I guess I'm just surprised you didn't tell me, and it makes me wonder if you have any time left over to have fun."

"Katy, we've only known each other for a week. I'm sure there are lots of things we both still need to learn about each other. And yes, I do have time left over for fun. You're still okay with going with me on Thursday, right?"

"Yes. But I was thinking it would be a half hour tour of the Gulf from a little airplane, not a trip to Tallahassee. What are we going to do all day while we wait for your business men?"

"I'm sure we can find something to do to fill our time. Have you ever been there?"

"No. What's there?"

"It's our state capitol; I'm sure we can find something to do. Or we could just find a nice warm spot and practice our kissing skills. Or, if you want to, we could fly on to Vegas and get married."

The man was unbelievably irresistible, and I was glad he'd just said that on the phone instead of face to face with me. I would have been tempted to take him up on the deal, right then and there.

*****

I picked Abby up at one like we planned. By the time we dropped the boys off and spent a few minutes with Mama Beth, it was three before we got to the mall. On the way, Abby asked me what kind of clothes I wanted to buy.

"I need a couple new pairs of jeans and some pretty tops. I'm getting tired of old tee-shirts. I don't know, maybe I'll try on something kind of sexy and dressy too."

She leaned over and felt my forehead. "I don't know whether to be worried about you or happy. Wait a minute…have you met someone?"

"Well…kind of."

"How can you 'kind of' meet someone? Either you have or you haven't. Come on, girl, out with it!"

"Okay, but let's go to the coffee shop first. Maybe if I tell you about him, you'll be able to tell me what kind of clothes I need."

We both ordered a latte and found a booth. I thought it would only take me a few minutes to tell her about Ben, after all, I had only known him for a little over a week. But we were still sitting there an hour and a half later.

I don't think I've ever seen Abby speechless, but she was, stopping me once in awhile to ask me a question.

When I got done, she leaned back and sighed. "Wow. I don't know what to say. Wasn't it just last Wednesday you were feeling skeptical about getting involved with anyone? And you had already met him and didn't tell me about him!"

"I know. And I feel like I'm in shock. It has all happened so fast. I like him so much Abby, and I really think I'm falling in love. Is that possible after only one week?"

"I don't know. I've never believed in love at first sight. Brett and I were just really good friends for a long time before we got serious. I suppose it's possible. Maybe it is because the two of you have both experienced something so personal and intense through Mrs. Johnson. That experience has shown both of you the true character of the other person. But to be honest, he sounds almost too good to be true; I think I should meet him. I don't want you to get hurt."

"I'm pretty sure he wouldn't hurt me. I mean, think about it. The first ten years of his life were with parents who appreciated the simple things in life, and they showed him true love. Then he lived with a grandmother who disciplined him with love. She showed him how to work hard and gave him a strong spiritual heritage. After high school, he spent four years in active duty, most of it in Afghanistan. Then he stayed in the reserves for the past eight years so he could learn to fly. He knew it was the only way he could afford to follow his passion. I'm not sure a man can get any more solid than that!"

"You don't think it's a little strange that he's thirty and never been married?"

"No, not really. Think about it. He had to have the past ten years to adjust to all the separation and grief he had in the first twenty years of his life."

"That's true. But I still want to meet him. When can I?"

"I want to wait on the family thing for awhile. I think we'll overwhelm him, there are so many of us. But I promise, you'll be the first, after my parents, okay? And can you let this be just between you and me for awhile? I think I need some time to wrap my head around it, before I bring in the rest of the family."

"Okay, but I get to meet him first. Don't forget! Now let's go find you something decent to wear to Tallahassee tomorrow."

****

My new clothes were spread out on my bed, and I had just decided on an adorable sweater set to wear with a new pair of jean the next day when the phone rang.

"Hey, gorgeous. I'm on my way to another accident, but wanted to tell you to wear old clothes tomorrow. And bring a sweat shirt and a wind breaker too."

"Why? Aren't we flying to Tallahassee?"

"Yeah, but I don't have time to explain. I'll pick you up in the morning at seven."

Chapter 13

True to his word, he was at my door at seven. And he looked so handsome-in dress clothes! His khakis looked like he had ironed them, (I don't even own an iron!) and his black dress shirt had a logo on the pocket. I had on my oldest jeans, an old sweat shirt and a wind breaker.

"Hey babe, you look beautiful this morning." He wrapped his arms around me and gave me a hug and an electrifying good morning kiss. When I had partially recovered from the kiss, I began to sputter.

"Did you not call me last night and tell me to wear old clothes?"

"I did."

"Then why do you have on nice clothes?"

"Cause I'm on business, remember? I have my old clothes in a bag. I'll change after we get there."

"So I'm flying to Tallahassee in these scuzzy old clothes with what I assume, will be two business men in suits, and a handsome well dressed pilot?"

"Yeah, but you look fine. Are you ready?"

"Ben, I don't want to wear these old clothes on the airplane. Your customers will wonder why a bag lady is flying with them."

"That's silly. Come on, you look wonderful."

"I don't want to go looking like this…with you looking like that. Can't I wear nice clothes and change into these when I get there too?"

"Oh for heaven sakes, I didn't think you had a vain bone in your body."

"I'm not vain, I just don't like looking like this…when you look like that!"

"Like what?"

"All handsome and professional."

I saw the sparkle in his eyes before the irresistible, dimpled grin. How dare he make light of my obvious distress! I sent him what my mom calls, my evil eye. He lost the grin.

"If it will make you feel better, go put on something else. But you need to hurry. And don't forget to bring your bag lady clothes."

I heard him laugh as I huffed into my bedroom to put on my new jeans and the sweater set. I stuffed the old clothes into a gym bag.

When I got back to the kitchen, he was lounging in one of my kitchen chairs drinking a cup of coffee.

"Oh look at you now! Maybe I won't take you deep sea fishing today."

"We're going deep sea fishing? I don't know how to do that."

"Good, I'll teach you. Now let's get moving, girl. The mechanic is warming up the plane as we speak."

Before we left the house, he pulled me into his arms and gave me another kiss. It was a good thing we had someplace to go.

The small airport wasn't far from where I lived, and we were there within minutes. He parked his car in a spot close to one of the hangars.

"You ready to fly, baby?"

"I don't know, can I trust the pilot?"

"With your life. I'll be extra careful today, since I have someone so precious on board."

I felt like my heart was going to burst. He thought I was precious!

He took my hand as we walked through the hangar and out to where a shiny little jet was sitting on the tarmac. His grip on my my hand tightened.

"You like it?"

He sounded like a little boy with a favorite toy. I could hear the pride and excitement in his voice. He had told me flying was not just a job for him, it was his love.

"Very nice!"

Above the sound of the engine, he introduced me to the mechanic, then helped me into the cabin.

"Just make yourself at home while I do my safety check. My other passengers won't be here for another fifteen minutes."

I was impressed. The company my dad worked for in Philadelphia had planes like this one. They had made them available to our family for trips to New York, so we could watch the Yankees play. But this one actually belonged to Ben. I wondered if it had been a profitable business for him. I knew planes and their maintenance were expensive.

I made myself comfortable in one of the four seats in the cabin and looked out the window at a couple other planes warming up. Once again, I felt like I was almost in shock. Two weeks ago I could not have imagined myself here today with a man who had me totally captivated.

I was so absorbed in my thoughts of him that I didn't realize he was standing beside me, until I felt his hand on my shoulder.

"You okay?"

"Of course. I just feel like I'm in a dream this morning, and I'm afraid I'll wake up, and you won't be here to spend the day with me."

"Then this is a dream come true for both of us. And if I have any control over our dreams, you're stuck with me every day for the rest of our lives."

"How can you be so sure, Ben?"

"Cause I've been looking for you for a long time. The minute I saw you, I knew you were the one. Come here."

He pulled me gently to my feet and kissed me again. This time it was a hungry kiss. I felt it in every part of my body.

"Oh, Ben…."

"I know, takes your breath away, doesn't it?"

"It does. So how long will it take us to get there?"

"About an hour and a half, we'll be there by nine."

"And we're really going fishing?"

"You don't want to? It's supposed to be a beautiful day and I thought it would be fun to charter a boat and spend the day on the Gulf. I'm sorry, I should have let you decide."

"No, I want to go. You've done it before?"

"Lots of times, and I love it. I'm an outdoors guy, remember?"

"I know. I think I like that about you. And my brothers are going to love you."

"Did you bring anything to read or do while we're flying? I'm going to be kind of busy up front."

"I'll be okay."

"I know you will. I need to go down and wait for my guys now. See you in Tallahassee."

*****

The flight was beautiful, and it was the smoothest airplane ride I had ever taken. I spent a little time getting to know the other two passengers, but they soon became engrossed in business talk. That was okay with me. My thoughts were on the pilot of the plane.

There was a limo and a taxi waiting when we arrived at the airport. The limo wasn't for us. Ben told me I could change into my bag lady clothes in the airplane, and leave my good ones there.

When I climbed down off the plane he was waiting for me with a huge tackle box.

"Are you happy you got to wear your new clothes for a whole two hours?"

"How do you know they're new?"

"You left the tag on the back of the sweater." He was grinning at me like a school boy who had just told a bad joke.

"I did not!"

"Yes, you did. I tore it off while I was kissing you this morning."

"I don't believe you."

"Why would I lie about something like that?"

"I don't know…cause you're a tease?"

"Okay, you're right. But I want you to know, I don't care what you wear, I like you. It doesn't matter what you have on."

"Thank you…so I can wear bag lady clothes all the time?"

"Not to bed after we're married."

"Who said I was going to marry you?"

"Your brown eyes say it every time I look into them. Let's go, bag lady. The fish are waiting for us."

Chapter 14

January merged into February with me falling more in love with Ben. I never imagined I could feel so intensely. Even though our work schedules were crazy, we usually managed to get together for one full day a week.

We spent them walking the beaches, biking the Pinellas trail, going to ball games and flying. If it was raining, we would stay at my house and play games or listen to music or watch movies. He loved old westerns and war movies, and I loved watching him watch them.

I grew up in a home where cards and board games were played a couple times a week. He was very competitive, and I actually found him reading a dictionary one day because he couldn't beat me at Scrabble.

We learned a lot about each other in those first few weeks.

After his grandmother died and he returned from Afghanistan, there was a short time when he felt like he had been abandoned in life. It was then, he threw his heart into learning to fly, and it became almost an obsession for him. He saved every penny he made so he could buy an airplane of his own. He started out with a single engine plane and flew it for years, for his own pleasure. But, because of the cost of doing it for pleasure, he knew flying would have to be his career.

"So now I have three flying jobs. I get to fly in the reserves, I get to fly the chopper for the hospital, and I have my own little taxi service for rich guys."

"That doesn't leave much time for anything, or anybody else, does it?"

"I haven't wanted anything or anyone else, until I met you. Do you think you can share my love and passion for it?"

"I think we can work something out. But I do worry a little bit about you being called back into active duty."

"I've thought about that. It didn't seem like a big deal before, but now that I have you in my life, I don't like the thought of having to be away for months at a time. And you need to know, there's a chance that could happen. We're just going to have to deal with it when the time comes. And it will come, Katy. You need to find a way to be okay with that."

"Have you considered getting out of the reserves?"

"I could, but it wouldn't be wise financially for me to do it. I've been in for twelve years. It has a good retirement plan if I stay in for just a few more."

"But it could be dangerous, and your life is more important than money."

"I know there's some danger when I get called back into active duty, but there's some risk in everyday life, too. We don't come into this life with a guarantee of a full eighty or ninety years. And money? I think it becomes more important when you've grown up without it. I want to be able to provide for my family better than my dad provided for his."

I wanted to tell him I could afford to take care of both of us with the trust fund my parents had set up for me. But I knew, in my gut, he would find that insulting.

I also knew I couldn't ask him to give up what he loved because it was too dangerous. I was falling in love with him knowing the risks. And I was letting him fall in love with me, without knowing the risk he was taking. My leukemia could come back before he ever went to war again. I knew I wasn't being fair to him, but what if he decided he didn't want the risk of losing someone else in life? He had already lost everyone he had ever loved.

On Valentines Day we went to Walt Disney World and pretended to be little kids. We did all the rides simply because he had never been there. The poor little boy from Texas never got the chance to even dream about such a thing. He was too busy grieving for his parents and living on a grandmother's Social Security check.

On the way home, I dreamed of a day we could bring our children back so he could experience it all through the eyes of a child.

*****

Abby wouldn't stop nagging me. I knew the day was coming when I would need to share Ben with my family, but I was being greedy. I wanted him all to myself for as long as I could have him. At the end of February, I finally told her I would bring him to her house for a cookout with my Florida family, if he felt like he was ready. But first, I wanted to to talk to my mom and dad in Philadelphia.

I call my mom a couple times a week, and still hadn't told her about him. I knew she would be happy for me. After talking to Abby, I dialed her number.

"Hey. Mom, it's me."

"Hey, Me…what are you up to today? Is it nice down there?"

"It is. Seventy-eight today, and the sun feels so good. I went to the beach this morning to walk."

"Ohhh, how nice. We had an ice storm here."

"I saw that on tv. Why don't you and dad come down for a few days of sunshine?"

"That would be lovely, but you know how busy he is."

"I know…but there's another reason why I need you to come down. There's someone I want you to meet."

There was silence on the other end.

"Mom? Are you still there?"

"Yes, I'm still here. You want us to come down there, just to meet someone? He must be someone pretty special."

"I think so. In fact, he's not just special. He's amazing."

"You're dating someone? How long have you been seeing him?"

"Not long. I met him the week you left after Christmas. But I think he's the one you've been praying I would meet. You've been praying for my future husband since I was in diapers, haven't you?"

"I have. I've always wanted God's best for you."

"Well, I think I found him, and I want you and Dad to meet him."

"Has the rest of the family met him yet?"

"No. For some reason I wanted you to meet him first."

There have been times, in the eight years since I left home, when I worried about my adoptive parents feeling left out. They said they understood my wanting to spend time with my birth mom and her family, but I never wanted them to feel like they became less important after I found Mama Beth.

"We would love to meet him, honey. Let me talk to your dad and see what we can work out. When were you thinking would be a good time?"

"Any time, hopefully soon. But Mom, just so you know, I haven't told him yet about my past health issues."

"Why not? Don't you think he would want to know?"

"Well yeah, but we're just having so much fun, and I didn't want to weigh down our relationship with all of that."

"I understand, but he still needs to know."

"I know; I'll tell him soon."

*****

My parents flew down the second week in March. They could only stay for the weekend, but it was long enough for them to meet and fall in love with Ben too.

Mom and I made dinner for the four of us, and he came over after a charter flight. He looked nervous when he walked in, but oh, so handsome. He gave me a kiss then looked flustered when he became aware that my parents were watching. I saw my mom smile, and my dad cleared his throat. I am their only little girl.

Dinner went smoothly. Ben and Dad spent some time afterwards talking about airplanes. My dad had contemplated buying one of his own but never had the time to learn to fly it.

"If you'd like, we could all take a ride tomorrow evening. I love the lights of Tampa and the bay after dark." We agreed to meet him at the airport the next evening at seven.

After he left, Mom and I spent half the night talking about him. I was glad my townhouse had two bedrooms so they could stay with me when they came to visit.

She could tell I was totally smitten, and I could tell she was happy for me. She and dad were one of those couples who had fallen in love at first sight too. They got married six months after they met. She told me there was only one time in their marriage when they went through a difficult time, and she wondered if their marriage would last.

It was after she found out she couldn't have children and their several attempts at in-vitro fertilization failed. She told my dad he was free to leave, so he could have a family with someone else. She said he got terribly angry. He wasn't the kind of man who would leave the woman he loved just because she couldn't have children. She knew that, but at the time, she was devastated by her infertility.

I came into their lives soon after that. I was their gift from Mama Beth.

The next evening was almost magical. Ben found a friend who was more than happy to fly his plane for him, so he could sit in the cabin and talk with me and my family. He pointed out some of the landmarks in Tampa. The coastline looked like it was wearing a necklace of bright diamonds.

After we landed, Mom gave Ben a big hug and told him how happy she was that he and I had found each other. Dad shook his hand but didn't say anything. He might be a big important banker, but he's sentimental when it comes to his kids.

They left the next morning after I went back to work. Before she left, when mom hugged me good-bye, she said "Katy, you need to talk to him. He deserves to know."

Chapter 15

Poor Ben. Once the family introductions began, they just didn't seem to end for him. The Saturday after Mom and Dad returned to Philadelphia, Abby insisted we come to her house for the cookout.

"I've waited long enough, and now that your parents have met him, it's my turn!"

We made plans for me and Ben to go over in the afternoon, to spend some time with her and Brett and the boys. Mama Beth, Alex, Carly and Jon would come over later.

I decided to tell Mama Beth and Carly about him before they met him. I didn't want both of them to be in shock. I went to their house on Friday evening after work.

"Katy, I've been missing you. When do I get to come to your house again? I haven't been there for, like, two whole months!"

"I know, Carly-girl, and I'm sorry. I've been so busy."

"Why have you been so busy?"

"I've had a lot of things to do and lots of places to go."

"Why didn't you ask me to go with you?"

"Carly! Your sister is busy with work and you have been busy with school. Now quit nagging her."

"I'm not nagging her. I just miss her."

I opened my arms and she came over and sat down on my lap. I knew the time would come, very soon, when she'd be too old to want to do that. I savored the feel of her in my arms.

"We'll make up for it when you go on spring break, okay?"

"Can we go to the beach everyday?"

"Maybe not every day, but you can bring a friend and I will too. How does that sound?"

"I'll bring Meagan. Who are you going to bring?"

"I have a new friend. His name is Ben. Can I bring him?"

"You're going to bring a boy? I don't think boys are very much fun."

"I think you'll like this one. And I think Mama will too. I'm going to bring him to Abby's house tomorrow so you can meet him, okay?"

"I suppose, but I still don't think he'll be very much fun."

"Carly, you need to go finish your homework. And don't argue. You can talk to Katy more tomorrow."

We watched her as she sighed and trudged up the stairs. Mama Beth smiled at me.

"I wonder sometimes if you were as obstinate at that age, as she is. I'll have to ask your mom the next time I see her. Abby told me they were in town last week. I'll bet it was good for you to see them again."

"It was. I wish we could have all gotten together, but they were on a tight schedule this time. I asked them to come down to meet Ben."

"Ben? So why haven't I heard anything about this new friend of yours?"

Like I've said, my birth mom is only sixteen years older than me, and there are times when she has felt more like a big sister than a mom. This felt like one of those times. I could see the excitement in the brown eyes that looked like mine.

"I wanted to get to know him before I introduced him to the family. And he wanted to wait awhile too. He doesn't have family, and I didn't want him to feel overwhelmed by mine. I think you're going to love him."

"If you like him, you know we will. What do you mean he has no family? How can that be?"

By the time I finished telling her about him, she was in tears. She is such a soft-hearted person; I've often wondered how she works as a social worker with a soul as tender as hers.

"Oh, Katy. He needs us in his life, doesn't he?"

"I think he really wants to be part of a family again. And I'm crazy about him. I never thought I would feel this way about anyone. It's so exciting, but kind of scary too."

"I'm happy for you, Honey. I've been praying God would send the right guy into your life. So you're bringing him to Abby's tomorrow?"

"He's coming, but he's a little nervous. When I told him he was the guy both my moms have been praying I'd meet, I think it freaked him out a little bit. He said with two moms and God on the same side he wouldn't have a chance of getting out of this, even if he wanted to. But I'm pretty sure he doesn't want out."

"So this sounds like a sure thing. Can you tell me why you think he's the one, if you've only known him for what, two and a half months?"

I told her the same thing I had told Abby. How I was able to see his true character by the way he treated Mrs. Johnson, and how much I appreciated his work ethics. Since then, I'd also seen his sense of humor and I loved it. "I just feel like I'm a better person when I'm with him, Mama Beth. Just wait till you meet him, you'll know what I'm talking about."

*****

When Ben came to pick me up on Saturday, I thought I was going to do one of those old-fashioned swoon things. Every time I saw him, he got more handsome. He was dressed casually in a pair of khaki shorts and a blue shirt. His hair was getting a little long and curled around his ears, and when he took me into his arms, my fingers were soon stroking it. It was so soft, and I pulled him closer. I felt like his meeting my family was the next step in our dance of intimacy.

He must have felt it too because he didn't seem to want to stop kissing me. He gave me one of those sweet, tender kisses that quickly deepened into one of those intense, hungry ones. The thought ran through my mind that I could finish our dance right then and never regret it.

He pulled back a little and looked at me. "You know I love you, right?"

"You do?"

"I do."

"Oh Ben, I'm so glad, because I love you too."

I felt like our two bodies could melt into one single one, if I would allow it. Our souls were connected, and I so wanted to connect with him physically, to show him how much I loved him.

I felt his arms leave me, and he gently pushed me away.

"We have to stop, baby. This is killing me."

"I'm sorry, Ben. It's difficult for me too. Why don't we just go? I made a chocolate cake. Can you take it to the car for me?"

"Yeah, sure. But can you look at something first?" I hadn't noticed the small bag he had brought with him.

"What's in the bag?"

"I bought these little airplanes for the boys. Do you think they are age appropriate for them?" He pulled two little airplanes from the bag. They had wheels on them, and little people in them that could be taken out and played with.

"Ben, they're adorable. They don't have these, and I'm sure they'll love them. It's good you got two of them, too. They would have fought over one."

"Good. I wanted to get something for Carly too, but I don't know what ten year old girls like."

How can you not love a guy like that?

"She would love it if you took something for her. When I told her about you the other day, she wasn't convinced I should have a new friend who was a boy. You know what? I have something I picked up for her birthday. We'll wrap it up, and you can give it to her."

When we got to Abby's, the boys were still napping so it gave the four of us time to sit and talk for awhile. Ben and Brett talked baseball, after Abby had done her interrogation of him. It was kind of funny to listen to the two of them talk. She was acting like a mother hen, and he knew he needed to win her approval. I knew that wouldn't be difficult for him to do.

She was finishing up a salad when the boys woke up.

"Can I go get them out of bed?"

"Yeah, but make sure you take Kyle to the bathroom before you do anything else. I have a couple of outfits laying out for them."

They had different bedrooms so I went to Kyle first. Abby had just finished potty training him, and it had been a battle.

He seemed happy to see me, and luckily, had not had an accident. I took him to the bathroom, and after he finished with his "bye-bye, poo poo" routine, he had to flush, "by myself." Three year olds can be so independent! I put his outfit on him. Today he looked like he was going on a safari. He was so cute with his dark hair and eyes like Abby's.

"Okay, champ, let's go get your brother now."

"I not champ!"

"Well, who are you then?"

"I is Dego!"

"Dego?"

"Dego is Dowa's fwend…he is a anmal res-s-s-cuer."

Kyle had obviously been watching a lot of television this past winter.

"Okay, Diego, let's go get your brother."

Konnor started to jump up and down in his crib when he saw us.

"Ka-Ka".

"Hey, baby boy. Ka-Ka's coming."

He was usually as laid back as Kyle was outgoing, and his looks were different too. He has blond haired and blue eyes like his dad, and he is still round with baby fat. He looked like sunshine to me. I picked him up, gave him a squeeze then changed his diaper and clothes. He had a belly laugh that was infectious, so of course I had to tickle his soft round belly. Just to hear his laugh. By the time I got both of them downstairs, Abby and Brett were starting the grill.

Ben was checking out Brett's golf clubs. I'll never forget the look on his face when he saw me and the boys coming toward him. He dropped the club he had in his hand and just stood there…watching me walk toward him.

"Hey, Ben. This is Kyle and Konnor."

"Wow, two little boys. Every man's dream."

Kneeling, so he could get down on their level, Ben held his hand out to Kyle, who suddenly became shy and tried to hide behind me.

"Hey, Kyle, I'm Ben. Do you like airplanes?"

Kyle looked up at me with a question in his eyes. Abby had already given him the stranger danger talk.

"It's okay, buddy. Ben's a nice guy."

In the meantime, Konnor was flapping his arms like a bird, and chattering like one too.

Ben smiled. "He must know what an airplane is. He's trying to fly like one. Should I go get their gifts now?"

"Sure. It'll keep them busy while we're getting supper around."

The airplanes were a hit, and Ben had two new friends in a matter of minutes. The rest of the family didn't arrive until it was almost time to eat. Introductions were made before we all sat down to eat the burgers and brats.

We were a lively group, except for Carly. I saw her glaring at Ben a couple of times. When I smiled at her, she didn't seem pleased. Maybe I had spoiled her a little bit too much. It was quite obvious she didn't want to share me, especially with a boy.

After supper we gathered around a fire Brett had made and watched the stars come out.

"Carly-girl, why don't you come over here and sit beside me?"

She seemed more than happy to sit in the seat between me and Ben for the evening. When her parents were getting packed to go, Ben pulled her gift out of his pocket.

"Carly, can I talk to you for a minute?" She looked up at me. I nodded my head and smiled at her.

"Go ahead. He really is a nice guy." She went over and sat down beside him again.

"Katy has told me how special you are to her. I was wondering, since I don't have any little sisters could you be my friend? Katy and I bought this for you…I hope it will remind you that you are special to both of us."

And just like that, Carly and Ben became friends too. It's true; the way to a ten-year-old girl's heart is through trinkets from the local dollar store.

Chapter 16

"So…now I've met everyone except your brothers?" He was sitting on my couch looking totally exhausted.

"And you survived!" I went over, sat down beside him, and took his hand in mine. "After the parents and sisters, the boys will be a piece of cake."

"That's a relief. So, do you think I passed inspection?"

"I have no doubts. Why wouldn't you? So handsome and smart and nice." I loved holding his hand and brought it to my lips to kiss. He grinned at me.

"Aw, shucks…it's just the Texas cowboy in me."

"Yeah, right. So what do you think? Am I lucky girl or what?"

"You are a lucky girl, and I'm a lucky guy. And now that I've met the family, we can get married. Right?"

Oh, Ben. I hope you still feel that way after I tell you what I need to tell you.

"Why don't we wait a little while? I need to find your faults first, and you need to find mine. We all have them, you know? And they can ruin a really good thing."

"There are no faults that love can't overcome, Katy. I honestly believe that."

"I hope you're right, Ben."

*****

At the end of March he returned from his monthly reserve duties looking a little haggard. I was beginning to get concerned about him. He never seemed to stop. Between the job at the hospital, his "flying taxi" (as he called it), and the reserves, I wondered when he was able to relax. One night, after he had fallen asleep on my couch for the second time in a week, I asked him about it.

"You worry too much, Katy. I'm fine."

"Can't you take a whole week off, and just relax?"

"I need to save my vacation for when I go to my two weeks of field training this summer."

"I thought employers were supposed to give you a leave for that."

"They would, but I've never felt the need for leisure time off."

"But you look exhausted."

"I'll make a deal with you. If you'll go on a honeymoon with me, I'll take two whole weeks off. Let's elope next month and go. Where do you want to go?"

"I can't elope, you crazy nut. My parents, all four of them, would be furious with both of us. Besides you haven't asked me nicely to marry you yet."

"What? You want the whole bended knee routine?"

"Yep, and you have to ask both my dads, not just one, for their permission."

"What am I getting myself into?"

"I think it's called love."

*****

He was bringing up the subject of marriage more often, and I knew I had to set him down and tell him the truth about my health before he actually popped the question. We both had the next weekend off so I decided to do it then. We would have time to talk about things, and decide how to proceed.

I asked him to come for dinner when he was done working on Friday night. It was the first three day weekend I'd had off in months. I cleaned all day and decided to cook him his favorite, a T-bone steak. I had learned you can take a boy out of Texas, but you can't take Texas out of the boy. And my Texan loved his beef!

He didn't get to my house until almost eight. He had stopped to buy me some daffodils—one of my favorite flowers and one we rarely see in Florida.

I didn't throw the steaks on the grill until he got there, I wanted them to be perfect. They must have been, he devoured all of his and half of mine.

When he was finished, I cleared the dishes quickly and put them into the dishwasher. Then I took him by the hand and led him to the sofa in the living room. I love my home, even if I'm not that good at interior decorating. I feel like it's a warm homey place. I had lit several candles before he got there and had a country music CD playing.

"You tired tonight?"

"Let's just say I'm looking forward to a long relaxing weekend with my favorite girl."

"I'm your favorite? I thought Carrie was your favorite?"

"You're silly. You know you're my only girl. Carrie's my favorite blond."

"I'm glad I'm your only girl. But if it's blonds you like, I could always dye my hair, you know."

"Don't you dare. I love your hair… and I love that you're young and beautiful too." (Not very original, Carrie Underwood was singing a song by that same title at the time.)

"I love you too, Ben."

He pulled me to him and smothered me with kisses. Sometimes I felt like I would drown in his love. It left me struggling to breathe.

"Baby, I need to talk to you about something. It's kind of serious."

He sat up straight and looked at me. I think he could hear the tension I was feeling in my voice.

"What? You can't be pregnant…unless my thinking about getting you pregnant can do it." His silly smile took the edge off my anxiety, and I had to laugh.

"Ben! Now be serious. It's something about my past, but it may be an issue for our future too."

"You don't have a skeleton of an old boyfriend in your closet, do you?"

I loved the way he could sense tension and so easily defuse it.

"No. I need to tell you about something that happened to me when I was sixteen though."

"Okay, I'm listening."

"When I was sixteen, I was diagnosed with leukemia."

"Leukemia? Oh, baby. How horrible for you! Why didn't you tell me this? But you're okay now, right? That was a long time ago."

"Yes, I'm okay now. It was a bad time, but the good that came out of it was that I got to meet my birth mom. And I got another family out of the deal."

"So that's how all of you got together. I've wondered why you haven't told me how that happened. Why haven't you told me?"

"I don't know, it's just kind of heavy and I like to keep it in the past. But like I said, it may be an issue in my future."

"Why would it be an issue in the future if you're cured?"

"Actually, I'm not cured. But I've been in remission for a long time, and that's a good thing. It's a really long story. Do you feel like listening to it?"

"Of course. Tell me all of it."

"Okay. If you're sure."

The blue eyes assured me as I went on.

"When I was diagnosed, my parents contacted Mama Beth to see if I had any half siblings who could be potential blood marrow donors, in case I would need a transplant."

"Carly! *That's* why she's so special to you."

"At the time, Carly hadn't been born yet. Mama Beth hadn't been able to conceive after she had me. That's why they became foster parents and adopted Jon. After she and Alex met me, they decided to see a fertility specialist so they could have a baby. They had always wanted one of their own and now they had another reason to have one. Their child would have the potential to provide marrow for me. God interceded for all of us. After Carly was born they harvested her cord blood and had it frozen. Cord blood is actually more effective for transplantation than regular marrow."

Ben's fingers were on my arm, and as I was talking, he kept moving them up and down, as if to reassure me and encourage me to continue my story. His touch was comforting.

"We didn't think I'd ever need it because I went into remission six months after I was diagnosed. I was on maintenance chemo for two years. Soon after I went off it though, I had a relapse and had to have the marrow transplant. It worked, and I've been cancer free for almost six years. With every day that passes, I'm that much safer from another relapse. If I can make it to ten years, without it coming back, I think I'll feel a hundred percent safe."

That's when he put both arms around me and pulled me close. With tears choking him, he made a promise to me that sealed our future.

"Katy, I'm so sorry you had to go through that. But, I promise you, darlin'…I'm going to take care of you for the rest of our lives." When Ben called me "darlin'" that night, I thought of his parents, and I knew it was a term of endearment he had learned from two people who had loved each other as intensely as Ben loved me.

"Ben? You need to know that loving me involves some risk. The leukemia could come back someday, and I could die."

"I'll take that risk, Katy. Just like you're taking a risk by loving me. I could die in a helicopter over Afghanistan or right here in Tampa. Life is uncertain. But you told me once, you've beat the odds. Now we're going to beat them together, okay?"

"There's one more thing. The treatment I had when I was sixteen?"

"Yes?"

"I may have a difficult time getting pregnant because of it. We women are born with all the eggs we will ever produce, and mine may have been damaged by the chemo and the radiation I had to have. When I saw you with Kyle and Konnor and heard you say two boys would be a man's dream come true, I felt like my heart was going to break. What if I can't ever give you children?"

"You told me your mom couldn't have children of her own, but she still has three who love her. There are obvious solutions to infertility."

"So you're okay with all of this?"

"I don't like that you had to experience such a horrible thing, and I'm sorry you've had to worry about it coming back, but we're going to beat this together, okay? Maybe Mrs. Johnson, who brought us together, will also be our guardian angel."

Chapter 17

It turned out to be the most amazing weekend of my life.

Ben fell asleep on my couch after our talk Friday night, and I didn't have the heart to wake him. I threw a blanket over him and went to bed. When I opened my eyes on Saturday morning, he was sitting in the rocker in my room, drinking coffee and watching me sleep.

"Hey, sleepy head, do you know you're beautiful, even when you sleep?" He got up, came over and sat down on the bed with me. Leaning over, he kissed me.

"Do you want some coffee?"

"That sounds wonderful."

"Stay there. I'll bring it to you."

After he left the room, I realized he had just seen me with bed head, and had kissed me with morning breath. I ran to the bathroom, brushed my teeth and combed my hair as quickly as I could.

He brought me a tray with some milk, a Danish and my coffee.

"Where did the Danish come from?"

"I went shopping this morning."

"What time is it?"

"Nine."

"I haven't slept this late in months."

"You're probably relieved, after getting all that stuff off your chest last night. I wish you would have told me earlier, Katy. I've had a feeling that there was something unsaid hanging between us."

"I know. I don't know why I was so afraid to tell you. It's just that you have lost so many important people in your life, and I was afraid you wouldn't want to take the risk with me."

"Just don't ever be afraid to tell me anything again, okay?"

"Okay. So what are we going to do today?"

"I have a couple of things I have to do this morning, but how about I come back at four? I was thinking maybe we could go flying tonight."

"Where we gonna fly to?"

"It's a surprise. Just be ready at four, okay? And you might want to bring an overnight bag, in case we don't get back until tomorrow."

"Come on, Ben. Tell me."

"Nope, I'm not gonna do it. Why don't you just relax today? Go get a massage or something. Call Abby; she'll go with you."

"A massage? I've never had a massage in my life."

"Well, it's about time you did. I need you good and relaxed for tonight."

"Ben Browning! I am not going to elope with you tonight! And I'm not going to bed with you, either."

"Darn it! You guessed my secret." He was grinning as he turned to leave. I thought I heard him say "I wish!" as he left my room.

*****

I finished my breakfast in bed, then stretched and lay back on my pillows. I had done it, I had told Ben my story, and it hadn't made a difference in how he felt toward me. He loved me, baggage and all. I was disappointed he couldn't stay, though. But I knew he had things to do on his days off. He had so few of them. So I got up and called Abby.

"What're you doing today?"

"Not a lot on the agenda, cartoons this morning, naps this afternoon, baths tonight. You know, the usual. What are you doing?"

"I don't know, but I'm feeling restless. Ben's busy today. Is Brett home to watch the boys so we can do something?"

"Yeah, he's home. What did you have in mind?"

"Did you ever have a massage?"

"A massage? I had one on my honeymoon, a hundred years ago. Why do you ask?"

"I was thinking about getting one today…if you'll go with me. I'll pay."

"If you're paying, I'm in, girl. How soon do you want to go?"

"Let me call around and see what I can find. You talk to Brett, I'll call you back."

I couldn't believe how many spas offered walk in massages. I found one fairly close and called Abby back.

"We're in at one for a hot stone massage. I'll pick you up at twelve thirty."

I had some extra time, so I packed an overnight bag and wondered where I'd be in twelve hours. My brain went into overdrive at that point, and I imagined all kinds of wonderful places I could go with Ben. I even thought of some not-so-wonderful places I'd be willing to go to with him. Honestly, I didn't care where we went tonight, as long as we were together.

When I got to Abby's, she was out the door before I got the car into park.

"Calgon, take me away!" She was so funny. I knew she loved being mother to her two little boys, but there were times when she acted like she couldn't wait to escape them. I had been around her enough to know that the poopy diapers, the constant picking up after them, and the crying could get to you.

I also knew there was nothing more precious than their little arms around my neck.

"So, what's going on? Why are we going for massages?"

"I don't know. I guess just because Ben told me to."

"Ben told you to get a massage? That's weird. Why would he do that?"

"I don't know that, either. Maybe he thought I needed a treat after I finally got up the courage to tell him about the leukemia and possible infertility issue."

"So you finally told him. That's good; what did he say?"

"You know Ben. He's just so calm about everything. He said things would work out okay. I hope he's right."

"You know, he puts on that whole I'm-cool-and-calm act, but I think he's like the proverbial still waters that run deep."

"I think so too. His feelings do run deep. I've known that from the beginning. I could tell, by how he treated Mrs. Johnson when we visited her. Is it just me, or is he a really amazing guy?"

"Well, I think you're a little prejudiced, but he is pretty amazing. I'm glad you two found each other. So what are you doing tonight?"

"I don't know. He said he would pick me up, and we'd go flying. I love watching him fly that plane. You can tell it's his passion."

"You make me sick. You get to go flying all over the country, and I'm at home changing poopy diapers."

"Hey, I remember when you and Brett were dating. I was so jealous of you. And you know he's still crazy in love with you and the boys. You're the one with the good life, sister. Ben says those little boys are every man's dream come true. Did I tell you he said that when we were at your house?"

"Aww, did he really? Well, maybe he can have a couple of his own in a few years."

"Oh, Abby...I hope so. But what if…" I knew I'd always live with a little bit of fear.

"We're not going there, Katy. You've met a lot of people in your support groups who have been able to get pregnant after having chemo. We're going to think positive."

When we arrived at the spa, they told us about a "sisters and friends" package that let us share the same room during our massage. It was so much fun. We started out giggling and chit-chatting, but about fifteen minutes into it, we just relaxed and let the hot stones do their jobs.

On the way back to Abby's house I felt as limp as a wet noodle. I hadn't realized that a good massage was so relaxing.

"What are you going to wear tonight when you go flying?"

"I don't know; probably just my jeans and one of my new shirts."

"Why don't you wear that skirt and silk blouse you bought when we went shopping?"

"No. I wanted to save that for something special."

"Oh go ahead and wear it. You looked great in it, and it will knock his socks off when he sees you. You can always buy more clothes later."

I didn't get back home until almost three, and was glad I had my overnight bag packed already. I took a quick shower, then on a whim decided to take Abby's suggestion and wear the new long skirt and silk top. And for the fun of it, I put some hot rollers in my hair and swept it into a messy up-do, with little tendrils hanging around my face. When I stepped back and looked at myself, I was actually pleased. I looked a little bit sexy and a whole lot relaxed. I made a note to myself to get a massage more often.

Chapter 18

Ben is a lot like Abby in one way. He's rarely speechless. But, when I opened the door for him at four, he was just that. He walked in, picked me up, and carried me into my bedroom. It was a good five minutes later before he actually said his first words.

"What are you doing to me, woman? You tell me you want to slow dance, then you greet me at the door looking like a sex goddess. It's a good thing we have somewhere to go or the slow dancing would have to end right now."

I got up and twirled around, like a little girl in her first party dress. "So you like?"

"Oh baby, I do like what I see."

I pulled him up off the bed. "I like what I see too…no, that's not completely true. I *love* what I see, every time you walk through my door. Ben Browning, you are the most handsome man I have ever seen. Do you know how much I love you?"

"I think I do, but don't ever stop telling me, okay? Now, come on, darlin', let's go flyin'."

Within minutes we were flying off into our sunset, just like his dad and mom had ridden off on their horses into theirs.

He still wasn't telling me where we were going, but I knew it was north because the sun was setting off the left side of the plane. About an hour into the trip, he asked me to get him a can of soda out of the little cooler he had in the cabin.

"If you're getting hungry, there's some cheese and crackers in there too. It's going to take us another couple hours to get there."

"Where we going? Alaska?"

"That sounds like fun. Maybe we'll go there on the honeymoon."

"Ben, tell me where we're going."

"Can't do it, pretty girl. You just sit back and relax. You did get that massage today, didn't you?"

"I did, and it was lovely. Thank you for suggesting it."

"My pleasure."

So, I sat back and relaxed. And fell asleep. I woke to the feel of the wheels touching down on the runway. I looked out the window and saw some other planes and small jets, but couldn't tell where I was.

"Welcome to Sevierville, Tennessee, my dear. Where it's a balmy sixty two degrees."

"Sevierville, Tennessee? You have to be kidding me?"

"I am not. And our limo awaits."

"Ben! What are we doing in the Smoky Mountains?"

"We're going exploring! But I hear they have some lovely little wedding chapels up in the hills. Come along now; we have places to go and things to see." I loved his playful side.

He took a beautiful shawl out of the small closet and wrapped it around my shoulders.

"April evenings in the mountains can be rather nippy."

"Ben, where did you get this? It's beautiful."

"Abby helped me pick it out for you. She said it would look great with that outfit you have on."

"Wait a minute. Abby knew you were bringing me here tonight?"

"She did. I told her to make sure you got that massage today, too. If you hadn't called her, she was going to call you."

Grinning like a little boy who had just played a trick on a friend, he grabbed our overnight bags and guided me down the steps and into the small terminal, where he picked up the keys for a car that was awaiting us in the parking lot.

Within thirty minutes we were sitting in a small, intimate restaurant at the entrance of the Smoky Mountain National Park.

I felt like I was in a fantasy world. I was in awe of the details Ben had worked out so I could have this experience, and I felt like this night would be something special. Something neither one of us would ever forget.

*****

We ordered dinner then he sat back and looked at me.

"Hey, how are you doin?"

"I'm not sure. This is all so…so surreal. I feel like Dorothy must have felt when she touched down in the Land of Oz. When did you plan all this?"

"I've been working on it for a couple weeks. After I found out we'd both be off for a long weekend, it seemed like the perfect time to surprise you with a little trip."

"Thank you for being so thoughtful. I've never been here, have you?"

"I've been here two or three times. I flew two different families here last summer. The airport in Sevierville was built for people who want to fly their small jets in here to vacation. It's more convenient than flying commercial into Knoxville. I imagine Dolly Parton has flown in a few times to visit her Dollywood. We can go there tomorrow, if you want to."

"I'm surprised you don't have something planned for tomorrow."

"Well, I thought maybe we could drive through the park. But if you want to do Dollywood, or go shopping here in Gatlinburg, we could do that too."

"No, I'd like to see the park."

"Good. There are a couple of waterfalls and a mountain top I'd like to see. We didn't have either one of those in Texas."

Our dinner came, and it was delicious. I felt Ben's eyes on me several times, but we ate in comfortable silence. Once when I looked up, he was smiling.

"What? Why are you looking at me like that?"

"Just enjoying the view."

For some reason I felt shy with him. Maybe it was just because we were in a different environment, but I think it was because after our talk the night before, I knew we were moving on to a more intense and meaningful relationship…if that was possible.

It was eleven before we left the restaurant, but I didn't feel tired at all; probably because of the nap on the plane.

"You tired, Ben? You've had a long day."

"I did have to get up early to fix your breakfast in bed, but I got a cat nap before I picked you up."

I didn't ask him where we were going to spend the night. He had planned everything so beautifully up to this point, and I trusted him to know what should come next.

As we drove down the main street of Pigeon Forge, I noticed it seemed to be one of those towns that doesn't close down at night. There were still crowds of people out walking the streets.

"I wonder if it's always this busy?"

"I read that a lot of people come in the spring because the mountain flowers are in full bloom. It's especially beautiful at this time of the year."

"Maybe we'll see some of them on our ride tomorrow."

We were soon on the outskirts of the little town, and Ben turned left off the main road. We began to climb a mountain road.

I have to admit, I did feel a little anxious. The road was hairpin turns and very dark. I didn't say anything though, hoping my silence let him know I trusted him. About fifteen minutes later, he pulled into the driveway of a small log cabin sitting on the side of a mountain.

"We're here. Sit still, I'll get your door." He walked around the car, opened the door for me, and took my hand.

"Welcome to your home away from home, for the next ten hours."

He grabbed our bags and walked behind me as we climbed the steps to the little cabin.

With the door unlocked, he stood back and held it open for me. A couple of small lamps were on, and a gas fireplace was burning. It was warm and cozy.

And Ben and I were alone. I took a couple deep breaths.

"It's beautiful, Ben. How did you find it?"

"One of the families I brought here last summer, told me about it. So you like it?

"I do. I just can't believe how beautifully you worked out every detail of this day, to make it so perfect."

It had started with breakfast in bed at my house in Tampa, and it was ending in this small love nest so far from home. I turned and placed my arms around his neck. I was feeling so emotional, I could barely talk.

"I love you, Ben."

"I love you too, Katy. And I will forever. No matter what the future holds."

He kissed me gently, like he needed to prove I was precious to him. Then he took my hand and walked toward a door off to the left.

"This is your room. Mine is over there across the hall, in case you need me for anything. But I'm wondering, before we go to bed, could we spend some time in front of the fire? Just for a little while? I promise you, I'll be a complete gentleman tonight."

I turned and put my arms around his neck.

"Ben, you know I would love to show you, physically, how much I love you, right? It's just that I made that commitment to myself and to God a long time ago."

"I know, baby. And we're going to honor that commitment you made."

I knew he would, but I wondered how I would ever get through this night without showing him how much I loved him.

I went into the bathroom and freshened up a little. By the time I got back to the living area, he was sitting on the sofa and there was a plate of chocolate-covered strawberries on the coffee table.

"Wow! You did think of everything. If I didn't know better, I'd think you were trying to seduce me."

"No, just wanted you to know how special you are to me."

"Well, you're doing an amazing job of that!"

He reached his hand out to me and pulled me down to his lap.

"It would be nice to live someplace where we could have a fireplace burning all the time, wouldn't it?"

"I grew up in Philadelphia, remember? I can tell you from experience, that it's lovely. Maybe we really could go to Alaska on our honeymoon. It would be fun to climb snowy mountains all day and come back to a blazing fire at night."

"Mmmm, that would be nice. But it would also be nice to go someplace tropical so I could just watch you lie around all day and all night with skimpy clothes on."

"Okay, whatever you want."

He picked me up then and sat me down on the sofa beside him.

"Katy, before we go anywhere on a honeymoon, you have to tell me that you really want to be my wife. If you'll do that, I'll give you what I have in this box in my pocket."

He went to his knees then, and handed me the box.

"Will you marry me and make me the happiest man who ever lived?"

I couldn't take it anymore. I burst into tears. This amazing man had planned the perfect day, and all I could do was cry. And say yes.

The diamond was beautiful, but it seemed insignificant, compared to the man who wanted me to spend the rest of my life with him. Ben was going to be my husband, my partner, my forever friend. We were going to be companions for the rest of our lives.

I fell asleep in his arms in front of the fire. When I woke up, I was in my bed with the blankets pulled up over me. The drapes were open, and I could tell it was close to dawn. I held my left hand up in front of me and saw the ring sparkle. Last night had been real.

Chapter 19

My clothes were a mess. They looked like they had been slept in. Actually, they had been.

I tiptoed to the bathroom, then out to the living area. The door to Ben's room was open, and I peeked in. From what I could see, he wasn't sleeping in his clothes. I closed his door quietly and went to the kitchen. It was stocked for breakfast. Whoever he rented the place from had thought of everything. I made some coffee and found a tray. He had served me breakfast in bed yesterday. Today it was my turn.

I put the bacon in the microwave and was scrambling the eggs when I felt his arms around me.

"If I had known a diamond ring would get you into the kitchen, I would have given it to you the first week I met you!"

"Hey, I was going to bring breakfast to you."

"You have to get up very early in the morning to do that! Besides, there's a beautiful view from the deck, and a table and chairs out there."

He helped me load the tray and take it to the deck. It was a beautiful view. We were high enough that we could see the sleepy little town of Pigeon Forge below us, and there were mountains all around us. There was a smoky haze hovering over all of it.

It was so serene, and I would have totally enjoyed the view, but I kept getting distracted by the fact that Ben had not buttoned his shirt. I seemed to have no control over my own eyes and I was mesmerized by the hair on his chest and the muscles in his arms. I wanted to skip breakfast and the view and go sit on his lap, feel his arms around me and the warmth of his body.

I was able to hold back when I realized I still had on the same skirt and silk shirt I'd worn yesterday afternoon, and I had slept in them. I doubted if I looked or smelled very sexy. So I just sat and enjoyed the view in front of me until we were done eating.

"Are we still going to take a drive through the park today?"

"Sure. We don't have to leave here until five. I watched the weather channel after you fell asleep on me last night, and the weather today is going to be perfect."

"I need to go take a shower first."

"Yeah, you look like you slept in your clothes, or something."

"Hey, you make fun of me and you'll have to do dishes."

"We don't have to do the dishes. The maid will do them. But before we leave, we should try out that hot tub around back."

"There's a hot tub out back? But I don't have a swim suit."

"We could go in our birthday suits." The eyes were having fun again.

"You wish."

"Actually, I have a swimsuit for you in my bag. It's Abby's, but she said it would fit you."

"I still can't believe she knew about all of this, and she didn't even give me a hint yesterday."

"She was excited, and I'm sure she's waiting to hear all about it."

"She has been the best friend and sister a girl could have."

"She's great. She has good taste, too. The swim suit she sent for you is a two piece."

"You sir, have a one track mind."

"I can't help it when I'm around you. Maybe we really should find one of those little wedding chapels today."

"We could, and not tell anyone. Then just have a big wedding in a few months."

"I'm ready if you are."

"I would…but we're slow dancing, remember? I think we would miss a few steps of our dance."

"You and your dance. I'm going to go crazy before we get to the final step of it."

"And that's why we better not do the hot tub. Actually, why don't you go soak in it while I take a shower and get ready? You'll have time."

"It won't be as much fun without you."

"I know, but I got a massage yesterday. You should get the hot tub today. We'll come back someday after we're married, and frolic around in it with just our birthday suits on, okay?"

"Promise?"

"Promise."

*****

I was actually ready to go before he was. Low maintenance has its benefits. I went back out to the deck to wait for him, and looked around me. Without Ben's bare chest distracting me, I could actually focus on my surrounding. It was magnificent. The plant life around me was in full bloom with some of the most beautiful flowers I had ever seen.

I was just getting ready to go down to smell some of them when I noticed some movement in the brush, a squirrel or chipmunk maybe.

"Katy…." I felt Ben behind me before I heard his whisper. "We need to walk backwards, very slowly and quietly into the house."

"Why?" I whispered back.

"I think there's a black bear in the bushes."

Did he say walk slowly and quietly? Not happening!.

I was back inside the cabin in less than three seconds. Ben was right behind me.

He closed the door and locked it, while I ran to the window… just in time to see a squirrel run up onto the deck railing. I heard him laughing. I turned around and pounced on him.

"You scared me to death, Ben Browning! You knew there was no bear out there, didn't you?"

"But I wanted there to be, so I could be your hero and save you."

"You were my hero before you pulled that dirty trick."

"I'm sorry. But you should have seen your face."

"Is life with you going to be like this all of the time?"

"Like what?"

"Full of surprises."

"Well, yeah. We certainly don't want it to get boring, do we?"

For some reason I didn't think it would ever be boring.

*****

The drive through the park the next day was beautiful. We were able to walk a few of the shorter trails that led to scenic waterfalls and spectacular views. Several times during the day I looked at the sights around me, and then at the man next to me and wondered if both were real. I felt like I was in a dream, and this was one dream I didn't want to ever end.

Chapter 20

Both of us were on the schedule to work the the next morning. We didn't get home until after midnight, and when I woke up at five-thirty I was so tired I wondered if I would be able to make it through the day. It had been an exhilarating weekend, but emotionally exhausting. As I was dragging myself out of bed, the phone rang. *It's probably Abby wanting to know about the weekend.*

"Good morning beautiful wife-to-be; how are you feeling today?"

"Oh, Ben…I'm so tired. I don't know how I'm going to make it through a full twelve hour shift."

"You aren't working today, sweetheart. Didn't I tell you? I found someone else to work for both of us."

"You did *what*?"

"Surprise! You have the day off."

"But, how did you do that? They won't let me have a day off unless I sign a PDO request sheet."

"Denny found someone else to work for you. I asked him last week if he would do it for you, and I forged your name on the sheet. I knew we would be tired and need a day to recuperate."

"You asked Denny to find someone to work for me?"

"Yeah, he was happy to do it."

"Did you tell him why I needed it off?"

"I just told him I was taking you away, and we might not make it home until today. It could have stormed in the mountains yesterday, you know. And we would have been stranded."

I didn't know whether to be relieved because I didn't have to go to work, or mad that he had interfered in my work. Then I caught sight of the sparkle on my left hand and smiled. How could I be mad at him? He really had thought of everything.

"Katy? You aren't mad at me are you? I just thought you would need the day to rest. I knew I would."

"I'm not mad, Ben. I just can't get over how you seem to think of everything. Do you always do everything perfectly, right down to the last detail?"

I heard the pleasure in his voice. "Not always, my dear. And I'm sure you'll soon find that out for yourself. But I wanted our engagement weekend to be perfect."

"It was. Thank you. And I am going to appreciate the day off."

"Why don't you go back to bed? I'll come over at noon, and we'll go to the beach."

"That sounds wonderful."

"Good. I want to see my future wife in this two-piece swimsuit."

I started to argue that my one-piece would work just fine, but he interrupted me.

"Come on, baby. I promise, you can wear it out in public without fear of me seducing you, unless we can find a really private beach."

"You're a crazy man! See you at noon, Ben."

"Love you."

"I love you too."

*****

I went back to bed thinking I'd be able to sleep a little more, but my mind was full. I was in love with the most amazing man, and thinking about him made it impossible to sleep. Ben was going to be my husband. I was going to spend the rest of my life with him, and I knew I had God to thank. As exciting as it all was, I had a sense of peace. I had learned one very important thing over the years. When I give the the details of my life to God, He works them out perfectly.

I dozed off after talking to Ben, but the phone woke me again at nine. This time it *was* Abby.

"I can't wait any longer. I need every detail."

"Oh, Abby. It was perfect. There just aren't words to describe it. And I can't believe you knew it was going to happen and didn't even give me a hint."

"Hey, I told you to wear the new outfit. Did he like it?"

"Yes, he liked it. I'm so happy. What did I ever do to deserve him?"

"You've waited a long time for him, Katy. God's timing is always perfect; you know that."

"I know. But did you ever have this feeling like life was too perfect and something was going to come along and ruin it for you?"

"I think I felt that way when I fell in love with Brett. It's a normal feeling. It's the euphoria of love that does it to us. You'll come back down to earth the first time you have to pick his dirty socks up off the floor."

"Well, that does put things into perspective."

"So, do you love the ring?"

"It's gorgeous. He has very good taste in jewelry. I'm telling you, Abby, the man is perfect."

"I think you're a little prejudiced." She giggled. "So did you talk about dates or plans for a wedding?"

"No, not yet. Maybe we'll talk about that today. Did he tell you he made arrangements with Denny for someone else to work for me today? Wasn't that sweet of him? I'm really glad too. I was exhausted. We're going to the beach this afternoon. How about if I tell you all about it when I see you on Wednesday?" I knew I was rambling, but couldn't seem to stop myself.

"I can't wait. Can I go wedding dress shopping with you?"

"Well, of course. You know you're my only fashion consultant. By the way, the shawl you picked out was beautiful."

"It *was* perfect, wasn't it? He and I had fun picking it out. He was so cute. He didn't want to tell you to wear something warm, because he was afraid you'd guess where he was taking you. So he asked me to find something I thought you'd like. When I saw that shawl I knew it would be perfect with that skirt and top you bought when we went shopping. Hey, did you get to wear the swimsuit I sent along too?"

"Oh, thanks for that too, sweet sister! No, I didn't wear it, but I have strict instructions to wear it today when we go to the beach. You know I don't like two piece suits."

"I know, but you look great in them. And he's going to love it on you!"

I had a feeling that between Ben and Abby, I was going to be married before I could figure out what hit me. And I was going to love it.

*****

Ben was early, as usual. I was out on my deck, relaxing in my recliner when he drove up.

"Hey, gorgeous. Are you enjoying your day off?" He leaned over and kissed me.

"I am. But I'm feeling confused today." He got a look of concern on his face.

"Confused? About what?"

"Well, the last two mornings, when I wake up, I have this gorgeous diamond on my left hand. I can't figure out where it came from. Do you know anything about it?"

He sat down, took my hand, and inspected the ring.

"It looks to me like someone might be in love with you. A rock like that doesn't just show up magically on a finger one morning."

"You think someone loves me?"

"I don't just think it-I know it! And now that you have that magical little ring, I'd like to know how long I have to wait to get a wife."

"It takes a long time to plan a wedding, honey."

"Do we have to do the big ol' fancy wedding thing? Can't we just have something small and intimate?"

"Is that what you want?"

"Yeah; short little wedding, and one very long honeymoon. Do you think we can get the honeymoon to last until we're like, eighty or ninety years old?"

"I can see that happening, Ben. The long honeymoon thing, I mean. I'm not sure about the short little wedding. Did you forget how many moms and dads I have?" He was still holding my hand, and I didn't want him to ever let go of it.

He groaned. "Well, can I at least see how my future wife looks in this two piece swim suit, before we start planning a huge wedding?

So I modeled the swimsuit for him, just to see him smile.

"I was right. You're a little skinny, but round in all the right places. Now cover up and let's go to the beach before I do something we can't do...yet." The man had willpower as strong as iron.

We spent the afternoon walking the beach and relaxing under a cabana. We talked more about a date for our wedding than we did about the wedding itself. He wanted it to be soon, and truthfully, I did too. I understood his desire for something small and intimate and was sure if we could keep it small, we could have it sooner.

I knew there would be people who would say we were moving too fast, that we should wait, and get to know each other better. But Ben and I were old enough to know what we wanted in a marriage partner, and we knew we'd found it when we found each other.

"How about a Thanksgiving wedding? The weather will be a cooler here, and the hurricane threats will be over. We could have it out here on the beach, and go back to the mountains for our honeymoon. It will be cool there, and you could have your roaring fireplace."

"Can we make love on a bearskin rug in front of the fire?"

"Anything you want, my dear."

"Nooo, Thanksgiving is too far away. How about a July fourth wedding? We can make our own fireworks after it's over."

"Ben, that's only two months away. I can't plan a wedding in two short months."

"What's to plan, baby? You go buy a pretty dress, we'll get the family together, and say 'I do.' It sounds pretty simple to me."

It did sound simple when he explained it like that; and I didn't want to wait. All I wanted was to be Ben's wife. I could become that with just my family around me. I didn't need the fancy dress and a reception with hundreds of people I barely knew.

"So if we make it small and intimate, do you think we could try to find your sister so she could come?"

"Honey, I told you. I don't think she wants to be found. It isn't like we've ever been that close. It's no big deal."

"But it would be nice if you had some family here."

"It's okay. I have your family now, and that's all I need. I do wish Gramma could see you though. She would love you." I saw him swallow hard and look away over the Gulf waters, toward the place where he had once lived. I had never had a grandmother who lived close. I could tell by the way he talked about his that I had missed something very special.

"Do you think you could take me to Texas some day and show me where you grew up?"

"There's not much to see there. Lots of dry, barren land, dotted with old oil rigs."

"But it's a part of who you are. I'd like to see it."

"We'll see. Why don't we just focus on getting married for now? So do you think we can work with the fourth of July?"

"It's going to be hotter than a firecracker out here on the beach on July fourth."

"We could have everyone wear their swimsuits and have one huge swim party for the reception!"

"Are you ever serious?"

"I'm serious about you. I love you, and just want to be your husband. All this other stuff is just fluff."

It's a good thing we were on a public beach. He was very close to irresistible today.

"Okay, we'll shoot for the Fourth. It seems like with two moms, we should to be able to get ready for a wedding in half the time."

"Just don't let them make it twice as long."

"I guess I better call all of them when I get back home, so they'll know we're engaged."

"They already know."

"How do they know? I didn't tell them."

"You told me I had to ask both your dads for their permission to marry you. I called your dad last week, and I talked to Alex and your Mama Beth last Thursday."

"Oh, Ben. You are amazing! I was just kidding when I told you that."

"You were just kidding? Do you know how hard that was for me? By the way, they are all very protective of you. Did you know that?"

"Yes, I know. So what did they say when you asked them?"

"They said I should insist on making love to you, three times a day for the first year, since you made me wait till we get married."

I couldn't resist. I had to throw a hand full of sand at him.

We ended up rolling around in the sand, totally oblivious to the stares from those around us. The sandy kiss he gave me was unbelievable.

Chapter 21

It was a perfect day for a wedding. Even though Ben had been going to church with me since we got engaged, we still wanted the ceremony to be outside under God's blue sky.

We had it at a beautiful hotel on St. Pete Beach that specializes in weddings. The ceremony and reception were outside, but they could have accommodated us inside if the weather had turned bad. It had been a challenge to bring everything together in such a short time. But with all of us working together, we did it.

Mom and Dad flew down twice in June to help me with the plans. They insisted I have everything I wanted for the wedding; they spared no expense. I was their only daughter, and they wanted my special day to be perfect, even if it would be small.

"All I really want is Ben."

"I understand that, honey. But some day your little girl is going to want to see pictures of her parent's wedding. You'll want her to feel breathless at how beautiful her mama was the day she married her daddy. I remember the day I showed you the pictures of your dad's and my wedding. You were about eight years old. You told me I looked like a princess, and you wanted to be a princess just like me some day. It's one of my best memories." So I gave in and let them buy me whatever they wanted.

Abby found a beautiful dress for me. The halter neck line and bodice were snug, but it flowed into soft delicate lace that came mid-calf in the front and was full length in the back. It was perfect for a beach wedding. And I did feel like a princess in it.

Abby and Carly were my only bridesmaids; their dresses were designed like mine but were royal blue. Brett and one of Ben's old friends from the reserves were in the wedding party, with Kyle carrying the rings.

Our guest list was a small one. Both my families were there, plus a few of our friends from the hospital, and some of Ben's friends and their wives from the reserves. They had been his only family for years. Ben called his maternal aunt to see if she had heard from his sister, but she hadn't. When he told her he was getting married, he asked her if she and her family would like to come, and they were thrilled. He hadn't seen them in over ten years.

Alex officiated, and my Dad walked me down the sandy isle where Ben waited for me. My two moms sat side by side, swiping at the tears I knew they would shed. I had come a long way from that hospital room where we had all been united into one family. Now I was bringing the love of my life into an extended family he had never known.

We said our vows on the beach, just as the sun was setting over Texas. My hope was that Ben could leave the sadness he had experienced in his childhood, to find nothing but joy and peace on this side of the Gulf waters.

The reception was out on the huge patio behind the hotel. We could hear the waves hitting the beach, and the fragrance from the hundreds of flowers was almost intoxicating. There were white lanterns on all the tables and set up around the dance floor. They made the night feel magical.

Dad was put in charge of the menu, and had insisted that his new son-in-law would have filet mignon.

When Ben and I had gone cake tasting, we took Carly with us and let her pick her two favorite flavors, chocolate and cherry. We let her pick out the topper for the cake too. It was a dancing bride and groom wearing cowboy hats. She had finally decided that my cowboy wasn't so bad.

We danced our first dance to a song Ben loved to sing to me. When he first sang it to me, I told him it was a cowboy song. But the words of it were perfect for us. I truly did feel like heaven was smiling down on us as we danced. The song was true; we had everything we needed in each other, thanks to the Keeper of the stars that shone above us that night.

Then I danced with both my dads while Ben danced with both my moms. Everyone seemed to be enjoying themselves, but I was totally focused on Ben. I could have danced in his arms all night.

"So, Mrs. Browning…is this the final step in our dance of intimacy?"

"I believe it is. It's been a lovely dance, hasn't it?"

"There's just nothing like a slow dance to get a guy ready for the love of his life. Are you ready for tonight?"

"I have to admit, I'm a little nervous. But I've learned to trust you. And you promised you'd take care of me. I know you will tonight."

"Don't be nervous, baby. We'll keep the dance slow as long as you need it." But from the intensity in his voice, I knew I had kept him waiting long enough. I had waited for a long time too, and I didn't want to wait any longer. A desire for him hit me with a force I hadn't felt before.

*****

Alex had told us about his and Mama Beth's honeymoon in the the Canadian Rockies, and we decided we would go there too. It would be too warm to have a fire in a fireplace in July, in the Smokeys. We rented a little chalet near Lake Louise, and didn't leave it for the first three days. We spent the rest of our two weeks exploring the mountains and making love on the bear skin rug in front of the fire. Ben insisted we buy one and ship it home, just in case we ever got a house with a fireplace and it ever got cold in Florida.

It was on the flight home from the honeymoon that we talked about children. We had talked about them soon after we got engaged, and decided we would do nothing to prevent pregnancy. We thought it would be nice to have a few months to just enjoy each other, but felt that God knew what we needed, and when we needed it. With the threat of infertility hanging over my head, I didn't want to do anything that would prevent us from having a baby.

I had gone to see my gynecologist prior to the wedding and after an ultrasound she assured me that my reproductive organs looked good. Since I was having regular periods, I felt certain I would be able to get pregnant when the time was right.

"So, do you think we made a honeymoon baby?"

I couldn't help but smile at him.

"Would you like that?"

"I would. The thought of holding a little girl in my arms,one who looks like you, makes me happy."

"I thought you said sons were a man's dream-come-true."

"Why don't we just plan on two of each?"

"That's a lot of babies. I would have to quit work and stay home with them. Are we going to be able to afford that?"

"We're both thrifty. We'll manage it.

"We'll have to get a bigger house. We could live in the townhouse with two babies, but not any more than that."

"We'll find a place out in the country so we can have horses too."

"Horses? Really? I didn't know you were still interested in horses. I thought flying was your passion."

"Every kid needs a horse. There's no greater feeling than getting on the back of one and sailing over the ground with the wind in your hair. I think you'd like it too."

"Babies, horses and a place in the country; you have lots of dreams, Ben. Are you still going to be happy if none of those come true?"

"Why wouldn't our dreams come true? We'll work hard, and make them come true."

"But what if we don't get the babies? Will you be okay with that?"

"All I need is you, Katy. The babies would be extra blessings."

Chapter 22

For the next three months, I felt like I was living in a fantasy land. Ben and I were totally focused on each other. We arranged our schedules at work so we had the same days and weekends off. We didn't pick up any extra days, because work took us away from each other. On the days we were off, if Ben had a charter, I went with him. We would spend the day together, exploring whatever city we were in. On the days when he didn't fly, we spent time planning our dream home or going to the beach.

The beach became our home away from home. Sometimes we would go in the early mornings, before dawn, to walk hand in hand. The sand was cool beneath our feet and the seagulls would screech around us. Many mornings we sat and watched dolphins as they jumped and played in the waters.

On one of those early morning walks, I shared with him the story of my birth. Mama Beth had told me about it with tears in her eyes. She had become pregnant for me with a high school boyfriend who offered her comfort one night after her alcoholic dad had beaten her mother. The boyfriend, my biological dad who paid for the abortion my mom never had, is a mystery to me. And I have no desire to meet him.

My Mama Beth named me "Dawn" when I was born. Her own mother had told her many times that "it's always darkest right before the dawn, and after that dark night, joy does comes in the morning". When my adoptive parents took me, they named me Kathryn Dawn.

"Kathryn Dawn…you know you're the joy of my life, right?"

"And our day has just begun, Ben!"

Some days we would take a picnic to the beach and spend the afternoon just soaking in the sun and talking about our future. Our dream for a family of our own was one we spoke of often, and I felt certain God would bless us with children. I wanted them more for Ben than for me. I wanted to give Ben the family he never had.

One night in early November, four months after our wedding, we sat out on the deck and watched the stars come out. It was quiet and peaceful and I had never felt so content. But Ben seemed restless.

"You okay, Baby?"

"I think I'd like to go for a walk."

"Ben… it's eight o'clock at night. Where are we going to go walking?"

"The beach. It's only ten minutes away. Let's go. But get your jacket; it might be cool."

The beach was deserted and the tide was out. There was a full moon that sent a path of light across the water and turned Ben's blond hair platinum. It was also a lamp that made it easy for us to see where we were going. Taking our shoes off, we ran through the cool water until my toes grew numb. When I complained, we sat down in the sand that still held the heat from the daytime sun, and Ben rubbed my feet until they were warm again.

He pulled me back to my feet then, and put his arms around me. "Dance with me."

How could I resist? The sound of the waves was the only music we needed. I had never felt so at peace in my whole life. I pulled back and looked at up at him, still amazed that God had blessed me with the man of my dreams. That's when I saw the tears in his eyes.

"You okay, baby?"

"More than okay. I have the most beautiful girl in the world in my arms."

"Oh, Ben…." Cherished. I knew what it felt like to be cherished.

"Are you cold?"

"No. I always feel warm when I'm in your arms." He stopped dancing and pulled me tighter into his arms. We had been married for four months and our need for each other had not lessened at all.

"I love you, Katy. You know that, right?"

"Of course. How could I not know that? You show me every night and almost every morning."

I heard him chuckle. "Yeah, I guess I do. I'm surprised you aren't pregnant yet-not that it matters right now. We have lots of time."

"It will happen eventually. In the meantime, I'm happy having you all to myself."

"It is nice, isn't it? I'm glad you aren't anxious about getting pregnant. I was worried you would."

"No. I think leukemia taught me to accept what life gives you, and make the best of it. You aren't worried about it, are you?"

"No. But right now, I kind of wish you were."

"Why?"

We were behind one of the hotels at the beach now. He sat down on one of the few cabanas that was still out, and pulled me down to sit in front of him. The hotel staff rarely came looking for trespassers at that hour of the night.

"It would be nice if you were pregnant right now. I think it would be good for both of us. We'd have something to look forward to."

I was sitting in front of him, and I felt him pull me back, closer to his heart.

"Ben, we have a whole life time to look forward to. But aren't you the guy who says we need to just enjoy today, and not fret about tomorrow?" I turned around to look at him.

The tears were in his eyes again. I couldn't understand them, and all at once I felt fear.

"Yeah. But…I have some news I don't think you're going to like."

I felt my pulse speed up and my stomach begin to churn. I didn't like the sound in his voice.

"What kind of news?"

"You know last weekend, when I was at training?" He stopped for a minute. I heard him take in a deep breath.

"Yeah?"

"They told us our unit may get called into active duty sometime within the next month. I was just thinking. If you were pregnant, our separation might not be so difficult for you."

I felt the tears begin to build behind my eyes.

"No, Ben! Not now! I don't want you to go. We're still on our honeymoon."

"We're going to be on our honeymoon for the rest of our lives, Baby. You promised, remember?"

"You have to get out of going, Ben. You can find a way, can't you?"

"We've talked about this, Katy. You knew it would be a possibility. There are soldiers still in Afghanistan who need to come home to their families for the holidays."

"But this will be our first Christmas. We should be together."

"I know, Baby. And it breaks my heart that we won't be."

"So it's definite?"

"Ninety-nine percent positive."

I couldn't talk about it anymore. I leaned back into him and cried until I couldn't cry anymore. He just held me close and let me cry. I felt his tears drip into my hair, too. Had I just told him that leukemia taught me we need to make the best of what life hands us? How would I ever make the best of this?

I heard once that when you're separated from someone you love, the significance of that person's absence was relative to the amount of time you had known each other. I knew now that wasn't true. I had known my husband for less than a year and just the thought of him being gone caused a pain so intense I felt like I couldn't breathe.

"Ben?"

"Hmm?"

"For how long?"

"Three to six months, probably six. You have your family here with you, and maybe you can work some extra days to make the time go by quickly. It will go fast."

"Yeah, I suppose." But why did I feel like my heart was breaking in two?

The drive home was a quiet one. Ben held me close all night, like he never wanted to let go of me. God knows just how much I didn't want to let go of him.

*****

He got the call the week before Thanksgiving. He would leave on December first. I tried my best to be supportive and positive, but I think he knew my heart wasn't in it. I felt like my life was being controlled by some unknown person who had a remote control. Ben kept telling me that the dangers in Afghanistan were not as high as they had been the last time he was there, but I watched the news and knew the risk.

I think what upset me most was that most Americans didn't even seem to care that there were still soldiers going to war in Afghanistan. Some people didn't even know it! But there were still mothers losing sons, children who had to grow up without a parent, and wives saying good-bye to husbands forever. Families were being torn apart by a long-term war in a country thousands of miles away. I understood. I too had been oblivious to all of it before I met Ben. But now it was totally changing my life and my dreams.

It no longer seemed important for us to have land of our own where we could have kids and horses running wild. All I wanted was for Ben to come back home to me. Occasionally, the thought of life without him would creep in, but I refused to let it take hold in my head or my heart. Ben would come back home to me. He had to! He was my dream come true.

Chapter 23

Thanksgiving was bittersweet. It was our first real holiday together and it was suppose to be the one we would look back on someday with sweet memories. It was going to be the Thanksgiving when I could thank God for bringing Ben into my life. I was thankful for that, but I was also angry. Not at Ben, just angry about the whole situation.

My family rallied around us that day. Mom and Dad hadn't planned on coming down for the holiday because Ben and I were planning to go to Philadelphia for Christmas; but they and both my brothers came. Mama Beth and Alex invited all of us to their house for dinner. The whole family was together. I think they all made a special effort to be there for us.

I found myself in tears a couple times during the day. Right before dinner my Mom found me outside on the deck, crying.

"Katy, you need to pull yourself together. This is one time when Ben needs you to be strong for him. You know he doesn't want to leave you; and I can tell by the way he looks at you that it's killing him. He needs to feel our support, our love, and our prayers-especially yours. He needs you to reassure him that you will be right here waiting for him until he gets home."

"I know that, Mom! But I'm going to miss him so much. I just can't imagine him not being here with me every morning and every night for the next six months. It's going to be so lonely. And....and...what if he doesn't come back?"

"We aren't going to think those kinds of thoughts. We're going to pray and trust God to bring him back to us."

She wiped the tears off my cheeks with her fingers. "You know from experience that God is with us during the difficult times in life, and He can always bring good out of them. When your Mama Beth got pregnant and couldn't take care of you, your dad and I were blessed by your life. When you were diagnosed with leukemia, your Mama Beth got to come back into all our lives." She had her arms around me now and I leaned on the woman who had always made me feel safe.

"Then, when you needed the marrow transplant, God was good and blessed us with Carly so you could live. His timing is perfect, sweetheart. And we can trust Him to take care of us."

"I know that. He even used poor, dying Mrs. Johnson to bring me and Ben together. I just can't see any good coming out of this."

"Katy, what does our favorite Bible verse say?"

"It says we are to put our trust in the Lord because He understands, even when we don't."

"And...?"

"We can have faith that He's directing our path in the way it should go."

"Remember when we used to say that verse every day when you were in the hospital?"

"Yes. I remember. Thank you for insisting I memorize it."

"Now believe in that promise again, baby girl. It's a promise that will hold true every day Ben is gone."

When Ben found me a few minutes later there were no tears...just prayers of thanksgiving for him and thankfulness for a mother who had taught me to trust in a God who loves us.

*****

We found other people to work for us the week before he left. I wanted to spend every minute possible with him. We didn't leave our apartment except to go to the beach to walk. We didn't talk much about where he was going; instead, we talked about what we would do when he came back. We would begin to look for land or a home in the country as soon as he returned.

Ben had to leave our house at six in the morning, on the first of December. He had everything packed the night before so all he had to do was dress, eat, and leave. I slept very little that last night, and every time I moved Ben pulled me close to him. I don't think he slept either. When the alarm went off at five fifteen I jumped out of bed.

"Katy, come back here."

"I want to cook some bacon and eggs for you."

"No, I don't want you to. I want you to come back to bed and stay here until I leave. I want to take the memory of you here in our bed with me. And when I get back this is where I want to find you, okay? Waiting for me."

"What will you eat?"

"I'm not hungry. And the auto start on the coffee pot is on. I'll take a cup with me."

We spent the next half hour just holding each other. Then he slipped out of bed. I watched him get dressed in the dim light before he came back to the bed and kissed me.

"Stay here until I'm gone, okay? When I walk out the door I have to focus my mind on what I need to do in the next few months. But I'm taking you with me… in my heart, okay?"

"I love you, Ben. And I'll be praying for you constantly."

"Thanks, baby. I love you too."

He turned away and left. But not before I saw the tears in his eyes. I heard the taxi honk its horn and the car door slam. I wanted to jump up and watch the taxi take him away, but he had told me not to.

I turned over and cried for what seemed like hours. I've always felt that everyone has their own personal trial in life-something that puts their personal strength to a test. I knew this was my trial, my test, at least for now.

I didn't feel like I had the strength to bear it.

*****

I heard the kitchen door open two hours later. My first thought was that he had reported for duty and they had sent him back to me. I jumped out of bed and ran to the kitchen. It was Mama Beth and Abby.

I saw the tears spring to their eyes as they rushed towards me and drew me into their arms. There is no better therapy than having people who will cry with you. They had brought my favorite Danish, and we made a new pot of coffee. They let me vent for an hour and consoled me the best they could. Then Abby took control.

"Okay, girlie. Dry those tears; it's retail therapy time.

"I'm not in the mood to shop, Abby. And I don't need anything."

"Yes, you do need something." Abby snapped at me. "You need a sexy new outfit for when your handsome husband comes home. We know you; you're going to work everyday until he gets back, and you won't take the time off to go with us later. So we're going today."

She was going through the ads in yesterday's paper while she talked.

"Let's see, six months from now will be May. We're going to look for something light and springy, even if it *is* December now. Then we're going to find you the sexiest negligee we can find. Ben's coming home again, and when he gets here he's going to find his wife sexy and waiting. Now go take a shower and put on some mascara; your eyes are a mess."

I had no choice. My sister can be such a bossy thing.

Chapter 24

My eight p.m. was Ben's five a.m. the next morning. That's when we talked, or Skyped, if it was convenient for him to do so. Most of the time the other guys were asleep at that hour, and he didn't mind getting up early to see or talk to me. The first few times I talked to him were both wonderful and painful. When I first saw him on the computer screen, I wanted to reach through it and drag him back to me. He looked so good. After we hung up I sobbed for hours. I missed him so much.

He was always upbeat and positive. When I would question him about his work, he would say, "I'm just doin' my job, baby. And I'm doing it as well as I can. I stay busy. It helps make the time go faster."

But then, I knew *that*. That's all I'd done since he left. I worked my own twelve hour shifts and any extra they asked me to do. There were some days when I would work an extra four on top of the twelve. I'd go home, sleep a few hours, then get back up the next day and start over. Since it was December, I had a lot of colleagues who wanted time off.

The worst part of the day was after work. The thought of going home to an empty house was almost unbearable. If I didn't work over-time, I went to see someone in the family, or to the church to do volunteer work.

They always needed help, and I'd been taught that loving God and serving Him were one in the same. I also knew the best way to help myself was to help someone else. I had let the serving God slip away a little since meeting Ben. But I felt like God understood. After all, He had given Ben and me to each other, and I was sure He wanted us to enjoy those first few months together. He had known what lay ahead for us.

I was still taking Wednesdays off to spend with Abby and Mama. The first week Ben was gone I decided to go to church in the evening to help with the youth group. When Ben called the next evening I told him about it.

"Do you think that's something we could do together when you get back? I see so many of the young guys struggling. You would be a good role model for them."

"I think I'd like that, especially if it's something we can do together. When I get back, I don't ever want to be apart from you again." I could tell he was having a difficult day.

"Does that mean you'll get out of the reserves?"

"I'm thinking about it. I miss you so much."

"I miss you too, but we can do this. God is helping us. Then we'll have the rest of our lives to spend together." He needed me to be the positive one that day, even if I didn't feel that way.

I stayed so busy at work I had to give money to Mama and Abby and ask them to go Christmas shopping for me. The only gift I spent time on was Ben's. I knew he didn't need much where he was, so I sent him food and an e-reader full of books.

I volunteered to work on Christmas Eve and Christmas Day then flew to Philadelphia to be with my family. I stayed with them until the first week in January. It was nice being able to spend time with mom and dad, and my brothers again. Both of the boys brought girlfriends to dinner on New Year's Eve. I liked the girls, but seeing the four of them together, having fun and enjoying their new love, only made me miss Ben even more.

It was while I was in Philadelphia that I realized how physically and emotionally exhausted I was. The past year had been a full one. I had fallen in love, gotten married, and then when life seemed perfect, I had to deal with the stress of sending Ben off to war. Being with Mom and Dad, and letting them take care of me was what I needed at the time. I slept a lot while I was there.

When Mom took me to the airport she scolded me.

"Katy, please slow down. I know work helps pass the time while Ben's away, but you can't afford to get so physically and emotionally exhausted. You know you need to take care of yourself. You're letting yourself get run down."

"I'm okay, Mom. Being here has been wonderful. Thank you for always taking such good care of me. Now that I've survived the holidays without Ben, I know I'll be fine for the next five months…if I stay busy and he stays safe. Besides, we can use the extra money we're both making to buy that little farm Ben wants."

"Katy, you know you don't ever have to worry about money."

"I know, Mom. And thank you. But we want to do this ourselves."

"I know you do. But God has blessed your dad and me so we can help others. That includes our family. Let us do what God wants us to do."

"I will, if we ever need it. But there are so many other people who could use it more. Ben and I want to take care of our own needs."

Ben and I had talked about my money only once before we got married. He was shocked at the size of the trust fund my parents had set up for me. When I told him that everything that was mine, would also be his, I saw how independent and strong-willed he could be. He was adamant that it not be used for our needs as a family.

"I hope I'll be able to supply not only everything you need, but everything you want in life," he said to me with great conviction. And since he was all I ever wanted or needed, it wouldn't be difficult for him to do that.

Chapter 25

By the end of January, I had missed my second period. When it hadn't come in December, I thought it was because I was so stressed out with Ben leaving. But by the end of January I knew-even without taking a test that I was pregnant. The exhaustion I felt in Philadelphia over the holidays didn't go away. There were some mornings when I woke almost too tired to get out of bed. And when I did get out, I just wanted to cry or throw up. There were other signs too.

I knew Ben and I were going to have a baby! I wanted to be happy. I really did. This is what we had dreamed about for months. But for some reason, I didn't want to admit it was true. It was *our* baby, not just mine, and I wanted to share every minute of this new life with him. He was going to miss the pink line on the pregnancy test, and the first doctor's appointment. He would miss the ultrasound, and he wouldn't be able to see or hear our baby's heartbeat for the first time.

I didn't even want to go to the doctor. I knew he would confirm what I already knew…but Ben wouldn't be with me when it happened. And I knew the minute it was confirmed by the doctor I would need to share the news with Ben. But I wanted him to be with me so I could see the joy in his eyes and feel his arms around me.

I tried to think about the positives. This was the one exciting thing I had thought might not ever happen to me. Ben would be thrilled, even though he wasn't here to share it with me. The knowledge of our coming baby would give both of us something else to think about except how lonely we were.

But what if I told him and then miscarried? He would blame himself because he would feel like his being gone had put extra stress on me.

I decided to wait until after I missed my third period before I went to the doctor. As a nurse, I knew I needed to get prenatal care as soon as possible. But I just didn't want to go without Ben. I also knew the chance of miscarriage would probably be over by then. In the meantime, I would just keep working, and sleeping, and throwing up all alone.

It was on a Tuesday, the first week in February, when Denny found me in the break-room crying and picking at my lunch. He came in and sat down beside me. He had become like a surrogate brother to me; not surprising, seeing as how we spent so much time together.

"You doin' okay?"

"Define okay?"

"What you aren't right now? What's wrong?"

"You mean besides the fact that my husband has been in Afghanistan for two months and I'm sick with worry and loneliness?"

"I'm really sorry, Katy. But you need to take care of yourself. You look awful and you're working like a crazy woman."

"I look awful? Now that really helps, you big lug! I'm okay."

"When was the last time you had a day off?"

"Last Wednesday."

"And your next day off?"

"What day is today?"

"Tuesday."

"Tomorrow. I have tomorrow off."

"And you have this weekend off too, right?"

"I'm going to work for Linda. She has something going on."

"Katy, you have to stop. I'm so worried about you that I'm tempted to get Ben's number and tattle on you. He'd be mad if he could see you."

"He just saw me. We Skyped last night."

"And did he see the black rings under your eyes?"

"No. He told me I was beautiful."

"I'll tell you what. I'll work for Linda this weekend if you'll take it off and rest up. Please? I like you for a partner, and if you keep this up you're going to get sick and not be able to be here to do my work."

"Ah ha! I knew you had an ulterior motive for all this concern."

But what he said sank in. I knew I was overdoing it. I could lose our baby and it would be my fault. So I took the next weekend off, stayed home, and slept.

*****

I called the doctor that Monday. What Denny said, put things into perspective for me. I had to think of my health. Ben's baby was depending on me. When I told the nurse I had already missed two periods she was able to make an appointment for me on Wednesday morning.

I called Abby and told her I wouldn't be able to come to her house until the afternoon because I had errands to run.

As I was getting ready for my appointment, the phone rang.

"Hey, Baby. It's me."

"Ben, what's wrong? You never call me at this time of the day."

"Nothing's wrong. But since I couldn't call last night, and I can't stop thinking about you, I decided to call this morning. I need to know you're okay. I've been worried about you. I think you're working too much. You looked tired when I saw you on Skype last week."

I couldn't have him thinking something was wrong and worrying about me. Especially when being pregnant with his bab was going to make everything right in our lives. I had to tell him. He deserved to know, and keeping it from him was wrong.

"Where are you right now?"

"I'm in our little command center."

"Is anyone with you?"

"Yeah, a couple of the guys. Why?"

"'Cause I need to tell you something that I think is going to make you happy and I want to know who you're going to share the news with after I tell you."

"What news? What's going on?"

"Ben, I think I'm pregnant."

He was quiet for a few seconds.

"Pregnant? Really? Why do you think that? Did you take a test? How far along are you? How long have you suspected it? Why didn't you tell me?"

I had to laugh.

"Hey, Cowboy... slow down. I can only answer one question at a time. I'm on my way to the doctor right now. I wasn't going to tell you until I had the ultrasound picture to show you. But since you felt the need to call today, maybe it's a sign I should tell you now. Actually, I'm glad you know. Now I know you'll be thinking about me while I'm at the doctor. It will make me feel closer to you. But I really wish you could be there with me."

"I wish I could be there too. So how far along are you? Do you know?"

"Well, let's see. The last time I slept with a guy was over two months ago. That means I have to be at least that far along." The sound of his laughter made my heart happy.

"Oh, Katy. I so want to be there with you. I'm sorry."

"Ben, it's okay. Why don't you call me again tonight? I'll have more information then. And I'll send you a copy of the ultrasound so you can see it. You just go to bed now and rest. When you wake up you'll know for sure if you're going to be a dad."

"A dad-I'm going to be a dad! Oh thank you, baby. I knew we could do it!"

"Ben? Take it easy. It hasn't been confirmed yet. I need to go to the doctor to get that done. So just calm down, okay? I need to go…I love you."

"I love you too… and our baby. What are we going to name her?"

"We have lots of time to decide that. You just take care of you, for me. No, you take care of you…for us."

Chapter 26

My appointment was at ten. They sent me to the lab when I got there, then I had to wait awhile before I was called in to see the doctor. While I waited I did some people watching. It has always been one of my favorite hobbies, and today I was in a place I had never been before. I was in an obstetrician's office and I was pregnant. New environment, new people, new experience!

I watched as women came and went. One of the first things I noticed was that I wasn't the only woman who sat alone. There were others. Maybe they were alone because the fathers of their babies were busy at work. There were probably some who were alone because the fathers of their babies were unconcerned, or not involved.

I thought of the story Mama Beth had told me about her pregnancy with me. She was sixteen at the time. My biological dad had driven her to the abortion clinic and dumped her off in front of it, telling her he would return for her in the afternoon. She sat alone, afraid, and in emotional turmoil because she didn't want to be there. At the time, she felt like she had no choice. She lived in fear of her abusive father. But she left the clinic that day with me still tucked safely inside her.

After she told her mother, both of them were able to escape from her dad's control. But because of her fear of him she gave me up for adoption, so she could continue to keep me safe.

Thinking about her made me realize what I was going through was nothing, compared to what she went through to give life to me. My baby had a daddy who loved it. He was also a man who wanted his own child and other children to live in a safe America. He was doing what his heart told him to do, and *had* been doing it long before we came into his life.

When my name was called I was feeling better about Ben not being with us. He would be with me if he could.

The blood test came back positive and my doctor told me she wanted to do the ultrasound before I left. When she took my health history and asked me about the father of the baby, I told her where he was. She offered to make a DVD of the ultrasound for Ben. I knew he would be thrilled.

As I watched the ultrasound screen, Dr. Palmer pointed out the beating heart of my baby. I was in awe that one so tiny could already reassure a mother that it was alive and appeared to be healthy. It was one of the most miraculous things I had ever seen. The joy I felt was indescribable. I didn't know how I was going to be able to describe it to Ben so he could understand the miracle of it.

The tiny feet and hands, and the beating heart were the result of our love. I couldn't keep the tears of joy back. I wished then that I had told my mom I was pregnant. She would have flown down, and she and Mama Beth could have both been with me. If I had not been feeling sorry for myself I could have shared the joy of today with them.

I knew I had to tell them. I would call Mama Beth on my way to Abby's house and ask her to meet me there. She and I would call my mom together.

Ben would be happy I shared it with them, even if he had to wait himself. At least he had been the first to hear the news.

"Katy, when did you say your last period was?"

"It was in November-a week or so before Thanksgiving. Why?"

"This baby's measurements are looking a little more mature than that. Do you remember if your period was light that month?"

"I don't remember. Some months are lighter than other months."

"I was thinking you were due in August, but it looks like this baby is big enough to come in July. We're going to estimate your due date at about July twentieth. When is your husband coming home?"

"They told him three to six months. But now we know he'll have to stay the whole six months. So we're planning on him being home by the end of May. He says if he gets home earlier it will be a pleasant surprise for both of us."

"So we know for sure he'll be here for the last two months of your pregnancy. That's good. Those will be your worst months because of the heat. You can make him feed you ice cream everyday."

Before I left the office, Dr. Palmer gave me a prescription for prenatal vitamins.

"They have some iron in them so take them. Your blood test shows your iron level to be a little low."

"I don't doubt that. I haven't been taking very good care of myself. I've been missing Ben so much. But now that I've seen our baby I intend to do everything in my power to have a healthy one."

*****

I left the doctor's office feeling so much better than when I went in. Seeing the baby had made him or her real to me. I decided even though Ben couldn't be with me, I would still try to enjoy my pregnancy.

On the way to Abby's house, I made my call to Mama.

"Hi, Honey. Abby said you're going to her house late today. You okay?"

"I'm good. But I was wondering…if you aren't doing anything special, could you meet me there? I'm going to stop and buy some double fudge ice cream."

"Mmm, double fudge. What are we celebrating?"

"Just that I'm not feeling so sad and lonely today. Can you come?"

"Of course! I would love to celebrate your "not so sad day" with you. I was going to do some cleaning, but I'd rather eat ice cream with my girls."

Abby had the boys in bed for their naps when I got there. Mama pulled into the driveway just minutes after I arrived.

"I didn't know Mama was coming too. And you brought double fudge ice cream! That's good. You've been looking a little puny lately. I'll put on a fresh pot of coffee." It was weird how all three of us had to have coffee when we ate ice cream.

"Do you have decaf?"

"What's the matter, you still can't sleep without your honey in bed with you?"

"Yeah. You should try it sometime, it's not fun!"

While Abby was serving up the ice cream, I took the DVD out of my purse. "Can you two watch this DVD with me while we eat?"

"What is it?"

"Something I found today. It looks like something we'd all like."

They both sat down on the sofa while I put the DVD in the player. I got my bowl of ice cream and sat down across from them. I wanted to see their faces when they recognized what I was going to show them.

"Where's the music? I've never watched a movie that started without music. Wait a minute…what is this?"

"It looks like some kind of an ultrasound. I had one when I was pregnant with Carly…oh my! Katy! Is this yours? Is this what we're celebrating?"

My smile was the only answer they needed.

They were so busy hugging me they didn't see the whole thing. So we had to watch it a second time.

"Does Ben know?"

"It was so weird. When I got up this morning I was feeling really bad about having to go to the doctor without him, and he called right then. He has never called me in the morning. It was like he knew something was going on. So of course I had to tell him, even though I was planning to wait until I could show him the picture."

"So, how did he sound? Was he very disappointed he couldn't be here with you?"

"Yes, he was disappointed. But I think he was just more excited that we are going to have a baby. I think it's going to be very difficult for him to be there now. He's going to call me later to get the details. I could tell he was excited, but kind of sad too, because he couldn't be here to go to the doctor with me." I had to stop and take a breath. I was so excited I couldn't seem to stop talking.

"But it's gonna be okay. The night he told me he was going to Afghanistan, he said he wished I was pregnant so I would have something else to focus on while he was gone. He got his wish."

Mama hugged me again. "You are both going to be such good parents. Did you tell your mom and dad yet?"

"No, not yet. I was actually thinking about trying to keep it a secret from all of you until Ben got home. But after I saw the ultrasound today and Dr. Palmer told me I was due in July, I knew I wouldn't be able to do that."

"And we would have been mad if you hadn't told us. So does this mean you're going to stop working so much? You have to take better care of yourself."

"I know. I already got that lecture today. So, yes. I will slow down-for the baby."

"We could go shopping and get the baby's room ready."

"No. I'm going to wait on Ben for that. He's already going to miss so much of this pregnancy, I don't want him to miss that too."

"Let's call your mom." Mama Beth was picking up our ice cream bowls and getting us more coffee. "We'll put her on speaker phone so we can all talk. I can't wait to hear her voice; she's going to be so excited. This is her first grandbaby. I bet she'll be down here before the week is over. Maybe it will be my first granddaughter. Kyle and Konner would love a little girl cousin. Wouldn't they, Abby?"

"Yes! And I would love to have a little niece to dress up in pretty clothes."

"Ben told me he would like a little girl too. But for some reason, I think it's going to be a boy. I want him to have a son. He can teach him to ride horses and fly airplanes."

"Little girls can learn to do those things too."

"I know…but I want a little boy like Ben."

Chapter 27

I made the call to my mom and turned the speaker on so everyone could share the excitement.

"Mom? It's me."

"Hi, me. How's my girl?"

It's funny; that's how we always start all our conversations. If they don't go that way, I feel like something's missing. I saw Mama Beth smile when she heard us. I think the fact that she was able to give my mom a daughter makes her happy now, even though it didn't in the beginning.

"I'm good. Are you busy right now?"

"Just getting dinner ready for your dad. What are you doing? No work today?"

"No, it's Wednesday. I'm here with Mama Beth and Abby. We want to show you something. Can you get on Skype so you can see it?"

"Sure. Give me a minute."

"Okay, we'll be ready on this end."

The three of us were giggling hysterically by the time we got connected with her.

"Well it looks like all of you are having fun today. I told your dad, just yesterday, we're going to have to retire down there because I'm missing out on too much fun. And…I've had my share of snow storms. So what do you need to show me?"

"It's a picture. Here it comes."

I held the ultrasound picture up to the screen.

"What is it, Katy? It looks like some kind of x-ray. You aren't sick are you?"

"Mom! Would we look this happy if I was sick? It's your first grandbaby! Look at him, isn't he cute?"

When she didn't say anything I had a fleeting thought that maybe the shock of it made her have a stroke or something. I should have prepared her.

"Mom? Are you okay? Did you hear what I said?"

"You're going to have a baby?"

"Yes, he's due at the end of July."

"He? It's a boy?"

"I don't know what it is, I just think that's what it is."

"Oh, honey. I am so happy for you and Ben. And us! I can't wait to tell your dad. He's going to be so excited. Now he's going to have to bring me down there on spring break. Goodness! Wasn't it just last year on spring break that you introduced us to Ben? Does he know?"

Once she got started, she couldn't stop talking either.

Oh, Ben...our baby is already bringing so much joy to our family.

*****

Ben called earlier than he usually did, which meant it was about three in the morning in Afghanistan.

"You're supposed to be sleeping."

"I couldn't stay in bed any longer. I need to know what the doctor said. Are you okay?"

"I am so fine, Ben! I'm having our baby! And guess what? I'm already over three months pregnant! Our baby is going to be here at the end of July."

"July? So I'll get to be with you for the last two months?"

"That's what the doctor said. You'll be here just in time for me to get really miserable. She said I'll have to insist you sit and feed me ice cream for two long, hot months."

"Honey, I'll feed you anything you want. So the baby looks good? Could they tell if it's a boy or a girl?"

"Not yet, silly. Besides, I don't want to know that until you're with me. Do you think we should wait until it's born to find out?"

"Do you?"

"Maybe. I already think it's a little boy who looks like you."

"But you know I want a little girl, with chocolate brown eyes like yours. Hey! Maybe we'll have both!"

"Not hardly. I saw the ultrasound; there's only one baby."

"I wish I could have been there to see it."

"The doctor put it on a DVD, and I got pictures. I'll send them to you in a little while."

"Katy?"

"What?"

"Thank you."

"No, thank *you*! You've made all my dreams come true now."

"And you and our baby are the family I've always wanted." I could hear the tears in his voice, and feel my own welling up in my eyes. Our baby was going to have two very sentimental parents.

Chapter 28

Every time we were able to Skype, Ben insisted on seeing my belly. For the first couple of months he was disappointed. He couldn't see any change. But by the end of April, it was beginning to pop, and I was feeling tiny kicks and flutters.

"I wish I could feel it kicking."

"One more month, Ben. One more month and you will."

"I think it will be the longest month of my life."

"For me too. But I'm feeling more energetic now so I'm going to work all I can this month. It will make the time go by faster."

"Katy…I've been thinking. I'd like for you to quit working when I get home. I think you should give them your notice this week, and tell them you won't be back after the end of May."

"I don't know about that, Ben. I love my work."

"I know you do. But you can always go back to it later."

"But we'll need the money if you're getting out of the reserves."

"I still haven't made up my mind about that. This separation has been horrible, but I feel good about serving my country. And you know how important the guys in my unit are to me. We all work together so well, and if one of us isn't here, the team isn't complete. It doesn't work as well. These guys were my only family for years."

"I know, but you have us now."

"And I'm so grateful I do. But leaving my unit would be like leaving family. And being a soldier is part of who I am."

"So…what? You'll keep all three of your jobs and I'll stay home with the baby?"

"Don't you want to stay home with the baby?"

"Yes, but I don't want to be a single mom. There has to be a better solution. I think it would be better if you gave up one of your jobs and I worked part-time. Being a nurse is part of who I am, too. And your son or daughter is going to need his or her dad, not just your paycheck."

I was confused. As much as he had talked about wanting a family, why wouldn't he want to be with us as much as possible?

"But I like the idea of you being at home with our baby while I'm at work. I don't want to leave him or her with a baby-sitter."

"That's why you need to quit one of your jobs. I could work two evenings a week and you could stay at home while I'm there. It would give you some one-on-one time with our baby." I was feeling some frustration at the way this conversation was going.

"Ben, you know I love being a nurse, and I'm good at it! Maybe I'll be like Mama Beth. She loved being a mom, but she felt like she needed a part-time job too. She always said getting away from the house a couple days a week made her appreciate her home and family more."

"A child needs his mom. You don't know what it's like-growing up without one." I heard something unfamiliar in his voice. It wasn't self-pity. It sounded like frustration or impatience.

"No, I don't know what that feels like. But I think a child needs a dad just as much! A dad with three jobs won't be around very much."

"But the dad provides for his family." Now I heard the stubbornness in his voice.

"Both parents can provide financially and emotionally. I want to share both of those responsibilities with you."

"Let's don't argue about this. Not now. But will you think about it?"

"I'll think about it, but you need to think about what I just said too."

"Okay, I will. Don't be upset with me. I was just thinking about how hard you work, and it makes me feel guilty that I'm not there with you to at least rub your feet at the end of your long days of work."

Now I was feeling guilty. The man was in hot, dirty, dusty Afghanistan, feeling bad that he couldn't be here. And I was arguing with him. But I had strong feelings about him getting out of the reserves. I was frightened with him so far away and in danger. And I didn't want our kids to have those feelings, the fear that maybe their dad would never come back. I tried not to think about that, but it was a possibility that was very real to me every minute he was out of my sight.

"I'll make a deal with you. I'll go on my pregnancy leave early. I was going to take six months off after the baby, but I'll tell them I want to change it to two months before and four months after. When you get home I'll be here full time and you can rub my feet every minute you aren't working. Besides, we have a lot to do before this baby gets here."

"I know we do. Have you even looked at any nursery furniture or decorations?"

"I've looked a little, but I'm waiting until you get home to decide what to get. So, what are you going to do about work when you get home?"

"I'll go back to the hospital, but maybe I'll wait until after the baby gets here to pick up any charters. I would hate to be hundreds of miles away when you go into labor."

"That sounds perfect. There's no way I'm letting you out of the labor part of this pregnancy!"

He sounded excited again when we hung up, but our conversations stayed with me for days.

*****

I had an appointment to see Dr. Palmer the next day. I had my blood drawn again and was going to have another ultrasound. I hadn't had one since my first appointment, and she told me they always did a second one at twenty-four weeks.

"We'll be able to see the sex of the baby this time. Do you want to know what it is?"

After much discussion, I had convinced Ben we should wait for that until we were together. Everything about my pregnancy that could be delayed until he got home, got delayed. The gender of our baby was an important thing. I wanted him to be with me, so we could find out together. I watched in amazement again, as my baby kicked and squirmed.

Just one more month, Ben. You have to stay safe so you can come home and see our baby. We need you...not just your paycheck.

Chapter 29

When I got home from the doctor I started to think again about Ben's suggestion that I quit my job. He had sounded adamant that I be a full-time mom. It was confusing to me. He had been so easy to live with in those first few months that I had begun to wonder if we would ever find anything to disagree about. Now we did. And this was a huge topic to not agree on.

I had seen a stubborn side of him on occasion. But I didn't think of him as being inflexible. He was probably just tired, homesick, and in need of being with me-as much as I was in need of him. When he got home, we could talk about it some more.

Being a nurse was all I ever wanted to do and I had just finished getting my Masters the summer before. What a waste of a good education if I quit working. And nursing is one of those jobs where things change all the time. If I got away from it for too long, I could lose my skills and get behind.

No, I couldn't stop being a nurse. And I was having a difficult time understanding Ben's reasoning. It just didn't make sense that I give up something I loved and do all the parenting. That would be like me asking him to give up flying, to become a full-time dad. It was definitely something the two of us would have to discuss more when he called back.

But Ben didn't call back that night. He had missed a few nights in the five months he'd been gone and I tried not to worry when that happened. He had warned me that there might even be several days in a row when he wouldn't be able to call because of his work.

Three days later, when he still hadn't called, I started to worry. Was he upset with me because I had argued with him about continuing to work after the baby came? But I knew Ben, he wasn't like that. He would never, not call just because he didn't agree with me about something. No, something else was keeping him from calling.

I turned the TV on and kept it turned to the twenty four hour news channel. But there was no news from Afghanistan. I began to feel afraid again, like I had been before he left. Why wasn't he calling me?

I thought then of my great grandmother. When I was very young and she was very old, she told me about a time during World War II when three of her seven sons had been oversees at the same time. She said she prayed for all of them from the time she got up until she went to bed. I'll never forget the tears in her eyes when she told me about the day a military car came up the dirt road they lived on. The news given to her that day was devastating. One of sons was missing in action. His body was never found and she assumed he was buried in France where he was last stationed.

I didn't sleep at all that night. I prayed and cried. And I came to the conclusion that keeping my job as a nurse after my child was born didn't seem important anymore. I just needed Bed to come home.

*****

The phone call came the next day. When I heard Ben's voice, I started to cry.

"Katy? What's wrong? Are you okay? I wanted to call you after your appointment the other day, but I couldn't get away to do it. Is the baby okay?"

"Oh, Ben! Please, don't ever do that to me again!"

"Do what?"

"Don't ever make me wait so long for a phone call! Where have you been? I've been worried sick about you."

"I've been right here, where I've been for the past five months. So, you're okay? The baby's okay? Why are you crying?"

"Because you haven't called me for four days."

"I told you that might happen sometime. It's happened before."

"I know. But…oh, never mind. I was just worried this time. The baby is fine and so am I, now that I know you're okay. Why couldn't you call?"

"Honey, you know I can't give you the details. But trust me, I missed you too. Hopefully, it won't happen again."

"So, you aren't mad at me for wanting to work after the baby comes?"

"What? You thought I wasn't calling because I was mad? I can't believe you'd think that about me."

"I'm sorry. I was just so afraid and I didn't know what to think. I know you're a better man than that. But, please…can we not argue again while you're there? It makes the separation more difficult."

"I'm sorry, too. I've been so busy that I haven't even thought about our conversation. And I didn't know it was so upsetting to you. We'll figure it all out when I get home. You just take care of yourself, okay?"

"Okay. You take care of you too. I love you so much. I think I would die if anything happened to you."

"Nothing is going to happen to me, so just put that thought out of your pretty little head."

*****

I did what he asked me to do. For the next three weeks I refused to think that anything bad would happen to Ben. But I couldn't stop thinking about what he had asked me to do. He wanted me to quit being a nurse. I didn't think that was something I could do, not even for him. But if it that's what the man I loved, wanted…how could I not consider his feelings? And I had told him I would think about it.

Nursing had been my pre-Ben and pre-baby goal and dream. It had been a wonderful way to make a living, and I felt like I had made a difference in many lives in the years I had done it. But now I had Ben and a baby on the way. I could feel my priorities changing every day. But why couldn't I have both?

I knew I needed to pray about it and let God lead me. I had let Him direct my life up to this point, and He had not failed me. I knew Ben was God's answer to my prayers and now a baby was going to complete my life. Did I really need to be a nurse too?

I sent an e-mail to both my parents and asked them to pray about it with me. Mama Beth had worked part-time as a social worker at the hospital ever since she had married Alex. She loved her work and was able to work around Alex's schedule. She told me she was the kind of person who needed to be out of her home for a few hours a week. She said she thought it made her a better mom when she got back home.

My mom had worked as a librarian in Philadelphia after she married Dad. She never *had* to work but had wanted to. Dad's parents were wealthy, and he had been successful in his career too. After they adopted me she never went back. She said she had waited a long time for me and she didn't want to miss one minute of my growing up.

Both my moms had done the mothering thing in a different way, but each had done a great job. Now I had to choose how I wanted to do it. I knew I was lucky to have that choice. There were so many women who simply didn't have a choice, they had to work. Abby was already talking about the day when she would have to go back to work so they could afford to send their kids to college.

But I had a choice. I could stay home with my baby, and it sounded like Ben wanted me to do that. I wanted to honor his wishes. But what if I quit, then decided I needed time away from home like Mama Beth had?

I knew I had to leave it all in God's hands. He would give me the wisdom I needed when the time was right. Life had taught me that God's ways are best and His timing is perfect.

*****

Two weeks later I talked to Denny about the possibility that I might not be coming back to work.

I had already given my supervisor the notice for my FMLA, and she had approved it. I would start it the week before Ben came home. That time was getting closer.

"So, who do you think you're going to get for a new partner?" Denny and I were in the break room eating lunch.

"I think I'm going to tell them I'll wing it alone until you get back."

"You know they aren't going to let you do that. Besides, I'm thinking I might not come back."

"Really? I thought you loved nursing and would be one of those career girls."

"Before Ben and this baby, that was my goal. But they have changed everything for me."

"So you think you'll be happy at home all the time?" Denny had a puzzled look on his face.

"Maybe. I could always find a part-time teaching job at the nursing school. I could do that with my Masters."

"I can't see you being happy with that. You love patient care."

"I know…it's confusing. Maybe I'll become a cowgirl. You know Ben wants to buy some land and get some horses. I'll probably end up with a whole farm full of animals to take care of." Just saying it sounded like fun, and I couldn't help but smile at the thought of it.

"A cowgirl! I can see you doing that too. So where are to going to look for land?"

"I guess we'll have to move away from the Gulf. I'm going to miss that. I love walking on the beach."

"Hey, my aunt and uncle are trying to sell their orange grove. Maybe you could buy that."

"An orange grove? We don't know anything about growing oranges."

"You could learn. I think they have about a hundred acres. Sixty acres of it is oranges, the rest is big, old oak trees. And there's a huge lake on the property too. You could still be close to water!"

"An orange grove…I'll have to pray a long time about that one. Where is it?"

"About fifty miles east of here. If you want to see it, let me know."

"Okay, but probably not. Growing oranges has never been in my dreams."

"Ben could have his horses and you could grow oranges and babies. Sounds like a lot more fun than checking in here every day."

Chapter 30

The seed had been planted and I couldn't get the orange grove out of my thoughts. But I didn't say anything about it to Ben. When he called the only thing on my mind was that he would be home soon. I could tell he was getting anxious too.

"Hey, baby! Ten more days! I can't wait…are you doing okay?"

"I'm feeling wonderful, Ben. But you may not recognize me when you get home. I've gained twenty pounds already."

"I bet you look beautiful. Let me see the belly."

"I don't think I want to show it to you anymore. Not until you can touch it, and feel our baby moving inside of me."

"Hey, that's my baby, and I have a right to see her. Now bare that belly, girl!"

So, of course I did. I loved my belly. I had talked to some of the nurses at work, and they told me they hated being pregnant because of what it did to their bodies. I didn't feel that way at all. I loved the way it looked and the way it felt.

"You look beautiful, Katy. I so wish…."

"Ten more days, Ben. We can do this! I have only three more days to work then I'm going to spend the rest of the time getting ready for you."

"You remember where you're suppose to be when I get home, right?"

"If I remember correctly, you told me to be in bed."

"Good girl!"

"But what if I want to meet you at the airport?"

"You don't want to do that, I promise you. I intend to make love to you within five minutes of seeing you. So unless you want to do it at the airport, then stay at home in bed."

"I'd like to know what happened to the man I dated? You know, the one who had self-control like iron?"

"The ring on my finger says I can make love to my wife anytime I want to. We'll still be able to…I mean, it's going to be okay to do it, isn't it?"

"Yea, of course. But maybe you won't want to when you see how big my belly is."

"From what I can see from here, you are sexier than ever."

I wondered if absence had really made our hearts grow fonder or if it was just the way we were. Every ounce of my body ached for him when I went to bed.

*****

When I wasn't thinking about Ben and our baby, I was thinking about being a citrus grower. The thought of it was intriguing to me, so I Googled the topic. Like most kinds of farming, citrus growing was a risky business, but one that could also be lucrative if done correctly. But it wasn't just growing citrus that appealed to me. I knew the grove would provide roaming space for my cowboy and our child on their horses. And the thought of providing Vitamin C to thousands of America's children sounded like it could be an extension of being a nurse. It would be a way of promoting good health.

The last day I worked with Denny I asked him if he would have time to take me to see his family's grove.

"You're really thinking about buying it?"

"I don't know. I just can't get it out of my head and I might as well go see it if you can take me."

"Yeah, sure! Aunt Lucy and Uncle John get lonely out there, and they love seeing my kids."

Denny, his wife, and two little girls stopped and picked me up the next Saturday. I had just three days until Ben would be home.

I fell in love again. The grove was beautiful with its long rows of perfectly spaced trees. The lake on the property was a picture of pure serenity. I instantly felt like Denny's Aunt Lucy and Uncle John were my family, too. They welcomed me with warmth, and their generosity was evident as soon as we shook hands.

We all piled onto two golf carts to take the tour. I was with Denny and his aunt. As we traveled the trails around the orchard and lake, she told me the history of the grove. I could tell she loved living there, and raising her family there.

She said the lake had a two-fold purpose. Besides being recreational; it provided irrigation, if needed, and warm mist if there was a threat of freezing. The grove was fully functioning and highly successful, with fruit buyers coming back every year.

"So, why are you selling? It looks like it would be a perfect place to live."

"It *is* a perfect place to live, but we're getting older and want to do some traveling in our retirement. We thought one of our children would want to take it over, but that isn't going to happen. What makes you think you'd like to be a citrus grower?"

"My maternal grandparents had a farm in Pennsylvania, and I loved going there when I was a kid. They had enough land for me and my brothers to roam on, and we were never bored. They had an apple orchard instead of an orange grove though, and they always had a variety of animals. I think they kept them around just to entertain their grandkids."

Unlike my paternal grandparents' mansion in the city, their home was warm and pleasant to visit, and I had fallen in love with country living as a child. But my life had always kept me in the city.

"My husband, Ben, would like to have land and horses like he had when he was a child. He says there's nothing better for a kid than climbing on the back of a horse and feeling the wind in your hair."

"Well, there's plenty of space to ride here!"

I was curious about the price, the taxes, and licensing fees. They were gracious about giving the information to me. It wasn't going to be a cheap purchase and I wondered if I would be able to talk Ben into letting me do it. It would also be a lot of work for both of us.

Lucy told me they had a group of local people who helped with some of the physical labor, and they had proven themselves to be reliable workers.

"My husband and I would be willing to stay around for a year to help the new buyers get established in the business-but only if we can find the right buyers."

Before we left, they showed me around the house, the barn, and the warehouses. It was a huge operation, and it would require me to work it full-time. The more I saw, though, the more at home I felt. And I knew I would be willing to give up nursing and use part of my trust fund to pay for it. Before I left, I asked about the nearest airport that could accommodate a small jet airplane.

"So what do you think?" Denny asked on the way home. "You gonna become a farm girl?"

"It was beautiful…but I'll have to talk it over with Ben."

After I got home that night, I laid it all out before God. As much as I wanted this for our family, I didn't want to do anything that would jeopardize the relationship between Ben and me. I asked God to work it out, if it was meant to be.

*****

My husband was coming home! His flight was due in at eleven p.m. on Tuesday. I was so torn. I wanted to be at the airport to welcome him home, but he reminded me, during our last phone call before he left Afghanistan, of where he wanted to find me. I knew he was serious about his little fantasy of me being at home waiting for him. I talked to Abby about it.

"I don't want him to get off the plane and not have a welcoming party waiting for him. Why does he have to be so stubborn?"

"Katy, having you at the airport probably isn't a big deal to him. He has come home before without anyone to welcome him."

"Exactly! Now he has a wife, so he could have someone. He wouldn't let me see him off, and now he doesn't want me there to welcome him home!"

"But this is the homecoming he wants. He's probably thought about it the whole time he's been there. You can't disappoint him. How would it be if Mama, Daddy, Brett and I go to the airport and give him a surprise welcome home party? He won't have to wait for a taxi, and we'll bring him straight home and dump him off."

"But that means you'll get to see him before I do."

"But you'll get the best of him. Let us do this for both of you."

I bought the balloons and flowers and told my family they had exactly thirty minutes to get him home to me after his plane touched down.

Before Abby left my house she wanted to know if I was going to be in the negligee we had bought the day he left.

"Abby, I'm seven months pregnant, that doesn't really work now. I look like a giant peach in it."

"I figured you would say that, so I bought you a different one. I think you're going to like it, and it will look amazing on you." It was pretty and fit my pregnant body beautifully. The bodice was fitted and flowed over my belly in soft silk. It showed off my legs, the only part of me that still looked the same as when Ben left.

"You are the best sister, ever! What would I do without you?"

"You'd be dressed in something frumpy when your husband gets home…now get ready, we're off to fetch your hubby!"

While I waited for him, I made a couple plates of his favorite hors d'oeuvres; stuffed baby portabellas with goat cheese stuffing and a plate of turkey and cheese wraps. I was sure he'd be hungry for something home-made when he got home.

At eleven thirty, I crawled into bed and waited for the love of my life to come home and find me right where he left me. This time, I had someone new with me though, and he seemed to be sensing my excitement, he rolled and tossed like a little acrobat inside me.

"Hold on, little boy. Your daddy will be here in a few minutes. I can't wait for you to meet each other. He's an amazing man and he's going to be a great dad for you."

I got up twice to look out the window. It was eleven forty-five when I finally called Abby.

"Where is he? Is his plane here yet?"

"We're still waiting. They say it won't be here for another fifteen minutes. Are you okay?"

"Just impatient; I want him now."

"We'll get him there, as soon as possible."

Okay. Maybe I need a cup of chamomile tea. It always seemed to relax me. I finished the cup and closed my eyes. I would just relax and he would be here soon.

Closing my eyes, I whispered, "Hold on baby, your daddy is coming home."

I woke to the feel of him next to me. He pulled me close and turned me to my back.

"Katy, I'm home."

I had no words. Just tears of pure joy as I pulled him as close to me as I could. He held me for several minutes. Then he pulled the sheet off me and began to examine my body with his eyes and his hands.

"Oh, Katy, you're more beautiful than I remembered." His hands caressed my belly, and he placed his head down to it. "Hey baby, I'm home. Can you talk to me?"

"He was just rolling around like a Sumo wrestler a few minutes ago. He must be as tired as I am. I can't believe I fell asleep, Ben. I'm sorry, I wanted to be awake to welcome you home with open arms."

"You are right where I wanted you to be, sweetheart."

"But you're probably hungry. I made some things for you to eat. Let me get up and I'll get it out for you."

"Later. Right now the only thing I'm hungry for is you. I just want to feel you in my arms."

*****

I woke in the morning still cradled in his arms. As I watched him sleep, I had to say a prayer of thanksgiving. God had brought him safely back home to me. The fear that had clenched my gut for the past six months was gone.

I slipped out of bed and went to the kitchen. I was at the stove when I felt his arms around me. He kissed my neck, sending a shiver of delight up my spine. He put his arms around my belly and caressed it, then turned me around and pulled me close. With my arms around his neck, I kissed him with a passion I had never felt before. How was it possible that loving him continued to evolve into something more amazing every day?

It was at that moment that our baby decided to kick so hard it made Ben jumped. "What was that?"

"Hmmm. I'm thinking your baby is telling you he or she doesn't want to be left out of this homecoming."

"Man, if he kicks a horse like that he's going to go on quite a ride."

"He? I thought you wanted a girl? Well, no matter what it is, I think we're all going to go on the ride of our lives in the next few months, Ben."

But before the ride into the future started, Ben and I spent the next few days catching up on precious days we had lost in the past six months.

Chapter 31

We spent the next two weeks working on the nursery. We had a difficult time deciding on the décor. Well…I did.

I love yellow and blue, the colors of sunshine and gulf waters. I thought about painting the top half of the room a sunny yellow then putting a wainscoting up and painting the bottom part blue. I knew Abby could and would love to paint flying seagulls on the top half, and fish and shells on the bottoms half.

Ben disagreed. "We can take him to the real beach anytime we want. Why make a fake one for him or her?"

"Well, how do you think we should do it?"

"How about blue on top and green at the bottom? We could have airplanes and clouds painted in the blues and a landing strip painted on the green."

"That doesn't sound very feminine."

"You said it's a boy. But if it's a girl she could grow up to be the next Amelia Earhart."

So we decided on animals. Not jungle animals though, Ben had to have farm animals. The first thing Ben bought was a rocking horse and a tiny pair of cowboy boots. If he had a little girl, she would have boots on for her first ride on the horse he would buy her someday. I made sure there was a little stuffed lamb in the crib. It had a pink ribbon around its neck. I told Ben it would bring out the nurturing side of our son.

When the room was ready, we stood back and wondered where we were going to put the baby. The high chair, play pen and toy box might have to wait until we got a bigger house because the desk, computer and file cabinets that had been in the baby's room were now in the living room. A two-bedroom townhouse gets a lot smaller when the baby stuff moved in.

I didn't want Ben to go back to work at the end of the two weeks.

"We can't live on love, Katy-girl…although it would be fun, wouldn't it?"

"I should have just worked until it was time to deliver. What am I going to do around here for the next six weeks if you aren't here?"

"I'm only working three days a week, I'll be here the other four."

"But they are long shifts."

"Not as long as the one in Afghanistan."

Ben always had a way of putting things into perspective for me.

*****

I found I had plenty to do while Ben was working. I was now going to the doctor every week, and Mom flew down so she could go shopping with me and Mama Beth. She stayed with me a few extra days and helped me get everything washed and put away. She said she and Dad were planning on coming down after the baby came.

"But I wanted you to be here for the birth, Mom."

"Oh, honey. I don't want to intrude on your and Ben's special time."

"Mom, you have to come. You never got to give birth to any babies of your own and I want you to have that experience through me."

"I thought maybe you would want your Mama Beth to be there with you."

"She already got to experience birth, twice. I'm sure she'll be at the hospital but I want you to be in the delivery room with me…if you want to be. I already asked the doctor and she said it would be okay."

"Oh, baby. I would be so honored. Is Ben okay with it?" I saw the tears in her eyes and I knew being there would be a dream-come-true for her.

"Of course. Actually I think he wants you there in case he faints."

"He isn't going to faint. With his job, he has seen it all."

"That's what I told him but he says he's going to be a mess if I have a difficult labor."

"How will I know when to come? I'll get a hotel when I get here."

"You don't have to get a hotel room. Mama Beth said you can stay in her guest room. Would that be okay? Since we had to turn the guest room into a nursery?"

"I don't want to put them out."

"I think she would be upset if you didn't stay with her."

"So…do you think I should come down about the fifteenth of July?"

"That sounds good, unless the doctor tells me different."

After Mom left, Carly moved in. Since school was out, she insisted she had nothing to do. In the eighteen months Ben and I had been together, she had grown into a young lady of almost twelve, and was counting down the days until she would be a teenager. She seemed mature beyond her years, maybe because she grew up surrounded by adults. She was so excited about the baby and really wanted me to have a little girl. She loved Kyle and Konnor, and was good with them, but she told me a little girl would feel more like a doll she could play with. (I think little girls who are in the process of growing into young ladies still want to play with dolls sometimes.)

When no one was around and I had time on my hands, I thought a lot about the orange grove. I still hadn't talked to Ben about it. The night we finished the nursery and were talking about how small our house was had seemed like a good time, but it just didn't feel like the right time. I wanted to focus on our being back together and the joy of preparing for the new baby. Not talking about a new and different adventure.

One day when I was coming from the doctor's office, I went into the trauma unit to visit with some of my friends. Denny was there.

"You thought any more about the orange grove? My aunt was asking me about you when I saw her last week."

"I've thought a lot about it. But I haven't talked to Ben about it yet. We've been kind of busy. Have they had any other lookers?"

"I think so, but no one has come up with the money yet. Not to be nosy, but where are you and Ben going to come up with that kind of money?"

"My dad has some money he wants to invest and I think I could manage the grove for him. I have a pretty good business head. I get that from him." It wasn't a lie. The money was originally my dad's.

"I thought you were adopted?"

"Sometimes environment works when biology fails. He taught me a lot."

"Don't wait too long. I know they're motivated to sell. They might even give you a deal since you're a friend of the family. I could put in a good word for you, even though you did desert me here in trauma."

Chapter 32

Ben and I celebrated our first anniversary on the fourth. We went out to dinner and Ben bought me a necklace. He knew I wasn't a huge jewelry fan so I was surprised. But it was perfect. It was a silver chain with a flat oval pendant on it. He had it engraved with the date and the words, "You complete me." It was simple, yet so meaningful. Something I could wear everyday for the rest of my life.

"If you weren't ready to pop, I'd have flown you to the mountains. It would be so nice and cool there compared to here. You could've soaked your poor swollen feet in the Little Pigeon River. Remember how cold it was when we were there?"

"That would feel amazing. Maybe we can go there for a week in the fall, and go hiking."

"Hiking with a baby?"

"Yeah. They have those sturdy carriers you strap on your back to carry a baby in. Don't you remember seeing it at the baby store? And I've read stories about couples who hike with their babies all the time. It would be fun."

"Where do you come up with these ideas, girl? Hiking with a baby? But I guess it wouldn't be that complicated since you have a built in food source for him. All we'd have to take is diapers. Maybe we'll do that. It could be his first ride in the airplane, too." Ben was now calling our baby a "him" too, even though he kept insisting he wanted a little girl who looked like me.

"Do you think we could go back to that same little log cabin we stayed in before? I think skinny dipping in that hot tub was on our agenda when we left there."

"Let me see what I can do about that. When do you think you'd like to go?"

"Maybe in October…when the leaves are turning colors? I do miss autumn in Pennsylvania sometimes."

"Sounds like a plan. I'll have to work around my schedule at the hospital and my reserve weekend though."

"About the reserves, Ben. Have you thought anymore about getting out of it? I know you get a lot of satisfaction from it, but maybe being a dad can more that make up for that."

"I still have three more months to decide if I want to re-enlist. I just hate to give up that retirement after all the years I've put in."

"It's your decision, but you know how I feel about it, right?"

"Yes, baby, I know. Now, is there anything else you want to do before our little bundle of joy gets here? Maybe go skydiving?"

"Very funny! Actually, I was wondering if we could go for a ride in the car tomorrow? The Valencia orange season is just wrapping up, and I'd like to go to a grove and get some before they're gone. Denny's aunt and uncle have a grove about an hour from here. Maybe we could go there."

"Fresh oranges—that sounds good. Why don't we take a picnic too? A day in the country sounds wonderful."

*****

"So you know where we're going? Denny gave the directions to you?"

I had to be honest with him. I had to tell him I had an ulterior motive for going to get oranges.

"Actually, while you were gone, I went with Denny and his family to visit this orchard. The Valencia oranges were just getting ripe then."

"When did you do that?"

"It was about the first of May, right after you talked to me about quitting work. Do you remember? You said you would like for me to stay home with the baby."

"I remember. I still like the idea."

"I know. I've been thinking and praying about it but want to wait and see how things go when my leave of absence is over. I still think I should keep mine and you should give up one of yours."

"Maybe we should both quit all our jobs and just stay home and take care of our baby. If only it was possible to live on love! But love doesn't pay the bills."

"Maybe it could, if we worked it just right."

"You've lost me, baby. But since you're the dreamer in the family, tell me how that would work." He grinned at me.

"We could become citrus farmers."

He started to laugh. He had to pull off the road because he was laughing so hard.

"You want us to become citrus farmers? That's funny. First of all, we don't own an orange grove. And even if we did, we wouldn't have a clue about how to run it. You just never cease to amaze me. How on earth did you come up with an idea like that?"

"In about ten minutes I'm going to show you how I came up with that idea." I was feeling a little defensive. How dare he laugh at my idea! "The grove we're going to is for sale."

"Katy, you can't be serious. We don't know anything about growing oranges. And where on earth would we get the money to buy an orange grove? They can't be cheap."

"Just promise me something? Keep an open mind. I've been thinking about this for over two months, and I think it could work. Just wait till you see it; you're going to fall in love with it, just like I did."

"You've been in love with an orange grove for two months and I didn't know anything about it?"

"Yep, and I adore the people who are trying to sell it. They are the nicest couple. I wasn't keeping it a secret, Ben. I just haven't had time to talk to you about it because we've been a little busy. You know, making up for lost time in the bedroom."

He just shook his head and grinned. "You never cease to amaze me, Katy-girl."

Chapter 33

Another thing I failed to tell Ben was that I had called ahead.

When we got close to the orchard, I told him to slow down. "It's right up here, on the left. Slow down and pull over so you can see how straight the rows of trees are. And if you roll down the window, you can smell the citrus in the air."

"I'm doing this just because I've read that pregnant women need to be pampered."

"I don't need pampered, Ben. I've thought a lot about this and I think we can make it work. I asked you to keep an open mind."

"My mind is always open to anything you say."

"Okay, good. Now slow down, it's right up here. There's a pull-off area where you can park. I think a lot of people pull over to look at it, it's so pretty."

He slowed the car and pulled into the worn area on the side of the road.

He didn't just open the window; he got out of the car, closed the door, and leaned on it. I let him stand there alone for a few seconds. I wanted him to soak in the sight, the smell and the amazing solitude of it.

I got out of the car, slowly, and closed my door quietly. It was so peaceful here, compared to the city. "So, didn't I tell you? It's beautiful, isn't it?"

He didn't say a word, just put his arm around me and pulled me close. I had known all along that he would love it. I knew Ben's soul. His was connected to mine.

*****

Aunt Lucy and Uncle John were sitting on their wide front porch in rocking chairs, waiting for us.

We weren't even out of the car when Lucy came running toward us. She opened my car door for me and held out her hands to help me out of my seat. Her hug made me feel like I was a long lost child who had finally come home.

"Katy, it's so nice to see you again. Oh my, it looks like that baby could come any minute now. Are you sure you should be out running around?"

"I still have over two weeks before I'm due, and I wanted to bring Ben out to meet you before we get too busy with the baby. How are you doing?"

"Well, harvest is over so now we can just sit back and relax for a few weeks. It was a great year for oranges."

"You still have some left, don't you?"

"A few, and they are delicious."

"Good, I'm going to want some to take home with me."

Ben came around to my side of the car just as John got there. He was a little slower than his wife. I think it was on purpose though. He knew he wouldn't get to talk until his whirlwind of a wife had made us feel welcome.

"Hi, John. I'd like for you to meet my husband, Ben. I was telling him all about the two of you on the way out here. Ben, this is John and Lucy Banks."

"It's good to meet you, son. When Katy was here in May she told us you were in Afghanistan. We sure are proud of you boys who leave your families and go away to serve our country. That isn't an easy life."

"It's nice to meet you, too. Katy tells me you have a beautiful place here."

"Well, it's been home to us for over forty years, and we love it. Would you like to have the grand tour?"

"I didn't realize it when we started out this morning, but I think that's one of the purposes of this trip." Ben grinned and put his arm around my shoulder.

John winked at me. "You have one of those wives who likes to spring surprises on you too? I'm telling you, boy, your life will never be boring. My Lucy is always coming up with some hair-brained idea to make our lives more exciting…even after forty years."

"John, we're going to have to take the golf cart. There is no way I'm going to let this girl walk all over this hundred acres." Lucy was definitely the take-charge person in their family.

"I'll go get it. Why don't you get the kids something to drink?"

"Come up to the porch and sit for a minute while I get you some juice. You can't come to the grove and not have a glass of it."

When we got to the porch, Lucy directed us to the chairs she and John had been sitting in, then left us to go through the screen door.

"So? What do you think? Aren't they wonderful people? And isn't this beautiful? Feel the breeze, Ben. Doesn't it smell good?"

Ben just shook his head again and grinned at me. "They are very nice, Katy. But I'm thinking we are here to get oranges, not buy the farm! We know absolutely nothing about growing oranges!"

"Open mind, Ben. You promised…."

Lucy returned with the juice just as John pulled up in the golf cart.

"We can take the juice with us if you'd like."

As we rode, John told us about the three kinds of oranges in the grove. All of them ripened and had to be harvested at three different times between November and the end of May. July was the time of the year when all three parts of the grove had old trees being removed and new ones being planted. We stopped for a few minutes to watch a crew of men cut down a tree. John said the trunk would be drilled out, new dirt brought in, and a new tree would be planted in the same spot. It would take four to eight years before the new trees would blossom.

After we explored the grove, John started on the trail around the lake. It was set in the middle of the great old oak trees. Some of them had Spanish moss hanging from them and provided a blessed relief from the hot Florida sun. This was the part Ben fell in love with. I could see it on his face, and I could easily imagine him riding a horse on the trails that wound around the lake and through the trees.

Our tour finally took us to the warehouse and to the irrigation and misting system. John explained all of it to Ben as we rode along.

When we finally got back to the house, Lucy invited us in. She had made an orange coffee cake and served us hot cups of coffee with it. I hadn't seen the interior of the house on my earlier visit, so she took us both on a tour of it.

It wasn't the grand, beautifully decorated house I had grown up in, but it was roomy and homey. Lucy explained that she and John had three children and since each of them wanted their own room, they had added a master suite thirty years earlier. There were now four bedrooms.

She had told me on my earlier visit that their children weren't interested in being citrus farmers. After touring the lovely home their parents had provided for them, I wondered where they went, and why they would want to leave.

When we stopped to look at family pictures in the living room, she told us about them. Their son was a lawyer in New York City. Their middle child, a daughter, was married to a man who owned his own hotel and casino in Las Vegas, and their youngest daughter was in med school.

"They're all successful and I'm happy for them, but John always wanted one of them to stay here and take over the grove for us. They all have many happy memories of living here, and enjoy coming home, but I don't think any of them will ever move back this way. We're pretty sure none of them want to be citrus farmers."

Ben and I looked at each other, and I wondered if he was thinking of Mrs. Johnson. She had come to the end of life without anyone; and now, here were two more people who had been left behind. But at least they had each other.

"So you really think you're ready to sell it?"

"Yes, it's time. We'd like to travel some. If the kids can't come here, we'll go to them."

"Where will you live if you sell it?"

"We're going to keep two acres of the land on the back road. We want to build us a little house to come home to when we aren't traveling. I'm not sure we can live without the fragrance of orange blossoms."

"So you'd be around and be able to do some consulting work for the buyer?"

"Yes. We told your wife we would do that…for the right buyer."

Ben looked at me and grinned. "Well, seeing as how my lovely wife just told me about you on our way here, I hadn't realized that."

"I told you, I haven't had time to talk to you about it. John, tell him how profitable the business is."

"With the right management, it's very profitable. We think our three kids had all their needs met, and most of their wants supplied."

"But how did you learn to be citrus growers? Did one of you grow up here?"

"No. We started from scratch when we first got married. We've put most of our time and energy into it, and have loved every minute of it. We would be more than happy to share our expertise with the new owner if they wanted it. Do you think it's something the two of you would be interested in?"

"We'd have to see the books and do some figuring of our own, but it sure would be a nice place to ride horses. And we'd have to come up with some financing, too. We have a few assets, but I'm not sure they are enough to get a loan, especially for something like this. How much are you asking for it?"

"A million and a half."

"Whoa! That's a lot of money."

"But look at what you're getting. And if there's a problem, we might be able to help you with the financing. I can promise you, it would be an investment that would pay off. People need their orange juice!"

"We'll talk about it and let you know in a few weeks. Of course, if you sell it before we get back to you we'll know it wasn't in God's plan for us right now."

"We know you both have a lot on your minds with the little one coming, and we're in no hurry. If you think of any other questions, you just give us a call. Or better still, bring that baby to see us when he or she gets here."

"We definitely will."

When I gave Lucy a hug, she whispered in my ear, "I think we sold him on it!"

Chapter 34

"Well, what do you think?" We hadn't been in the car for two seconds and I had to know.

"It's beautiful, Katy. But there's no way we have the money for that, even with their help with the financing. And all it would take is one bad harvest and we could lose it!"

"Don't think about the money now. Just tell me what you liked best about it."

"I loved everything about it. The property is beautiful with the oaks and the lake. And you can tell the grove has been taken care of. The house is a little old and could use some work, but it sure was roomy. I loved it…all of it. But we don't have the money."

"We do have the money, Ben"

"We've had this discussion. I will provide for my family."

"And what am I suppose to do with all the money sitting in the bank with my name on it? Ben, if it was your money you know darn well you'd use it to buy that property. And you'd insist that it would be ours, not just yours."

"That's different. Men are supposed to support their families."

"That is old-fashioned and narrow-minded thinking."

"But it's the way I think. I will not have your family thinking I married you for your money."

"Ben Browning! I can't believe you just said that! My family loves you and they know you love me. I've told you a dozen times. They feel like God blessed them financially, so they can help others. They would be thrilled if we took our money and bought something wonderful for our family. And I'm positive my dad would think it's a great investment."

"No, Katy. We're not using your money and that's final."

"It isn't *my* money, it's *our* money! Why do you have to be so pig-headed?"

We drove in silence for at least a half hour, both of us in our own little world. We were almost home when I turned to him.

"I have one more question for you."

"Okay…but the answer is still no."

"If, after the baby is born, I decided I wanted to use *my* money to go back to college to become a doctor, would you have a problem with that or would you insist on paying my way?"

"I wouldn't understand why you'd want to do that with a new baby. But you know I'd never stand in your way. I would do everything I could to support and help you. Since it's your money, you should use it to advance your career if that's what you want. You would make a great doctor."

"So, you'd let me use my money to pay for a new career?"

"Honey, you can use your money to do anything you want to do."

"I would be a good doctor, wouldn't I? But I don't want to be a doctor. I want to be a citrus grower. And I want to use my money to do it. But I can't do it without your help and support, Ben. I need to know…will you help me be the best citrus grower in the state of Florida?"

He continued to look straight ahead, but I saw the dimple deepen in his right cheek. Lucy was right. We had sold him on it! And I learned that sometimes you have to use a little trickery when you are dealing with bull-headed cowboys.

*****

Ben had the next day off, too. I had a doctor's appointment so he went with me. It was two weeks before my due date and this was the appointment when I would be checked to see if my cervix was dilated. Ben sat beside me and held my hand while the doctor did the exam.

"Katy, I think I'm going to have to do another ultrasound. I don't feel the baby's head and you aren't dilated at all. The baby might be breach. I need to know that before you go into labor."

"That's okay. Now Ben can see the baby." I smiled at him but he wasn't smiling back.

"But I don't want the baby to be breach. That will make the delivery more difficult for you, won't it?"

"Let's not get ahead of ourselves, Ben. The ultrasound will tell us if we need to worry about anything."

I stretched out on the table and the doctor put the warm lubricant on my belly. I had seen this before. What I wanted to see now was Ben's face when he saw his baby on the screen. I wanted to see the joy on his face when he saw the heart beating and those precious little hands and feet punching and kicking. I smiled at him again. "It's okay, Ben." He gave me a weak smile back.

I watched him as the doctor began to roll the ultrasound paddle over my belly. When I saw his gorgeous blue eyes light up, I knew what he was feeling. That first glimpse of your own baby on an ultrasound screen is exhilarating.

"Katy, look! Is that a hand up against your belly?"

"Looks like it. Maybe that's the one he's been boxing me with."

Dr. Palmer was studying the screen and didn't seem to be paying any attention to us.

"Well, I have some good news and some bad. He is butt down, but it doesn't look like he's engaged in the birth canal yet. Can you see his legs up against Katy's abdomen, Ben? His feet are up by his head, and he has his arms around his legs. That means he's a frank breech baby. He's bent like the letter V. Katy, I can try to do an external version, to see if I can get him turned around."

"What is that? Will it hurt either one of them?" I saw the worry in Ben's eyes.

"It's a procedure where I try to turn him from the outside. I have to take him in my hands from the outside and try move to him around a little bit. It may be a little uncomfortable for Katy. And we'll monitor the baby's heart rate while we do it. If it causes too much discomfort for her or if his heart rate changes, we'll stop."

"You keep calling him a him. Does that mean it's a boy?" Ben was the one who wanted to wait until birth to find out the gender. Obviously, his curiosity was getting the best of him.

"Didn't I already tell you it's a boy?"

"No. So, it is a boy?"

"Sure is. I'm sorry…I had forgotten you didn't want to know until birth."

"It's okay, Katy! We're going to have a son! At least we know why he's being obstinate already. He's just like me, right?"

"Ben, it's our little boy. I knew it! And he isn't being obstinate; he just wants to do things his own way. Kind of like you do sometimes."

Ben was studying the screen now. "Is there any chance he could turn on his own since he isn't engaged yet?"

"That's a possibility. But if he doesn't, any external version I attempt later would be less effective. Once the baby is engaged in the breech position I usually just plan a C-section- especially if it's a first baby and a big one—like this one seems to be."

Ben looked at me and I could see what looked like fear in his eyes.

"Honey, it's going to be okay. Dr. Palmer, can you give us a little time to talk about this?"

"Sure. I'll be back in a few minutes."

"Katy, I'm so sorry you have to go through this. I just wanted you to have a normal, easy delivery."

"Ben! Stop it. Everything's going to be fine. You made it through Afghanistan. I survived six months of loneliness. And this baby is going to make it through the birth canal just fine. Millions of babies have done it; ours will too. And I don't care what I have to go through. I just want a healthy baby when we're done." I reached up and pulled his head towards me and kissed him.

"Now, let's talk about what's best for the baby. I'm usually one to let nature take its course with as little outside interference as possible. But I'm thinking we should let Dr. Palmer try the external version. If that doesn't work, we'll just have to pray he'll turn on his own before a C-section would have to be done. What I don't want is to have labor start with him in this position, then get stuck and go into some kind of distress."

"You know more about this than I do. Whatever you think is best. I just don't want her to hurt you today."

"Better a little hurt today than a lot more pain later. Are you going to be okay in here?"

"Yes, I want to stay for you. I'll be okay. I promise I won't faint."

"That's good. I don't want to have to tell your son that his big ol' cowboy dad whimped out on us before he was even born."

"I'll be okay. Let's just get this over with."

"Ben, I'm really glad you're here with me today. I would hate doing this without you."

"I'm glad too, baby."

*****

Dr. Palmer did her best. She even gave me some medicine that was supposed to relax my uterus to make it easier. But the child would not move. Maybe he was a little obstinate. We planned the C-section for the fourteenth and hoped our baby would turn himself around in the meantime.

Chapter 35

I went home and called my Mom. I was so disappointed; more for her sake than my own. I wanted her to be able to experience the miracle of a normal natural childbirth.

"Hey, Mom. It's me."

"Hi, me. Are you calling to tell me to get on the next flight?"

"Not the next one. But you might want to be here by the fourteenth, unless I go into labor before that."

"Why the fourteenth? Didn't you want to wait and go into labor naturally?"

"Yes, but your grandson has other ideas."

"My grandson? It's a boy? And what do you mean he has his own ideas? What's wrong?"

So I gave her the story without going into any detail that would make her worry.

"So, what will happen if you go into labor before the planned section?"

"They'll do another ultrasound to see what position he's in. If he turns, I can do natural labor. If he's still in the breech position they'll go ahead and do the C-section."

"So maybe I should come before the fourteenth. I want to be there with you."

"Mom, you can come anytime you want to. I would rather have you here early, than not have you here when it's time."

"Good. I think I'll come this week then."

*****

Dr. Palmer had shown me some exercises I could try that might encourage the baby to flip around on his own. She also gave me a website called "spinning.com". Ben was determined we were going to do all we could do to get our baby to turn on his own.

For the next several days I did the exercises with his help. I did everything but stand on my head to get our bull-headed little guy to flip on his own.

One evening while I was lying on the couch with my swollen feet propped up on some pillows, Ben knelt down on the floor beside me.

"I need to talk to my son, if you don't mind."

"He likes it better when you sing. He goes right to sleep."

"Nope, we're talking this time."

He kissed my belly and started to talk to it. I started to laugh so hard it made the whole couch jiggle.

"Okay, little guy. It's time for our first little father-son chat. I have to tell you, I am a little frustrated with you right now. Your mother has done everything in her power to get you flipped around head first, and you aren't moving. So, here's the deal. You get your butt flipped up before we get back to see the doctor, and we'll move to a citrus grove. I promise, you can have the prettiest little pony you've ever seen. Now, that's as sweet a deal as you're going to get so you better start moving."

That night I woke up to movement. Not just hands and feet. It felt like my baby had rolled himself into a ball and turned completely over. I knew, and Dr. Palmer confirmed to me later, that breech babies do that. But Ben is totally convinced his son heard him and did it for the pony.

*****

Eight days later my water broke.

Abby and I had taken her boys for a short walk on the beach early that morning before it got too hot. The humidity was still smothering. I was happy to get back home and into the air conditioning.

I was standing at the kitchen sink getting a drink when I felt a gush of warm water running down my legs. I looked down and saw a puddle forming on the floor. I just stared at it. I couldn't figure out what it was. I thought I would go into labor first and my water would break sometime after that.

When it finally hit me what had happened, I didn't know what to do. Ben was at work and my Mom was at Mama Beth's house. Abby had just left.

While I stood there and watched the puddle get larger, I felt my heart start to beat faster. I was scared, but excited. I knew this was the day our baby would be coming. I wasn't sure what to do though, so I grabbed a dish towel and put it between my legs. Then I felt the first pain. It was like a severe cramp that started in my groin, moved up to my lower back and made my belly tighten up. I gasped and clutched the counter top.

When it was over, I knew exactly what to do! I dialed Ben's cell phone number. He didn't answer so I left a message and dialed my mom's number.

Within twenty minutes Mama Beth's car was in my driveway. I am quite sure she broke speed limits to get to me. I was still standing at the sink and was breathing through my second contraction when both of my moms rushed through the door. While one mom cleaned up the kitchen floor, the other one helped me into clean clothes.

Minutes later, they grabbed my suitcase and helped me into the car.

I was sure I still had plenty of time, but it worried me that my water had broken. I knew the baby's cord could fall into the birth canal and become compressed with each contraction. Sometimes being a nurse and knowing what can happen is a curse.

While Mama Beth drove, Mom called Ben's cell number again. He didn't answer. That meant he was probably on a trauma run. We all decided he would get to the hospital faster if we let the hospital find him and get him to labor and delivery.

We went through the trauma department and I quickly talked to the receptionist there. She promised me she would page Ben and tell him to go to Obstetrics as soon as he landed.

By the time I was admitted to my birthing room, the contractions were fifteen minutes apart. Dr. Palmer strolled into the room with a smile on her face.

"I hear our little flipper is ready to see his Mom."

"I think he is. But now his daddy needs to get his butt out of a helicopter and in here, pronto. He promised me he would be home for this and I'm not letting him out of it."

"I just called trauma myself and told them to direct him here as soon as he lands. They said he was about fifteen minutes away, so I think he'll get here in plenty of time. Why don't I check you before he gets here? That way, we'll know how far along you are when he arrives?"

While Dr. Palmer was checking me, I looked up at both of my mothers. Mama Beth had gone through her labor with me all alone, except for her own mother at her side. My adoptive mom had *never* been through this. What the three of us were experiencing today was new to each of us, and I was glad we could do it together. But what I really wanted was Ben. He had promised me when he was in Afghanistan that he would be here for this. Where was he?

"Good news and bad news again, Katy. Bad news is that you're only three centimeters dilated and you'll probably have a few more hours of this. Good news is that Ben will be here for all of it." She had seen him peeking through the small piece of glass in the door and waved him in.

"Now that Dad's here, I'm going back to work and the nurses will call me when you're ready to deliver. Everything looks good. But if you need me before then, they'll call me. You are going to do well. I know you will."

"Dr. Palmer?"

"Yes?"

"Did you remember that we want to harvest the cord blood?"

"Of course I remembered. You are here today because of cord blood and I know you want your baby's harvested in case someone else needs it. I wouldn't forget something as important as that!"

"Thank you."

My moms told me they would be in the waiting room so Ben and I could be alone. Dr. Palmer told both of them they could be in the birthing room with me when the baby was born. For now, I was happy it was just Ben and me.

We were both excited, but nervous. We were about to become parents and start on a completely new adventure. Ben had packed our favorite music and we both tried to stay relaxed between the contractions. When a contraction would come, Ben would breathe through it with me.

We were five, very long hours into the labor when my back began to hurt so bad it brought tears to my eyes. Ben rubbed it and put heat on it. Then he rubbed it some more and put ice on it. I knew nothing was really going to relieve it though until our baby was born. But I did appreciate his efforts. Well, I did until I got into the transition part of labor.

Dr. Palmer had told me when I got to about seven centimeters, the labor would change and so would I. She was right. The contractions got harder and I got a little bit mean. I had planned to deliver by natural childbirth and had refused an epidural in the beginning. Now I begged for it.

I told Ben several times in the weeks leading up to the labor that I needed him to be strong for me, and encourage me to finish the delivery without medication. When I started to beg for some relief he had tears in his eyes when he reminded me of our deal.

"But if you need it, I really think you should take it. I hate seeing you hurting this much. It's okay if you want it. Do you want me to tell Dr. Palmer?"

By then the contraction had stopped and I told him no. We went through that whole dialogue many times in the next couple hours. Finally, the nurse told us it was too late to get the epidural. The baby would be coming very soon. It was time to push.

"Ben, why don't you sit behind her and prop her up while she pushes?"

Ben climbed up on the bed behind me and I rested against him while I waited for the next contraction to hit. It felt good to have him behind me and his arms around me. I leaned back and he kissed my cheek. He had been so patient with me.

"Katy, I love you and am so proud of you. We'll have our baby in our arms in just a little while."

I felt the next contraction begin to build and the desire to push became intense.

"Okay, now take a deep breath and push…that's it, you're doing it. You are strong and you can push this baby out. Don't stop. Keep pushing."

I pushed until I felt the desire to do so go away.

"That was a good one. A few more like that, and we'll have our baby."

He was such a good coach, and I was glad once again that he had returned from Afghanistan in time to go to the birthing classes with me.

A few more pushes. Another hour passed.

"Ben…I just can't do this anymore. I'm too tired."

"You can do it. Your moms were just in here and told me they are ready to come in and hold their new grandbaby. Is it okay if they come in now?"

"Will their coming in make this go faster? Are we getting close?"

"The nurse just called Dr. Palmer and told your moms they could come in. So, I think we're almost ready. Just a couple more pushes and our boy will be here."

"It hurts, Ben."

"I'm so sorry, baby. We don't have to have anymore babies if you don't want them."

Then I heard Dr. Palmer's voice. It seemed to come from far away as the contraction took my body into its control.

I tried to breathe through the burning pain and the pressure of my baby's head as it pushed against the small opening of my body. Then some one told me to push again. I felt like I was being ripped in half, but I knew with that push my baby's head had been delivered. Within seconds I felt the rest of his body slip into the world. It was one o'clock in the morning. I had been in labor for fourteen very long hours.

I felt Ben's arms tighten around me and heard my moms oohing and aahing. Then I heard him cry.

I opened my eyes and watched as Dr. Palmer placed my baby on my stomach. He was red. And he was mad. I saw his arms and legs flailing until a nurse picked him up, wiped him off and brought him to me.

She placed him belly down on my chest and when I pulled him close he stopped crying. Ben's arms were still around me, supporting both of us. I turned my son a little bit so I could look at his face. He looked back at me with dark blue eyes like his daddy's. I touched his dark hair that was the same color as mine. Ben was still behind me and I felt a tear land on my shoulder as his hand curled around our son's dark head.

"Ben. He looks like both of us. He has your blue eyes and my dark hair."

"He's amazing."

"Hey Sam…I'm your Mama. I'm so glad you're finally here. We've been waiting a long time for you."

Ben slipped out from behind me while the nurses pushed pillows behind my back. He came to my side, and I watched as he took his son into his arms and showed him to my two moms. Watching them, I knew my son would never suffer from neglect or lack of love.

"You named him Sam?" That was the one thing Ben and I had kept a secret after we learned our baby was a boy.

"Samuel. It means "*asked of God.*" We asked God for him and God gave him to us."

"It's a beautiful name for a little boy."

After my moms held him, I asked if I could have him back. I held him close again and kissed his head. I took one of his hands in mine and watched his tiny fingers wrap around my thumb. He moved his head towards me and opened his mouth. I felt my breasts begin to ache and I knew my baby wanted to eat. My body was responding to his needs already.

The nurse came over and helped him latch onto my breast.

"Nursing makes him happy and it helps your uterus contract so your body can get back to normal faster."

"It makes me happy, too." I pulled him closer and looked up t my two mothers standing beside my bed. They had tears in their eyes and I realized at that moment, nursing me was the one thing neither of them had been able to do for me.

Chapter 36

I was exhausted. When my moms left, Ben told me to try to rest. The nurses had taken Sam to the nursery so the pediatrician could do his routine exam.

"When they bring him back I'll watch over him while you sleep."

I looked up into Ben's face and knew the past few hours had bonded us to each other in a new way. He had been so patient and strong. And even though I had been in pain, I had felt so cherished. He was looking at me now in a way I had never seen. It was almost reverence.

"Ben, I'm so glad you were here with me. I don't think I could have done it without you."

"You're the strong one, Katy. You were so brave."

"I didn't feel strong. It was hard, but so worth it. Our Sam is here and healthy. Isn't he beautiful?"

"Yes. But not as beautiful as his mother. I love you so much, Katy."

"I love you too."

"Now get some rest, okay? I'll take care of Sam when they bring him back."

"Wake me up if he gets hungry, okay?"

Two hours later I woke up to the sound of his crying. Ben was holding him and trying to soothe him.

"I'm sorry. I was hoping you'd be able to sleep a little bit longer, but I think he wants to eat again."

"It's okay." I sat up in the bed and Ben placed our son into my arms again. As I pulled him closer he began to root around, looking for food. Ben smiled at me.

"Guess that's the one thing I'm not going to be able to do for our boy."

"Tell you what. As soon as my milk comes in I'll let you feed him a bottle every morning and every evening. *If* we can get that expensive breast pump to work."

"Sounds like a good deal to me."

I stroked Sam's cheek, the one that lay closest to my breast, and guided him to the food he wanted. He clamped on and sucked so forcefully I was shocked. He knew he found what he was looking for and began to move his cheeks in the pattern nature had taught him. Sucking, then breathing, sucking then breathing…and again I was amazed at one more of God's amazing designs for his ultimate creation.

*****

Ben and I were able to squeeze in a few more hours of sleep before the whole family invaded my birthing room that evening. Dad had flown in from Philadelphia to join my mom, and Alex came with Mama Beth. And of course Carly came. After holding him, she decided he was "probably better than a girl" as long as she got to babysit. Abby and Brett came, leaving their boys at home with Jon who volunteered to babysit. He sent word he would visit when I got home.

I'm always amazed at how a baby can bring new life into a family. Everyone agreed he looked just like Ben, except for the dark hair. Mama Beth said it might change when he got older. Her brother had dark hair when he was born, but it eventually turned blond.

As I watched and listened to my family all around us, I felt bad that Ben had no family to talk about what he looked like when he was a baby. I made a mental note to ask him if he had any pictures of himself as a baby or a child. I don't know why I hadn't asked before.

After everyone left, Ben sat down in the rocker next to my bed and held our boy close to him. As I watched the two of them together, I felt a sense of pride. I had just given Ben a gift that no one else could have given him. I gave him a child who was the unique combination of the two of us. When he looked up at me and smiled, his blue eyes were glistening.

"Isn't he amazing?"

"He is. He's our gift from God…and I'll be forever thankful for him. And for you."

"We did well, didn't we?"

"We're a good team. But I think you need to go home and get some rest. You've been awake for most of two days and a night, and I can tell you're exhausted."

"I was going to stay the night and help you with him."

"I have nurses to help me tonight. I need you to be rested so you can help me tomorrow night when we're at home."

He argued with me but finally gave in when I told him I would be ready to go home when he returned in the morning.

Before he left, though, he tucked his son into bed then came to me.

"Need to tuck my son's momma into her bed, too. You sure you don't want me to stay?"

"I want you to stay, but I think I'm going to need you more tomorrow night. You go home and sleep in our bed and get your rest."

We were both exhausted and I hoped we could get some sleep. The nurses said they would take Sam to the nursery and take care of him for me but I wanted him to stay with me. I was getting up without help and wanted him close beside me. I told them I'd call if I needed help.

At one a.m. I heard him whimpering. It had been three hours since he'd eaten and I had a feeling he wasn't going to go back to sleep until I fed him. I sat up on the side of the bed, pulled his crib close to me, and started to change his diaper. He stopped crying and looked at me so intently his eyes began to cross. It made me laugh.

"Hey, little man. It's just you and me tonight. Are you hungry?"

He just kept staring at me. "I hope you know you're my miracle baby. There was a time when I didn't think I would ever be blessed with a child. But I asked God for you and He answered my prayer. And you need to know…if I never do anything else with my life but love your daddy and give him a child, I'll know I've done what God wanted me to do. I feel like I was born to give life to you, baby boy. I know you don't understand that, because I didn't even know it myself until you were born. Oh, Sam. I love you so much already."

I liked thinking he understood what I was saying to him and was burying it deep in his heart. But he had enough talking and just wanted to eat. He let me know about it, too. My son had lungs and knew how to use them!

Chapter 37

I fed him again at four. When I woke up at seven Ben was sitting in the rocker, holding him.

"Hey, handsome cowboy. You were supposed to sleep in today. Did you get any rest at all?"

"I did. But the question is, did you?"

"He only woke me up twice. Both times he ate and went right back to sleep. I think he's going to be a good baby as long as his belly is full. How long have you been here? Was he awake when you got here?"

"I got here about a half hour ago and he was squirming around. I took him for a walk out in the hall and the nurse gave me a pacifier for him. She said it would be okay for him to suck on it until you woke up; or until he got tired of it. He's been awake and looking at me. I'm not sure he knows who I am yet. He looks puzzled."

"Oh, I think he knows who you are. And he isn't going to forget that promise of a pony. Do you think he wants to eat yet? It's been three hours."

"He does seem to be getting a little frustrated with this pacifier. Do you want him?"

"Of course! I can't seem to get enough of him. I'll feed him then go take a shower. That way when Dr. Palmer comes in to discharge me, I'll be ready and we can go home. Won't it be nice when we can all three be together in our own home? All my dreams have come true, Ben."

Ben brought him to me and I scooted over in the bed so he could sit beside me while Sam nursed. I was excited that the nursing had gone so well. I had talked to a few moms who said they had a difficult time getting their babies to latch on. Sam didn't seem to have that problem. Now I just had to worry about whether I would have enough milk.

"Ben?"

"Hmmm?"

"He's a beautiful baby, isn't he?"

"He is, and so healthy. I was checking out his fingers and his toes while you were asleep. They're all there."

"I'm glad. I was just thinking about something Mama Beth said to me after I recovered from my bone marrow transplant. She told me there is no greater joy than having a child. I was amazed she could say that, seeing as how she had to give me up when I was a baby. Now I know what she was talking about. This little guy has already brought me more joy than I thought I was capable of experiencing."

"I was thinking about him last night after I went to bed. The instant love I felt for him when I held him in my arms…it's just unexplainable. The love I feel for him is just as intense as the love I feel for you, but they are different kinds of love."

"I know. Isn't that strange? And you know what?"

"What?"

"I think the best gift we can give him is to love each other. I think if he grows up knowing his parents love each other, he's going to be one lucky boy."

"Then he's going to be one *very* lucky little boy."

*****

I was just coming out of the shower when Dr. Palmer came in.

"How are you feeling this morning?"

"Like I'm ready to go home!"

"That's good. But there's a couple things I need to discuss with you before you leave. The nurses will talk to you about how to take care of the baby and yourself when you get home. But I did want to talk to both of you a little bit about birth control."

"But I'm nursing. Isn't that a natural birth control?"

"Nursing advocates will tell you it is, but I encourage all new mothers to use another method. It's called abstinence. Until you get back in to see me in six weeks, I'd like for you to not have sexual intercourse at all, so your body can heal. I know that can be difficult but it will be best for you."

I looked at Ben. Dr. Palmer didn't know I had a man with willpower like iron. If he could abstain before we got married just because I asked him to, he would do it this time too.

"We understand."

"I know you do. But I can't stress enough the importance for your body healing completely before you become pregnant again. A second pregnancy would put a lot of pressure on you, physically and emotionally. I would suggest you get some condoms before you come back to see me, just in case. We can get you something more effective when I see you."

"So I can go home now?"

"Of course. If you promise me you'll get plenty of rest. Nothing should be more important than taking care of yourself and your baby. Ben? I know I can count on you to make sure she does that!"

Chapter 38

It didn't take Sam very long to let us know who was in control of our household. The sweet little baby I saw my last night at the hospital turned into a howling night owl when we got him home.

Nothing seemed to help. When I tried to nurse him he would suck for a few seconds then pull away and start to wail. We tried the pacifier, we tried walking him, and we tried giving him a soothing bath with lavender. Nothing helped.

At four in the morning I called Abby.

"What am I doing wrong, Abby? He's been screaming all night and we are at our wits end. I'm sure the neighbors think we're torturing him."

"Did you try putting him in a car seat and taking him for a ride?"

"A ride? It's four in the morning!"

"We know that, but he doesn't. Take him for a ride. It might help."

"Okay, if you say so."

"Katy?"

"Yes?"

"You're going to be fine and so is he. It just takes a little time for everyone to get adjusted."

Of course he went to sleep. When we brought him back into the house we left him in the seat and propped the foot of it up so he was lying flat in it. We were afraid if we moved him he would wake up again. Both of us crashed. When he woke us up three hours later he was as content as he could be.

Ben went off to work with dark rings under his eyes and I decided I would definitely be sleeping while Sam slept during the day.

*****

Once he figured out that night was for sleeping and day was for playing, Sam turned out to be a very good baby. By the time he was two months old he was waking up only once between ten p.m. and five a.m., and he always fell back to sleep after he ate. Abby said I was lucky and could give birth to her next kid, if I promised to have one for her who liked to sleep. Her boys were still not good sleepers at night.

When Sam would wake up at five, Ben and I would both lie quietly and watch him and listen to him. He usually didn't cry right after waking up. Instead, he would make some cooing sounds for a few minutes. We would watch him start to wiggle, and soon he would begin to move his arms around until he got his fist into his mouth. We could hear him sucking it for a few seconds, until he realized there was no food coming out of it. Then he would begin to fuss.

Ben would get up and change him for me before he went to the kitchen to make coffee. He'd bring his cup back to the bedroom and watch Sam nurse while he drank his coffee. He called it his "having breakfast with my son time".

They would both get done about the same time so Ben would hold him for a few minutes before he went off to work. It was a good time of the day for us.

If Ben didn't have to work at the hospital, he usually had a charter booked. So, most days I was at home alone with my boy, and I loved every minute of it. What I didn't love was that Ben was working all of the time. I was still thinking I should go back to work part-time, so he could quit one of his jobs.

The alternative for both of us was the orange grove.

By the end of September our lives had settled into a routine and I knew it was time to have a serious talk with Ben about the grove. The more I thought about buying it, the more convinced I was that it was the right thing for us to do. We hadn't talked about it much since Sam had come into our lives, but I knew it was because we hadn't made the time to talk about it. It was on a Tuesday, when Ben was flying a charter to Miami, that I decided the time was right. I went to the store and bought two T-bones steaks. Then while Sam napped, I made a pecan pie. If his favorite steak and a pecan pie couldn't slow him down and put him in the mood to talk, nothing would!

When he arrived home at six, I had already fed Sam and he was in his swing. Dinner was ready and Sam behaved himself while we ate. Ben played with him for awhile before I fed him again and put him back to bed. With both my men fed and satisfied, I asked Ben to go to the deck with me to watch the stars come out.

We hadn't been to the beach to watch the stars come out for weeks. We were always too tired, so the deck became the place where we escaped in the evenings.

"So, how was your flight today?"

"Nice. But they're saying there's a hurricane out in the Atlantic that might make some trouble for us. I'm glad I got to make a little extra money today. If it comes this way I may not get back up for a couple of days."

"It won't be a threat for a couple of days?"

"Not until the weekend, they said."

"And you're working at the hospital on Thursday and Friday?"

"Yep."

"So you have tomorrow off?"

"I do. Did you have something in mind? Seems like we haven't done anything but work and take care of Sam for months! But they have been good months, haven't they?"

"They have. And yes, I would like to do something tomorrow. I'd like to take Sam out to meet John and Lucy at the citrus grove."

"So you haven't forgotten them."

"No. And I haven't forgotten the grove either. I think we should talk about it. Do you remember what you told them when we left in July?"

"What?"

"You said if they sold it before we got back we would know it wasn't in God's plan for our lives right now."

"And?"

"It hasn't sold. I called them today."

He didn't say anything for a few minutes.

"You still want to buy it?"

"I do. And I want it to be a family venture. That means maybe you can give up one or two of your jobs, Ben. You can't keep doing all three of them."

"Which one do you want me to give up?"

"It isn't my choice. But you know how I feel about the reserves and this is the month you need to decide to either quit or go on. I would think between the hospital and your charters you would have enough flying to keep you busy. Or, if you want to stay in the reserves, then maybe you should give up the job at the hospital. Giving up just one of those would give you more time with me and Sam. And we need you, Ben."

"I know you do, baby. And I did promise Sam a pony if he did that flipping thing in utero." He stopped and smiled at me. We were sitting on our glider at the time and he put his arm around me and pulled me close. I leaned back and looked up at him. He was still so handsome to me and I loved him more every day.

"So does this mean you want to give up being a nurse for the rest of your life and be an orange grower instead?"

"I want both of us to be orange growers right now. We'll let the future take care of itself. If John and Lucy could make a living for their family, I don't know why we can't do it too. Maybe—eventually—you could give up your second job and just do charters. That makes the most sense to me since you'd be able to do your own scheduling."

"A citrus grower. Never in my wildest dreams did I ever think I would be that!"

"You also get to be a horse rancher if we buy the grove. That you can imagine, can't you?"

"I can. And if you're sure this is what you want to do, then I'm with you. We'll go tomorrow and talk to Lucy and John. I hope they're still planning on being around to guide us through the transition, though. Do you know how much we both have to learn in the next few months?"

Chapter 39

Lucy and John were sitting outside on their front porch and were at the car before we got the doors open. Again, I felt like I was home. Lucy gave me a hug and John shook Ben's hand and told him how happy he was to see us.

Sam was asleep from the car ride, of course, so we carried him in the car seat and sat it down on the front porch beside Lucy, who couldn't take her eyes off of him. There were several wooden rockers on the front porch to sit in, and a nice breeze blowing in from the grove.

I love October in Florida. The blanket of humidity that hangs over the state for months seems to lift. And although it's still warm, we aren't suffocating.

Lucy had a pitcher of lemonade and some cookies set out on a small table. The four of us sat and talked, mostly about Sam, for quite a while. They didn't have any grandchildren yet and I could tell our son would be a total delight to them when we became their neighbors.

"I'm so glad you brought him to see us. But I do wish he would wake up so I could hold him."

"I can promise you, when he wakes up you'll know it. He seems to be hungry all the time, and he'll want to be fed. I brought a bottle along. You can feed him if you want to."

"Oh, I would love to. It's been years since I've fed a baby. He looks like he's eating well. Look at those rolls on his legs already. How much did he weigh when he was born?"

"He was exactly eight pounds, but when I took him to the doctor this week he weighed thirteen pounds, six ounces. They say he's perfectly healthy."

"God is good to us, isn't He?"

"He is. Ben and I talk about that all of the time. So you are Christians too?"

"Goodness, yes. I don't know how people without faith get through life. It has gotten us through some difficult times."

"And we're glad for God's guidance in our lives, too. Do you remember what Ben said when we left here three months ago?"

"Yes. He said if we sold the grove before you made it back, you would know buying it wasn't in His plans for you."

Ben and I looked at each other and smiled. God wasn't going to have to hit us over the head with this one.

"So, do you still feel that way? Do you think it's in God's plans for you?"

"Have you sold it?"

"No. We haven't even had anyone look at it since you were here."

"Then it looks like we might become citrus growers and horse ranchers."

I saw tears in Lucy's eyes, and John reached over and took her hand. Their hands were old and gnarled from years of hard work, but their eyes were still full of life and promise. I could see them becoming like parents to Ben. God wasn't just providing us with a new way to make a living; he was providing us with more family. My husband, who had come into my life with no one, now had God given mothers and fathers. Lucy reached over and gave me the biggest hug.

"Oh, Katy honey. I'm so excited. It will be wonderful to have all of you here. John, God answered our prayers."

Holding my hand, she went on to explain that they were so afraid the grove would be bought by a large corporation. "And that isn't what this grove is meant to be. It started out as a home for a family and we wanted it to stay that way. Thank you, God!" And she lifted her hands and her eyes heavenward.

The excitement of the moment woke Sam and he began to wail. When I took him out of the car seat, he stopped crying and looked around with his big blue eyes. His eyes landed and focused on Lucy. He smiled.

"Ben! Did you see that? He smiled! And he has a dimple just like yours when you smile!"

"I saw it. Lucy, his first smile was for you. I think you're going to be very special to this little guy of ours."

That's all Lucy needed to hear. While John talked business with me and Ben, Lucy sat on the front porch and fed and played with our son.

John told us his contract with his realtor had run out the month before, and he hadn't relisted the property. Because of that, he could sell it on his own and would deduct the realtor's fee from the price.

"If you think you need some help with the financing, I can do that. Lucy and I are just so excited about keeping it family-owned that we would be willing to sell it on land contract."

"We won't need your assistance with the financing, but we do need something else from you."

"And what would that be?"

"Your help and your expertise. We understand your desire to travel after the sale, but we'd like to hire you for a year…to manage it while we learn from you. Do you think that's a possibility?"

"Definitely. We've already purchased a travel trailer and will plan on living in it while we build our new home on the back road. It will take until next spring to get the house built, so we'll be here all during harvest season. By next summer you'll have the hang of it and we'll be free to go to the mountains for the hot summer."

We spent most of the day with John at the grove office while Lucy insisted on watching Sam. She called me on my cell phone twice to tell me he was hungry. I took the golf cart back to the house long enough to nurse him, then she sent me back to the office. I had no doubt our son would have an onsite baby sitter available at all times.

When we left that night we told John and Lucy we wanted one more week to think and pray about it. There were so many things to consider. We had to sell the townhouse and Ben had to decide which one of his jobs he wanted to give up. I knew that would be difficult for him.

And we had to tell my parents about our plans. I knew Mom and Dad would be okay with it, especially Dad. He had been making business deals his whole life. I could see Mama Beth being excited about it too. She and Alex were both what I call "earth people." They would be thrilled with us raising our family in the country.

I wasn't sure how Abby was going to take it though. She and I had been able to see each other whenever we wanted to, and now that was going to stop. And Carly wasn't going to be happy either. To pacify her, I would have to offer her a whole summer at the ranch to help with Sam.

We decided to make our decision without the influence of our family though. This was our future and we felt like we had to do what was best for us.

In the end, Ben made a decision that I wasn't completely happy with. He decided to give up the job at the hospital and keep his position with the reserves. He felt like it would be better to be away one weekend a month and two weeks every summer, than to be away for three long days a week. With commute time to the hospital, he figured his days would be fifteen hours long.

The monthly weekend and yearly two-week training sessions, I could deal with. But the chance that he could be called back into active duty at any time was almost unbearable to think about. I knew he loved being a soldier—and the benefits that went with it, but I couldn't understand why it was so important to him. I asked him to explain it to me.

"I don't know why being a soldier is so important to me. It just is. Maybe because it's something Grandma wanted me to do. Maybe because the guys in the unit were the only family I had for a long time. They are like brothers to me and I like being with them. After all these years, we are a team and we work well together. Like I told you before, if one of us isn't there, the team doesn't feel whole. We have each other's backs—here, and when we get deployed. We depend on each other."

"I understand, Ben. But what if you get deployed again?"

"We'll deal with that when, and if, it happens. But now that we're going to be at the grove, I feel good that you'll be there with Sam during the times when I'm gone. And knowing you have him gives me comfort. You'll never be alone like you were when I was gone this past winter."

"But unlike the hospital, it's a commitment you can't get out of if you need to."

"Why would I need to get out of it, honey?"

"I don't know. I just wish you would reconsider. Why don't you just do the chartering? If you do that full time we'll be okay financially. And maybe, eventually, you could get a cargo plane and deliver our produce yourself."

"I'll think about it. I still have two weeks before I have to give the reserves my final decision."

But in the end, he stayed in the reserves.

Chapter 40

The transition turned out to be an easy one. John had a lawyer draw up the papers for the sale, and Dad made arrangements for the money to be taken from my trust and put into an account that would be used exclusively for the business of the citrus grove. We decided to call it "The Browning Family Farm." We also decided to rent the townhouse, rather than sell it. Because it was close to the hospital, two nurses were thrilled to get it.

Lucy and John moved their furniture out of what we were now calling the "ranch house," and into storage. They moved into their camper on their new home site on the back road of the grove.

We found ourselves moving into our new home the first week in December, exactly one year after Ben left for Afghanistan. Our Sam would spend his first Christmas in the house we hoped would be his lifetime home. Ben insisted that Sam's name be put on the deed.

After the townhouse, the four bedroom ranch seemed humungous to us and we didn't have enough furniture to fill it. Lucy and John didn't want to take all of theirs with them since their new home was going to be smaller. So they left one of the bedrooms furnished, and their family room furniture. With an extra furnished bedroom and some air mattresses in the other one, we could entertain our families.

I called Abby and asked her if she could come out and help me with the interior decorating. I told her to bring the boys and just plan on staying a week. She was more than thrilled to help me. Actually, she did almost all of it. Interior decorating was not my thing and I was as just as thrilled to let her do it. I told her I would much rather be out in the grove watching my oranges ripen and playing with her boys.

Ben left his job at the hospital at the end of November. He scheduled no charters in December. The harvesting of the oranges had already started and I wanted him to be with John and me as we went through that.

After months of him working all the time, it was wonderful to be working alongside him on a daily basis. Lucy spent most of her days with us too. Between the four of us, Sam had all the attention he needed. He was usually riding in the backpack we bought when we thought we were going to hike the mountains with him.

Hiking in the Smoky Mountains and cavorting in a hot tub with my husband would have to wait. But it was okay. We were on a new adventure we hoped would bring us a lifetime of happiness and a sense of security.

Ben and I asked our family to join us for Christmas in our new home, since we finally had one big enough to accommodate everyone. Mom, Dad and my brothers came in a couple days early from Philadelphia so they could spend extra time with us. The rest of the family came from Tampa on Christmas Day. They had helped us move, but couldn't wait to come back. I had a feeling our little orange grove ranch was going to be a peaceful respite spot for everyone. After only four weeks, it already felt like home to me and Ben.

It was a wonderful Christmas. At five months old, our Sam was interacting with others and loved the attention he got. Abby's boys were growing up fast, and she told all of us they were expecting again in August. Carly was like a big sister instead of an aunt to all three of her little nephews. All of her nurturing characteristics were put to good use. My step-brother, Jon, brought a girl with him and my other two brothers both had steady girlfriends. There was talk about possible weddings in our family's future in the coming year.

When the day was over I was exhausted, but thrilled with the blessings God had given me in the two short years since I'd met Ben. I was looking forward to the year ahead. We already had so many plans for it. We had oranges to harvest until June, and Ben was already planning on buying Sam his pony for his first birthday in July. We wanted to go back to the mountains in the summer while John and Lucy were there. Mom and Dad were insisting we make a trip north too.

On New Years Eve, Ben and I had a time of reflection. Both of us had experienced our share of difficult times in life. Ben lost both parents then his sister and grandmother. But he survived it and come out a stronger man—a man who not only loved and wanted to care for me and our son, but wanted to do his part to protect his country.

And although I had been the recipient of the love and guidance of two sets of parents, I too had gone through a trying time of my own. A diagnosis of leukemia at the age of sixteen had been devastating. But God had been gracious and given me a little sister who provided me with life saving donor marrow. I had been in remission for almost eight years since my bone marrow transplant. I felt like I could finally start feeling at ease about living a long life free of any further relapses.

Ben and I both felt like we were better people and more appreciative of each other and of Sam because of the struggles we had early in our lives. We knew the old saying "into every life some rain must fall" was true, and felt like ours had already fallen. Our life now was the rainbow at the end of the storm. The dawn of our new day was a beautiful one. And hopefully, new storm clouds would not form.

But unfortunately, we don't always get what we hope for.

Chapter 41

The first harvest was a good one. There were only four nights during the winter months when the low temperatures could have damaged the oranges. With John and Lucy's guidance, they had been saved. By the end of May, all of them had been harvested and gone to market.

John helped us identify the old trees that needed to be taken out, and new ones were planted in their place. All of our employees had been paid except John and Lucy, who refused any money for their guidance during the year. They said the joy they got from Sam was the only pay they needed.

Ben resumed his charters in January, and since he didn't have to plan around his hospital schedule he was able to pick up more clients. I wanted to go with him on a couple of the overnight trips, but felt a need to stay with the harvest.

At Easter we flew to Philadelphia. My brother David had gotten engaged on New Year's Eve, and since he and his fiancé had already dated for years, they didn't have a long engagement. It was a beautiful wedding and I was happy David was planning on staying in Philadelphia. Maybe my mom and dad would end up having grandkids who lived close by.

One evening in June, while we were on the deck, watching the stars come out, Ben and I talked about having another baby. Even though Dr. Palmer had tried to talk me into birth control, Ben and I agreed we should take whatever children God would give us, whenever He wanted to give them to us…at least until we had two.

But we had not conceived. We weren't purposely trying to. We weren't doing the whole day counting thing, and taking temperatures, but we hadn't done anything to prevent it either.

"So do you think I should start taking my temperature so I know when I'm ovulating? We could have a lot of fun on just those days. Or should we just let it go for awhile?"

"Katy, I'm happy with the way our family is right now. I would like for Sam to have a sibling, but I don't think we should go to extremes trying to get him one. Not yet, anyway."

"I want him to have a sibling too, and we aren't getting any younger. Maybe I should go back to Dr. Palmer and see what she says."

"It's about time for your yearly appointment with her, you can ask her then. Right now, I think we should just go to bed and have some fun…you never know what might come of that."

*****

After harvest, our lives slowed down a little bit and we had the hot months of Florida's summer ahead of us. Ben asked me if I wanted to go anywhere special for our second anniversary on July fourth. But I couldn't think of any place I wanted to be, except at home. My new home with my husband and my son was everything I wanted and needed.

"We could fly up to the mountains and rent that little log cabin again. I think when we left there you promised me we would go back and go skinny dipping in that hot tub. We could take Sam along and take him hiking. He liked riding around the ranch in the back pack this past winter. I'm sure he would like hiking a trail."

"That sounds like fun, but I think I'd rather wait until later in the fall when the leaves are turning. It'll be so much prettier then."

"But it would be so cool up there right now; the heat this summer is suffocating!"

"That's true. But it's almost time for Sam's birthday and I want to have a big party for him. I need to start planning for it."

"Katy, he's gonna be one year old. He doesn't even know what a birthday is yet."

"I know. First birthday parties are really for the parents because the kid doesn't have a clue what's going on. But I want to have a big one for him—to celebrate what a blessing he has been to us."

"So you want to give up an anniversary trip with your husband to plan a birthday party for our one-year-old son who doesn't even know what a birthday is? I guess I know where I am on your list of priorities!"

I knew he was just kidding around with me, but I promised him I would definitely go to the mountains with him in the fall.

"Okay. If you promise me that date in the fall, we'll stay home right now. I need to go get his birthday present soon anyway."

"What birthday present?"

"The one I promised him when we wanted him to do his flip in-utero act…the pony."

"Don't you think he's a little young for a pony?"

"He'll grow into it. Besides, I already found one. I saw an ad in the farm magazine last month for a ten month old colt. The owner wanted to sell it with its mother, a five year old mare. I thought it would be cool to get it since it'll be one year old the same time Sam is. They can grow up together."

"Uh-huh; and how convenient that it comes with a horse you can ride too."

"I thought it sounded like a perfect deal. You want me to get one for you too? Then we can all three go riding."

"I think we should wait on that. I like the golf cart. But I'm glad you're finally going to get your horse, cowboy."

He grabbed me around the waist and lifted me up to kiss me.

"Every cowboy needs a cowgirl as much as he needs a horse."

"I'm all yours, cowboy...."

*****

For me, Sam's birthday was more than just the celebration of his first year of life. To me it was also a time to celebrate our new home, the new friends we had made, and the success of our first harvest.

Our families came and we also invited some of our new neighbors. Friends we met at our new church came with their kids. John and Lucy even paid Ben to fly them home from the mountains for our boy's birthday. They had learned to love our child as much as his grandparents loved him. Our Sam had been blessed well with grandparents. He didn't seem to mind that all of them were not blood related.

Soon after Ben and I bought the grove, I sensed again that John and Lucy were going to become more to us than just friends. John and Ben were almost like a father and son by the end of the first harvest, and Lucy had simply fallen in love with Sam. I think my two moms were a little jealous that Sam preferred Lucy over them, but they understood it was because of his familiarity with her. And I think they were glad Lucy had been so available to help us during our first year of training in the business.

Now that he had his ranch, Ben decided we should have a hog roast for the party. He also thought since Sam was getting his pony, we should have a western theme. The man who had made fun of me for wanting to have a big party for our son's first birthday became almost obsessed with the details of it.

Since it was so hot out, Ben cleaned up one of the warehouses and brought in large fans.

The centerpieces for the tables were cowboy hats filled with fruits that held down the helium balloons the kids were going to release at the end of the party. We had bales of hay for people to sit on, and country music playing.

As I watched Ben getting ready for the party, it suddenly dawned on me: perhaps this had been one of his own childhood dreams that had never come true. He and his sister had lived such isolated lives in Texas with his parents. And then, it had been just him and his grandmother. A large group of family and friends was a new way of life for him, and he seemed to revel in it.

The best part of the day for me was when Ben set Sam on top his new pony and walked him around. Sam liked the pony…well, at least he wasn't afraid of it. But of course he had no clue how important it was for Ben. It's true. First birthday parties are more for the parents than they are for the kid. But the older kids at the party loved the pony rides and the hundred pictures we took of the day are proof that it was a party everyone seemed to enjoy.

Chapter 42

Two days after the party I woke up drenched in sweat. It felt so hot in the house I wondered if the air conditioner had gone off. Then I realized I was probably hot because I was curled up with my back against Ben's chest and belly. His right arm was flung over me and I could feel his warm breath close to my neck, stirring my hair along my shoulders.

I had been waking up like this for two years now and it still gave me a feeling of pure bliss. I reached up and stroked Ben's hand. Since moving to the ranch it had become hardened and more tanned. When he wasn't flying, he was usually out in the grove doing some kind of manual labor. He must have sensed me touching his hand because his fingers closed around mine and he pulled me closer to him.

I felt so safe within his arms. As I lay there curled up against him, I thought about how I had been redefined by him in the past two years. Before Ben, I was just Katy; a daughter, a sister and a nurse. I was still all those people, but since Ben, I had become everything I had ever dreamed of becoming—a wife and a mother.

As I lay there in his arms, I knew my sense of contentment was also due to the fact that I had redefined Ben too. Before me, he was alone and now he wasn't. He had told me recently that he felt disconnected from everyone after his grandmother died, but now he belonged to me and Sam. I knew Sam and I had made him feel happy and completely fulfilled.

It was just before dawn, and through the baby monitor I could hear Sam begin to move around. He was still a content little guy and would sometimes play in his bed for several minutes before he began to call for us. His first word had been Da-da of course. He and I had practiced it everyday right before Ben was expected home. I listened to him now as he began to call for his Da-da in his sing-song voice. Ben heard it too, and sat up in the bed.

"Should I go get him?"

"Yeah, bring him back so we can snuggle with him for a few minutes."

As I listened to them through the monitor I could tell the second Sam saw his dad. I knew he had pulled himself up to the side of his bed and was jumping up and down. He was so close to walking, and might even do it before the week was over.

""Hey, little man. You're awake early today. Do you need a diaper change?"

There were toy airplanes flying above the changing table and I heard Sam's deep belly laugh as Ben sent them twirling above his head. He thinks that is so funny.

"You wanna go see Mama now?"

"Mom-mom-mom."

Holding him above his head, Ben "flew" him into our bedroom. The boy already knew what an airplane was, how it took off and flew high above everything. Soon he would know what a horse was too, and his dad would teach him how to ride it.

"Fly to Mama, Sam!"

I held out my hands and caught him as Ben guided him into my arms. His eyes were just as blue as the day he was born, and he still had some of Ben's facial features. But his hair had stayed dark brown like mine. He was a perfect combination of the two who had created him, and now loved him so intensely.

His favorite game in our bed was tent making. Ben and I would hold the sheets high with our legs and he would crawl down under them and sit and grin at us. He now had two little teeth that stuck up from his bottom gum, and in the dim light of the lamp they looked like two little pearls.

The three of us played for awhile—until he grew tired of it or noticed he was hungry and started to climb off the bed by himself. That was our signal that playtime was over and it was time for breakfast. Ben scooped him up and the three of us headed for the kitchen.

Life could not have been more perfect, but for some reason, in the heat of that sultry July day, I felt myself shiver. And the thought went through my head that life may have its perfect moments, but it doesn't stay that way forever.

*****

I had scheduled my appointment with Dr. Palmer for the second week in August. I thought about getting another doctor, one closer to our new home, but still hadn't done it. The hour drive to Tampa wasn't that bad and I still liked going to the city. It was where my family lived.

Mama Beth and Carly were going to watch Sam while I went to the doctor. After the appointment I was going to go see Abby's new baby girl. She had been born a week after Sam's birthday party.

When I got to the office, the nurse sent me off to the lab for my yearly blood tests. After years of seeing doctors non-stop, it felt good that I hadn't seen one for myself since having Sam. The oncologist I saw for years after my leukemia diagnosis had shared my old records with Dr. Palmer and decided I didn't need to see him again unless something unusual showed up on my annual blood tests.

I was asked to meet Dr. Palmer in her office before my exam.

"You're looking good, Katy. Are you having any concerns?"

"No. Except I'm not pregnant yet. We haven't done anything to prevent it, but nothing has happened. We would really like for Sam to have a sibling."

"What's been going on in your life this year? Have you had a lot of stress?"

"Well, yes. But most of it's been good stress."

I told her about my decision to give up nursing, our move to the ranch, and the new adventure in citrus growing. And of course, there were my ongoing worries about Ben being called back into active duty with the reserves.

"Well, it's no wonder you aren't pregnant, girl! Your body is still in recovery from having Sam and all the changes in your life. Your body just isn't ready for any more stress. Give it some time; once things settle down, you'll probably be pregnant in no time."

"So I don't need to worry about infertility?"

"Not right now. You got pregnant easily with Sam, so I have to think the chemo you got year ago didn't do any damage to your eggs. You just need to slow down."

She picked up my labs and began to look at them.

"Didn't you have a low iron level when you were pregnant?"

"Yes."

"Well it's still low. Probably because you've been so busy and aren't eating enough iron enriched foods. Citrus fruits don't have much iron in them, you know." She grinned at me when she said it.

"Yeah, but I'm married to a cowboy, remember? So I promise you, I'm eating my share of red meats."

"Let's get you on an iron supplement again and you can come back in three months to have it rechecked. We need to build you up before you get pregnant."

Chapter 43

For the second year in a row, we didn't go to the mountains in the fall like we planned. On the day we planned to go, Ben's unit was put on stand-by alert due to a hurricane in the Atlantic. It hit several islands and was headed toward the gulf waters, where they thought it would turn and head back to Florida.

Another unit had been sent to Haiti earlier in the year, because of an earthquake, and conditions in Afghanistan weren't getting any better either.

I suppose we could have flown to the mountains for a short trip, and come back if he was called; but I was still irritated that Ben had chosen to stay in the reserves. It was only a three-year commitment, and one year was almost over, but it just seemed to complicate our lives. His monthly weekend training and the two weeks a year he had to go away made me resentful of how our lives had to revolve around it. I resented the time and energy he spent on the reserves. Then I would feel guilty about feeling resentful, because I knew it was a good thing. He did it because he was so patriotic.

But there was always that constant threat of activation hanging over our heads.

Soon after I saw Dr. Palmer, I came down with a cold. I hadn't been sick in years and had a feeling she was correct. I had been on the go for so many months that I was just worn out. Fatigue had depleted my immune system. I felt bad for about a week so Ben took Sam to Lucy on the days he had to make a charter run.

It was difficult to feel bad for very long though.

As it always does in October, the humidity lifted and the weather was beautiful with warm days and cooler nights. Since we hadn't moved to the grove until December the previous year, we had missed out on the Hamlin orange harvest that starts in October. As they began to ripen, it felt like Ben and I were giving birth to a whole new season of oranges.

It was still fascinating to me how growing oranges had become so important to Ben and to me. The early season, mid season, and late season harvests were each as unique to us as the four seasons of the year were to my family in the north. Each kind of orange became like a special child to us, a child we had nurtured and watched closely. October to June was when our babies came to harvest and I felt a need to be with them.

We would get up early in the morning and make our rounds of the grove in the golf cart. Ben would usually drive and Sam and I would sit on the back seat. It was a family adventure, unless it rained. That fall it rained a lot, but it was okay. It meant the orange harvest would be better.

It was amazing to me how the two of us had so smoothly transitioned from life in the city to country living. It was like we were born to be a part of the grove, and our previous life had just been a waiting ground for what we were meant to do in life.

Ben had his ranch, I had my oranges, and together we had Sam. And we seemed to fall more in love everyday. There were days when I became conscious of him watching Sam and me with what can only be described as devotion. He made me feel like I was the most adored creature on earth. He had grown into the caring man I'm sure his Grandmother dreamed he would be. One who valued family more than anything else in life.

As October eased into November and we began to prepare once again for the holidays, I felt the urgency to have another baby grow stronger.

Sam was walking and chattering like a little magpie. And he was spending more and more time in the barn with Ben and the horses. I loved watching them together, a man and his son, as they shared the things they loved. But now I dreamed of a little girl of my own.

I couldn't understand why I wasn't getting pregnant. I was now watching the calendar closely, and had even started to take my temperature to see when I was ovulating. I didn't tell Ben I was doing it; I had read how the need to "perform," just to produce a baby was sometimes frustrating to men. But on the days I knew I was ovulating, he always got beef tenderloin and a pecan pie. And I made point of wearing the sexiest clothes I had.

*****

On the second Tuesday in November, I went back to the doctor's office to get my blood drawn again. I had been taking the iron tablets like Dr. Palmer had prescribed and really wondered if the test was even necessary.

After the test I went to Mama Beth's house to spend the day with her. We spent much of the day talking about the holidays and how we would celebrate them. My parents had asked me to come north, since they had come south last year, and we had agreed. We were hoping they would have snow and we could introduce Sam to it.

So we made plans to have Christmas with our Florida family the week before we left. Mama said she enjoyed the time at our house the Christmas before but was hoping we could do it at her house this year. Jon had told her he was getting ready to propose to his girlfriend, and now that Abby had the three kids it would probably be easier for her to have Christmas close by.

I liked the idea of Sam being able to spend the holidays in his grandparents' homes too.

Right before I left Mama's house to go home, Dr. Palmer called and said there was a mix-up in the lab. She needed me to come back in to get the test redone. It was frustrating, and meant I would get home late. But I did it since that was the reason I had gone to Tampa in the first place.

Ben had flown a charter to Miami that day and wasn't planning on getting back until the next evening. Mama told me I could stay in town, but I wanted to go home. We had a neighbor who took care of the horses when Ben was gone but Sam and I always slept better in our own beds. Home was where I wanted to be. Besides, it was ovulating time again and I wanted to be relaxed and waiting for Ben when he got home the next evening.

*****

"Hey, Baby. I'm home."

I had put Sam to bed early. I knew Ben would want to see him since he'd been gone for two days, but he would have to make up his time with him the next day. I needed Ben to myself for the night.

"I'm in the kitchen."

"Where's my boy?" When he walked in, I caught my breath. One of the things I had recognized about Ben, right from the beginning, was that he didn't realize how handsome he was. His sandy-colored hair was even lighter now that he was outside so much, and his year- round tan made his blue eyes even more vibrant looking. The hard work of the citrus grove had hardened his body and he looked like some kind of Greek god when he came through the door.

He pulled me into his arms and kissed my forehead as I burrowed my head into his chest.

"Sam's in bed already. He was tired. Go see him, but don't wake him up, okay? I need you all to myself tonight."

"I thought I smelled the tenderloin when I came through the door. We gonna make a baby tonight?" He grinned at me as he turned to go. I guess he had caught on to what I was now calling my fertility trap.

"I just need you tonight, okay?"

He stopped and looked back at me.

"You've been crying. What's wrong?"

"Let's go see our boy. Then we'll talk."

He took my hand and together we walked into Sam's bedroom. Sam was asleep on his belly with his chubby little legs pulled up under him. His head was to one side and a little drool was leaking from his mouth. His dark hair was still damp from the bath I'd given him earlier and in his hand he clutched the stuffed pony that had become his constant companion.

Ben leaned over and gently touched the round little cheek to his own. Straightening up, he whispered, "I think he grew while I was gone."

The tears were running down my cheeks by then. As I watched Ben stroke the dark head, I knew in my heart that this was the only child I would ever give my husband.

Chapter 44

I turned and left the room. I was afraid the sobs building up inside me would spill out and I would wake our son. Ben was right behind me. As he pulled the door closed to Sam's room with one hand, he reached for me with the other. I fell into his arms and leaned my head against his chest. I could feel the thumping of my own heart and it seemed to be keeping time with the drum of his as it beat against my ear.

"Katy, what's wrong?"

I wasn't a crier like Abby, so when the tears came he knew my heart was burdened by something important. He led me to our bed and pulled me onto his lap. Just like he'd done the night he proposed to me.

"Oh Ben…it's back."

"What's back?"

"The leukemia. It's back."

He said nothing for a few seconds, but I felt him pull me closer.

"No! Oh God, no. It can't be." He whispered, and I felt the shudder of a sob come from deep inside of him.

"Why do you think its back, honey?"

"The blood test I had done…it's abnormal."

"It could be a mistake. You haven't even been sick. And besides, they don't diagnose leukemia with a simple blood test. Even *I* know that!"

"Ben! They ran the test twice. And once you've had leukemia, it isn't difficult to identify it when it returns. I have a low red blood cell count. I have a low platelet count and there are too many immature white cells in my blood.

"But those results could mean something different, right?"

"They could, but it isn't likely. I've had some other symptoms too. I woke up a couple times lately with night sweats. And the cold I had a few weeks ago left me feeling tired and lethargic. After Dr. Palmer called today, I checked and found some swollen lymph nodes just like I had before. And the bruises…you saw them last week after I tripped over that bale of straw in the barn."

"But you haven't even seen a doctor. All you're going on is a blood test and some symptoms."

"Ben! I had these same blood test results and symptoms two other times. I know what leukemia does."

"Well, I'm not going to believe it until you go see your oncologist. What did Dr. Palmer say?"

"She called me today and said she already made an appointment for me with my old oncologist at the university hospital. You don't get referred there, Ben, unless you need it."

"I don't care what she said. It's something else; it has to be. You'll see. It will be something completely different. When do we go so we can know you're okay?"

Denial. It's the first stage of grief. And grief is the response to loss or anticipated loss. I had been through it before, and even though Ben didn't talk about it, I'm sure he went through it when his parents and his grandmother died. It's a coping mechanism we depend on until we can summon the courage to accept what is real.

*****

When I was diagnosed with leukemia at the age of sixteen, I lived in Philadelphia with my adoptive parents and they used their significant resources to make sure I got the best care available. They hired the best oncologists who consulted with the best hematologists, cardiologists, and gynecologists. I was under the care of infection control specialists and pulmonologists. I had private rooms at the hospital and private nurses. If money could have bought healing, I would forever be in perfect health.

What their money couldn't buy three years later when I had a relapse, was the perfect bone marrow for transplant. Fortunately, soon after I was diagnosed the first time, God extended His hand of mercy to us when Mama Beth got pregnant with Carly. When I relapsed, I had her harvested and frozen cord blood that could be used for a transplant. It wasn't a perfect match, but it was usable. Cord blood doesn't have to match as perfectly as donor marrow.

The year following my transplant was both worrisome and exhilarating. I lived with Mama Beth and Alex during that time and they were so supportive, but it was still difficult at times.

During the first eight weeks after the procedure I was in the hospital and exhausted from the chemo and radiation I'd had before the procedure. I was in isolation because of my compromised immune system and there was a seemingly endless infusion of blood products and antibiotics. There was also the worry that my body would reject the donor cord blood.

After I was well, people would often asked me if I would ever go through it again. I told them I didn't think so. But I'll never forget the excitement of being alive after being so close to death.

Although I have tried to put it out of my mind in recent years, there has always been a nagging worry, that relapse would occur; or that I'd have some kind of secondary malignancy pop up. I was monitored almost constantly for the first five years for complications that can occur from chemo, radiation and the the transplant.

The year before I met Ben, I had reached the five year survival mark after transplant and had breathed a partial sigh of relief. When I met Ben and he said he would take care of me forever...I wanted to believe his love would keep me safe.

Chapter 45

My appointment with the oncologist was scheduled for the week before Thanksgiving. Ben went with me. As we drove to Tampa, my thoughts went back to the Thanksgiving two years earlier. I had been devastated about Ben leaving for Afghanistan and his being gone over our first Christmas. That seemed so insignificant now as I wondered if this would be the last holiday season I'd ever spend with him. And I knew, if I could trade another holiday separated from him for another fifty with him, I'd gladly do it.

Mama Beth was going to watch Sam for us. I told her we wanted to do a little shopping for Christmas before things got crazy at the grove. I didn't want to tell her the real reason for our trip into the city. Not until I knew what we had to deal with. No sense worrying her if I didn't have to.

She was always thrilled to spend the day with her grandson, but I should have known she'd take one look at me and know something was wrong. I was her daughter, after all.

"Doing some Christmas shopping already…that's a change. Usually you wait till the last minute."

"Hey you can get some good deals if you wait till the last minute. But without John helping us this year, Ben and I are going to be busy. I thought maybe we should get a head start on Christmas. I can't believe how many orders we've already filled for gift baskets going north for the holidays!"

"Can't you get some help with that? You look like you've lost some weight and you didn't have any to lose. You need to slow down a little bit, sweetheart."

"I'll be okay. You know I love working the grove and Sam has so much fun when he's outside with us. You should see him, Mama. He runs around and picks up all the oranges on the ground. Last year we were carrying him in the back pack and now he's a picker for us!"

Mama smiled as I was talking, but I could feel her eyes on me. It was like she had x-ray vision and could see what was going on inside of me. I needed to leave before I fell into her arms and told her what was breaking my heart.

"Bye, Sam. You be good for Gramma." I captured him before he began to explore and gave him a kiss and hug. *My baby…I hate to leave him, even for a few hours.*

*****

Doctor's offices never change. The straight backed chairs are still hard and uninviting, and their outdated magazines are still torn. You wonder how many germs are on them. The smells, a mixture of the sterile and the sick, are nauseating.

"Good morning, Katy. I was hoping I'd never have to see you again."

"Hi, Dr. Robinson. I was hoping I'd never have to see you again too. This is my husband, Ben. Ben, Dr. Robinson."

Ben got out of his chair to shake hands but he didn't flash his usual smile. "Good morning, Doctor. I noticed he didn't say, "it's nice to meet you."

"Katy has told me how well you took care of her a few years ago. Thank you. It looks like we may need you to do it again."

"Well, we need to find out what we're dealing with first. I have the lab results from Dr. Palmer and they do indicate the need to do a bone marrow aspiration. Do you need me to explain it to you again, Katy? Or do you remember how we do it?"

"It's pretty difficult to forget that one. I'd just like to get it done and over with, if you don't mind."

"After I talked to Dr. Palmer I figured you would want it done as soon as possible, and I think that's wise. She did tell you not to eat anything before you came, right?"

"Yes. I've had nothing since last evening."

"We might as well get started then. Since you're going to be sleepy when we're done, I'll tell you now that we have you scheduled for a return appointment on the Monday after Thanksgiving. We can go over the results then, if that will work for you?"

"Sure…and thank you."

Ben wanted to come with me but I asked him not to. It would have broken his heart to be there. A bone marrow aspiration requires some sedation, but the patient still feels it.

*****

I remember waking up and Ben helping me to the car.

"I think you need more time to wake up before we go back to get Sam. Would you like to go to the beach?"

"That would be wonderful. We haven't been there for months. Why haven't we been there, Ben? We should be taking Sam with us so he can collect shells for his sandbox at home."

"We've been busy, Katy. We're parents now, and citrus growers. And I have a charter business, remember? When would we have had time to go?"

"We should have made time. The beach is a special place for us."

"I know. We'll go today and bring Sam back some other day."

With some lunch and a cup of coffee in me, I felt wide awake by the time we arrived. It was just as beautiful as I remembered it. We seemed to be the only ones on it. But then it was a Tuesday in November. All the noisy teenagers were in school and the snowbirds were still up North. There is nothing as peaceful to me as a beautiful, deserted beach... unless it's a quiet night in the middle of an orange grove.

"Remember the night you brought me here and told me you were leaving for Afghanistan?"

"Yeah. It seems like the beach calls our names when our hearts are troubled, doesn't it?"

"So do you want to talk about it?"

"Today, at the doctor's office? It became real to me, Katy. But it also made me more determined to never give up hope that God will give us a full life together. I need you to promise me something…promise me you'll never give up on us."

"Ben, I'm a realist. I have no doubt that those tests are going to come back positive. As a nurse, I know what the odds are for me right now, and they aren't good. But I promise you, Baby, I'll never give up hope for us."

He pulled me close to him and kissed me on the forehead.

"But you have to know, Ben; what lies ahead of us is not going to be easy. They'll put me on a regiment of chemo that's going to wipe me out. We need to talk about how we're going to handle that."

"We're going to handle this like we've handled everything else up to this point. Together. I'm going to be with you every step of the way."

"I know you will be. But things are going to move fast, Ben. You're going to be busier than usual because you're going to have to pick up my share of the work at the grove. And you're going to have to be more available for Sam when I don't have the energy for him."

"I can do it. This isn't going to last forever. You'll be well again, soon."

"It won't be soon, Ben. It takes a long time. I know you think you can do it all, but I think we need to get some help. As soon as we have the results I'm going to call my mom and see if she can come down and stay with us. To help with Sam. She's gone through all of this with me before and she knows what to expect. She was always so positive and she helped me—not just physically, but emotionally."

"But you have me now. I can do those same things for you."

"And I'm so happy I have you. But like I said, you're going to be very busy. I want you to focus on Sam and the grove, and let her help me with this. Just because she's experienced with it. Is it okay if I call her and ask her to come down?"

"Can we wait until after Christmas?"

"I have a feeling they're going to want to start my chemo as soon as they get the results back, and this is our busiest season. I think we need her before then."

"Let's wait and see what the doctor says."

"Okay. And Ben?"

"What?"

"Thank you for not being afraid to talk to me about this. There are some men who deal with stuff like this by closing down. I'm glad you aren't one of those guys."

"Didn't I tell you once that you should never be afraid to talk to me about anything?"

"Yeah." I had my arm around his waist and pulled him close. "But I don't think you had this in mind at the time."

"That's true. But we're in this together, and don't you forget it."

"I won't. I'm glad John and Lucy are back home too. I know they'll help you at the grove."

"They're great, aren't they? I feel like John has become the Dad I never had. We don't even have to talk and we still know what's on the other's minds."

"I'm glad. He's a good man."

We were walking down by the water now with our shoes off. The water was still warm from the hot summer we'd been through, so it felt good on my feet. As I looked out over the water, I could see the huge, white fluffy clouds reflected in the water. Suddenly I wanted to be above them with Ben. I wanted to fly away from the heaviness of this day. He must have been reading my mind.

"Katy, do you think we could go to the mountains next week? We've put that off for two years now and I want to make love to you in front of the fire again."

"What about the harvest and all the Christmas orders we have to fill?"

"They'll still be here when we get back."

"I don't think it'll be very good weather for hiking and Sam will be bored in that tiny little cabin."

"Let's leave Sam with Mama Beth or Abby."

"Ben, I don't know if I can do that. He's never been away from us at night. Mama has to work, and Abby will be busy. And it will be Thanksgiving; we should be with family."

"If they can't watch him, I'll ask Lucy. We'll go this weekend and be home by Thanksgiving. I'll make all the plans. I do that well, remember?"

I had to smile at the memory. He did make our engagement weekend perfect.

"A weekend date with my husband. Now how can I say no to that?"

We both knew it might be the last chance for awhile. My chemotherapy could go on for months.

Mama watched Sam while Ben and I went to the mountains. He was able to rent the same little cabin we rented for our engagement weekend. As breathtaking as that weekend had been for me, this one was even more so. But in a different way. The intensity of the love we were feeling was almost as overwhelming as the pungent fragrance of the orange blossoms in the spring and the heat of the Florida sun in the summer. Ben's love still left me breathless at times.

We ventured out of the cabin to do some hiking in the cool fall air, but the warm fire and our love drew us back to the cabin to lose ourselves in each other. I loved Ben so much that weekend it actually hurt. And when he wasn't watching, I let the tears come… to wash the pain away.

If Sam hadn't been waiting for us, I think I could have stayed there forever. But Sam *was* waiting and our hearts led us home.

Chapter 46

By the first of December we had shared the results of my tests with our family. They came back as I expected. My leukemia was back and I was scheduled to start chemo the next week.

Christmas plans had to be changed and were done so without complaint. Our plans to take Sam to Philadelphia to experience a white Christmas in the snow would have to wait until the next year.

When I told Mom about my relapse, she didn't hesitate to come immediately. And it only took two weeks of treatment to make Ben grateful she was there.

My first treatment as an outpatient started on the tenth of December. On the twentieth I had to go to the hospital for my first blood transfusion. The poison called chemotherapy not only wipes out the bad cells, it wipes out the good ones too. The transfusion at that time was good, though. It gave me the energy to enjoy Sam's second Christmas. He was the perfect age for the magic of the season.

Mama Beth hosted both families for the holiday. And even though we always had a good time when we were together, there seemed to be cloud hanging over the whole day. We all did our best to ignore it, but I allowed myself, just one time, to think about the possibility that this could be my last Christmas on earth. And I wondered if any of the rest of my family had that thought. We were all pretty optimistic people, but occasionally, reality sets in for all of us.

After the day together, Dad and Mom, my two brothers, and sister-in-law, Keisha, returned to our house.

We all tucked Sam into bed and returned to the family room to play some of our old favorite board games. Before we could get started though, my dad told us we needed to have a family meeting. We had done that often when we were kids, but hadn't done it since Ben became part of our family.

"Your mother and I need to talk to all of you about something. You kids know that you've always been the most important part of our lives, right?" He looked around at all of us as we nodded our heads in agreement. "We wanted you to come home for the holidays this year because we wanted it to be a special Christmas. It was going to be our last year in the home you grew up in. But sometimes plans change, and that's okay." He was sitting beside me and reached over and took my hand.

"It was going to be our last Christmas there because I filed my papers for retirement in October. We are planning on moving down here, to Florida, in February. I guess now we understand why God has been leading us in this direction." He squeezed my hand.

"Oh Daddy, are you sure you're ready to retire? You don't have to quit working just to come down here and take care of me."

He laughed. "I'm seventy years old, girl. I couldn't be more sure! And your mother has been nagging me to do this ever since Sam was born. She and I both want to be closer to you. But before we invade your lives, we wanted to make sure it was okay with you and Ben. Some kids don't like their parents so close."

It was Ben who answered their question. "I think it would be great to have you living in Florida. Are you planning on living close by? If you want, you could have some property on the back road beside John and Lucy. They would love it, and it would be great for Sam to have all of you around. It would be great for me and Katy too."

"I agree with Ben. If you're going to move down here, you might as well be close. Dad, I will even buy you your first pair of overalls so you can help with the ranching."

"That sounds great. And I might even have time to take some flying lessons."

My mom wasn't saying much, but from the tears shining in her eyes I could tell she was happy we wanted her nearby.

"I just love that Lucy. I think it would be great fun to be her neighbor. Maybe we could build a small house like theirs, too. I'm so tired of cleaning that huge house we've lived in for years. You never know. We might even buy an RV and go to the mountains with them too."

"I told you years ago to get a maid, so don't be complaining about cleaning."

"I'm not complaining, I just said I'd like less to clean."

Ben and I grinned at each other. My parents were known for the good-natured squabbling they did in private. As professional people, they always had to be dignified and proper in public, but behind the doors of home they were just like any other couple. Unlike some well-to-do couples though, their love for simplicity and their warmth as human beings had always shone through.

My brothers hadn't said much up to this point, but they were looking at each other.

"So…you are abandoning us?"

"Excuse me? I think the two of you have abandoned us! Running off to get married and to visit girlfriends all the time! We never see you."

My sister-in-law dug her elbow into David's side. "Hush up, you big lug. If they live down here, we can vacation here."

It was Doug who came up with the best idea of all. "Hey, if you get an RV, Dave and I can use it as a guest house when we come to visit!"

My brothers were obviously not too worried about being "abandoned" in Philadelphia.

Chapter 47

The plan for treating leukemia is long term. After the four week induction phase of my therapy, called "Course I", Ben and I sat down with Dr. Robinson to discuss what was to follow. The picture she painted for us wasn't a pretty one and Ben came away from that appointment very quiet. I knew he needed to think things through before he talked about them. And I knew he did his best thinking on his horse or while he was flying. I would give him a few days to process everything we had been told..

The protocol for my treatment included five different courses of chemotherapy. The first one had been four weeks, the second one would take eight weeks, the third one was twelve weeks, the fourth one was eight weeks and the fifth course was prolonged maintenance and could last up to twenty-four months. That meant I would have intense, almost daily therapy that included IV treatment, injections and many pills for the first eight months. That would get me through the end of August.

I knew if I could stay healthy during those first months, and not come down with any life- threatening infections, I would be alive to see Sam turn two years old. I knew my best chances would be found in short term goals. Things I could look forward to, things that would get me through the torture of chemotherapy.

Dr. Robinson had already put me on the list for a bone marrow transplant, but my donor would have to come from the donor bank. None of my family members, not even Carly, were potential donors.

"How about Sam's cord blood that was harvested when he was born? Surely that will work, won't it?" The hope in Ben's voice when he asked the question was almost heart-breaking.

"I'm sorry, Ben. It's not a close enough match for Katy. We'll hold onto it though. It may save another life someday."

She was honest and told us that seventy percent of leukemia patients never find a donor.

"I need to know the latest statistics for someone who's had two relapses and has just a thirty percent chance of finding a donor, Dr, Robinson."

"Those are discouraging numbers, Katy. You know that." I did know that, but I wanted Ben to hear it from her. "But you never know. The cure may be right around the corner. We're going to do everything in our power to have you here when that cure is found. If we can't find an HLA-matched donor, we'll enroll you in clinical trials. That's an additional option we have."

"Katy's a fighter, Dr. Robinson. When we first met, she told me she's good at beating the odds. And now she has me and Sam to help her fight, so we're optimistic."

"That's the way to think about it, Ben. Katy is fortunate to have many people who love her and support her." Ben may not have noticed, but I did. No promises of a cure were made.

*****

Mom and Dad made their transition to Florida without looking back. Their house in Philadelphia was for sale, but with a depressed housing market the realtor said it might take a while to sell it. The boys moved back in until it could sell.Mom and Dad lived with us until their new home was completed in June. Their presence was a blessing to all of us as the second phase of my chemotherapy was started.

One spring evening while Mom and Dad were working on their house, Ben and I went to the deck to do our star gazing. The fragrance of the orange blossoms was heavy, and the sounds of the night were like music. When Lucy had owned our home, she had used her master landscaping skills to produce the most beautiful tropical garden all around our home. It was as comforting to me now as Mama Beth's garden had been when I was going through the recovery from my transplant.

"I'm really glad it worked out that your parents could be here these past few months, Katy. Just knowing your mom has been here to help with Sam and do some of your work has been a relief for me. I know she's making sure you're getting your rest, and I just feel like the chemo can work better in a rested body than in a fatigued one."

"She's been wonderful. She lets me do the things I want to do with Sam. Then, when she senses I'm getting tired she just takes over. She's a wonderful woman, Ben. As much as I love the Mama that gave life to me, I sometimes think that my adoptive mother was the one I was suppose to grow up with. I appreciate her wisdom and her inner strength so much."

"Your dad's been great too. For a man who spent his life behind a desk, he's a hard worker. With him and John helping me here at the grove this winter, I haven't had to worry about turning down any of my charters."

"Ben? You know we could afford for you to give up the charters. The grove is doing very well. And the health insurance from the reserves has covered almost all my medical expense. We're so blessed. I become more aware of that every day I spend in the treatment center. There are so many people there who have so little support."

"We're going to get through this, baby. I just know we are. And we're going to spend the rest of our lives enjoying, and sharing with others, the blessings God has given us."

He pulled me close to him, slipped the scarf off my head and kissed the top of my bald scalp. "I do miss running my fingers through your thick, beautiful hair though…not that you aren't beautiful without it."

"Yeah, I miss it too. But it's only hair, and it does grow back

Chapter 48

The good thing about short term goals is that every time you succeed in reaching one, you feel like a winner.

That summer, Ben and I celebrated our third anniversary with a trip to Texas. Even though he kept insisting there was nothing to see, I wanted to see where my husband had come from. We flew into Dallas, rented a car, and headed west. I loved it; maybe because it was so different from Philadelphia, and the Tampa Bay area of Florida.

The home he grew up in wasn't there anymore, and I felt some sadness for him. It was like the first ten years of his life hadn't even existed. The people he spent those early years with were gone too, along with the house he had grown up in. He said it was okay.

"I have my memories. But more important, I have my life now with you and Sam.

We visited with his aunt and uncle who had come to our wedding. They had bought his grandmother's house when she died. Ben told me later it was as close to "going home" as he knew he would ever get. Even though they had totally remodeled and added on to it.

His aunt told us his sister had shown up several months ago and stayed for a few hours. She had asked about Ben, and they told her about our wedding. They gave her the address of the grove but hadn't heard from her since. And she hadn't left an address where she could be contacted.

"Ben! Now that she has our address, maybe she'll get in touch with us."

"Don't hold your breath, sweetheart. She was always an independent kid and I doubt if she has changed as an adult." I just couldn't comprehend that. I don't know what I would have done without my family this past year.

As we traveled back home from Texas, I felt more strongly than ever that God had brought Ben into my family, so he could once again have one of his own.

******

Sam's second birthday was even more fun than his first one had been. He was probably too young, but we took him to Disney. I think Ben and I enjoyed watching him more than he enjoyed the magic of it. But all the pictures we have of him with Goofy and Mickey Mouse show him smiling. I'm glad he wasn't afraid of them.

We celebrated the end of my eight months of aggressive chemo and the beginning of my next sixteen months of maintenance chemo with a family trip to the beach. The whole family went along for the day. We had a picnic and collected enough sea shells to fill a half dozen little boy's sandboxes.

On Carly's thirteenth birthday, Mama Beth, Abby and I took her to New York City for two days to see a Broadway show and go shopping. It was a fun trip, except for one evening when she wanted to talk about my leukemia. She said she'd been reading about it and was wondering why she couldn't be a bone marrow donor for me.

I didn't know if I should share the whole story with her, but Mama Beth nodded her head at me.

"Honey, you already did that once… when you were a baby."

"I did? Then why can't I do it again?"

"It's kind of hard to explain. Do you know how a baby is attached to its mother before it's born?"

"Yeah. By an umbilical cord. It's why I have a belly button."

"Right. Well, when you were born, the doctors took the blood from that cord you didn't need anymore and froze it, in case I would ever need it. Cord blood is a very special kind of blood. It can do things regular blood can't do. When you were two, I got sick again and they used it to make me well. If it wasn't for you, I would never have had the time to get to know you, or to meet Ben and have Sam. What you gave me was eight years of healthy living and I will always be grateful for that."

"So if my blood worked then, why won't it work now?"

"Because now I need bone marrow and that is different than cord blood. Bone marrow has to be a better match than cord blood."

Mama Beth put her arms around Carly. "Honey, you were able to give Katy a gift that none of the rest of us could give her. You gave her time to live."

"No, you gave her the best gift, Mama. You gave her life." That was a story Mama Beth and I had already told her…when she asked why she and I had the same mom, but not the same dad. Even the most beautiful lives can be complex.

We all came home with beautiful memories. Memories I hoped would be with my little sister forever.

Chapter 49

At Christmas time, a year after my relapse, Mom, Dad, Ben and I took Sam north, and he got to see snow for the first time in his life. Mom and Dad's house had not sold after a year, so David and Keisha were buying it on land contract. Doug was still there too, but was planning to get married in the spring. He and Janelle had been dating for three years, so we all thought it was about time.

Keisha had the house beautifully decorated. While we were fixing Christmas dinner she told us she was pregnant. Sam would now have a cousin on the other side of the family. Mom was thrilled that her new grandchild would grow up in the same home her son had grown up in.

Sam loved the snow. We all took him sledding on the same hills I went sledding on as a kid, and when we got home we drank hot chocolate. Ben built a fire in all three fireplaces in the house. The man loves fireplaces.

When we returned to Tampa we had Christmas with the other side of the family. As I watched Mama Beth rocking Sam, I felt a sense of gratitude. She was able to nurture him and I hoped it made up for those early years she had missed with me.

I thought back to the story she told me about going to the abortion clinic on that cold January day when she was sixteen. She had saved my life that day, and with my life I had brought new life into the world. And now, our Sam was bringing so much joy to me and Ben and to my Mama.

I had no doubt that there is a purpose for every life. And I felt certain: God's timing for each life is perfect.

*****

In January, four years after I met Ben, Dr. Robinson called and asked me to come in to the office. She said I needed to bring Ben with me. I had been in the maintenance phase of my chemo for six months.

That evening, after she called, Ben asked me if I wanted to take a walk to the lake.

"Can we go in the golf cart? I'm a little tired tonight."

"Sam's gonna be mad if he finds out we went for ride in the cart without him."

"He's having fun at Gramma's house tonight."

We headed towards the lake.

"Wanna go for a ride in the boat?" Ben had bought an old paddle boat so he could take Sam fishing in it.

"Sure, but no skinny-dippin' tonight."

"Now you're even reading my mind. How do you do that?"

"I know you pretty well, Ben."

He helped me into the boat and started to paddle out into the middle of the water. The night was still, except for a soft breeze that stroked my cheeks and stirred Ben's blond curls.

The moon was full and it shone through the old oak trees, casting long shadows across the surface of the water. It was one of those nights that would have been beautiful and romantic, if our minds hadn't been on other things.

"Do you think they found a marrow donor for us?"

"I don't know, but I doubt it."

"Why do you doubt it?"

"I think she wants to talk to us about something else."

"What?"

"Maybe the maintenance dose isn't holding."

"Why would you say that?"

"I don't know…maybe because I haven't felt very good lately."

"Maybe you're just worn out from the trip up north and all the Christmas excitement."

"Could be, but my bones are hurting. And I'm starting to get short of breath when I'm up too long. Just the thought of walking down here tonight was too much."

"Sounds like you need another blood transfusion."

"Or a new body."

"Come on, Baby…you can't give up on me now. You'll feel better after a transfusion."

*****

Dr. Robinson was buried in papers when her nurse showed us into her office. She looked as tired as I felt.

"So, how are you feeling these days, Katy?"

"Worn out."

"From the looks of your blood test, it's no wonder. We'll get you transfused before you go home today."

"So have you found us a marrow donor? We thought maybe that's why you called us in today." I could hear the hope in Ben's voice.

"I wish I could say I had, Ben. I actually wanted to talk to both of you because the maintenance chemo doesn't seem to be working. I think we need to go back to the induction phase again."

"Oh, Dr. Robinson. I don't know if I can do that again." I felt the tears spring to my eyes. I had known it in my heart; her words made it reality to my brain.

"I know, Katy. But I don't have any new clinical trials for you right now, and we haven't found a donor. This seems to be our only option."

"How long do I have…if I don't do anything?"

Ben grabbed my hand. "That isn't an option for us, Katy. You promised you wouldn't give up on us."

"Ben, honey…I'm not giving up on us. But I'm tired of fighting."

"You can't stop fighting. Sam needs you."

"He has you, and all his grandmas. Besides, what good am I to him when I'm so sick from the chemo? I can't even take care of him."

"Fighting gives us time, Katy. The cure is right around the corner, remember?"

So, for Ben, because he was still fighting for me, we decided to go on.

Chapter 50

Intensive chemotherapy is a form of torture. You go to the treatment center four days a week for three weeks in a row. Then you get a week off so you can rest up to go back again. Every day you go, you spend six hours there and get up to eight IV bags of medicine and fluids. You feel sick and exhausted all of the time.

It makes you feel like you're going to vomit nonstop, even though they give you medicine to stop it. Nothing seems to help the diarrhea or the constant tingling in your fingers and toes. You can't eat. And even if you could, the food tastes like salty metal. The chemo makes you get sores in your mouth; sores that bleed all the time and change the taste of everything. Because you can't eat, you begin to resemble a skeleton.

Perhaps one of the worst things about getting chemo is that you do it with others who are as sick as you are. They become almost family. Then one day you come to therapy and you hear that one of them won't be coming anymore. Not because he or she is cured, but because they gave up and are dying.

Before we restarted the induction chemo again, Dr. Robinson decided I should have a Central line inserted into my chest. The PICC line that had been in my arm from the beginning, needed replaced anyways. Through the central line, I could not only get the medicine, I could also be hydrated. I needed it because when you throw up and have diarrhea all the time, you can get as dry as Texas sagebrush.

For the next six months our lives once again revolved around my being flat on my back or hanging over a toilet to vomit. Sam was with Mom most of the time, and Ben left the grove to my Dad and John so he could be at my side. He was with me almost constantly, although there were a few times when he would leave me with my mom and disappear for an hour or two. Mom told me he had hung a punching bag up in one of the warehouses. After denial and bargaining with God, anger came next for him in the steps of anticipatory grief.

And the grief was taking a toll on him.

I could see he was losing weight. And since he was inside with me all the time he was as pale as I was. My heart ached for him. Even though he came to bed with me every night and held me in his arms, we hadn't made love for months. He said he didn't want to hurt me.

It made me sad, but I was glad he didn't want to. I knew I wasn't sexy-looking any more. I could see that my skin was now a yellowish color and I didn't have any hair on my body at all. I was nothing but skin and bones.

I didn't have to look in the mirror anymore either. I had cared for patients who looked like I felt; I already knew what I would see. Cancer and its treatment change a person on the inside, and on the outside. I thought often of the early days when we were dating and Ben teased me about being round in all the right places. Now that roundness, that softness, was gone.

I knew, physically, I was just a shell of my former self. But as long as I had any fight in me, I refused to let cancer change my heart. I had lived my life with passion, loved intensely and I had dreamed dreams until they came true. And most important, I had kept the faith when all seemed lost.

I had lived well. But now, even though Ben wasn't ready to admit it yet, I knew I was going to die. I was determined I would die well too.

I knew something else too. I knew that even though I would not be present, life would go on without me.

*****

"Ben? Did I ever tell you about the day in nurses training when I saw the beginning of a new life and the end of an old one, all in the same shift?"

It was an unusual summer evening. The air was cool. He had carried me out to the deck and set me on the glider he had padded with blankets and pillows. He sat beside me now, rocking us gently and holding me against him.

"No, I don't remember you telling me about that."

"I was working in the emergency room. Soon after I started my shift, a woman who was having her third child was brought in by her husband. She said her doctor told her to come in as soon as she knew she was in labor. Her previous labors had been easy and quick." I had to stop talking for a few seconds to catch my breath.

"When she came through the doors, she told us she felt the need to push and before we could get her up to OB, she delivered her third baby in the elevator."

"It would be nice if our next baby came that easily."

Oh, Ben. If I could have another baby for you I wouldn't care how long the labor was.

"Then right after lunch that day, an older man was brought in by ambulance. He was having chest pain and was nauseated. We were getting ready to send him up to the cardiac unit, but before we could do that he went into shock. He had come in with a signed "Do Not Resuscitate" paper, so all we could do was let him go. The doctor said he probably had an aneurism that had burst."

"A witness to birth and death in twelve hours…. Not too many people can say they've had that experience."

"I know. I learned something that day, Ben."

"What did you learn?"

"I learned that as significant as the moments of our birth and death are, it's the life lived between those two moments that counts the most. Some people get a long time between birth and death and never choose to live well or love. I feel sorry for them. I might not have as much time on this earth as I wanted, but I can say I lived well and loved to the max."

"We have both loved with all God gave us, Darlin'" He pulled me closer to him.

We sat and watched as the stars slid into view. At first, it was one at a time, and then the sky was full of them. There were the summer fragrances; the smell of the moss that hung from the oak trees was pungent when the orange trees weren't in blossom. There were the night time sounds: the cicada and frogs, a crooning bird. And there were the gentle movements of the still night. The trembling of leaves in the soft breeze, the rocking of the swing, and Ben's breathing as I sat with my head on his chest.

"Ben?"

"Hmmm?"

"I want you to get married again."

"Katy, I can't. I can't talk about this."

"We must, Ben. Just hear me out."

"Honey, you may be getting comfortable with your not being here, but I'm not. I don't want to talk about the future. I just want to be here with you, today."

But I had to talk about it. There wasn't much time left, and I didn't know if I'd have another chance.

"I hate the thought of you being alone."

"I'm not alone."

"You will be someday, and I don't like the thought of it. I want you to love again. It would be a compliment to me, you know. I like to think our marriage is so good that you will want to do it again."

"Please, Katy. I can't do this."

"Okay, but we will talk about it again. Now I need to talk to you about Sam."

"Sam is fine. He has a mom and a dad who love him."

"Of course he does. But when I'm not here, I need you to make sure he gets good discipline." I had to stop again, to rest. It was getting difficult to breathe and talk at the same time.

"Don't spoil him…just because his mother died. And he's going to need something else. He needs to know you aren't going to go away too. I'm begging you, Ben. I need for you to get a hardship discharge from the Reserves. I want you to go and file your papers. Tomorrow."

"It's already done, Katy. I don't ever want to be away from you and Sam again."

"One more thing. About Sam. When I get to the end, I don't want him to see me if I can't talk to him. So I have a plan. You know how once he's asleep, nothing wakes him?"

"Yeah, I don't think dynamite would wake him up once he's asleep."

"Yeah…so when I get too weak and can't talk to him anymore—when he's sound asleep—could you bring him into our bed and tuck him in next to me, just so I can feel him beside me? But you have to stay awake when he's with me. If he even looks like he's going to wake up, you need to take him back to his own bed. I don't want him to see me unresponsive and unable to love on him."

Then I couldn't talk about it anymore. And Ben's head was in his hands. He was sobbing.

I had more to say, but knew we'd both had enough for today. My hospice nurse was writing in my journal for me every day, I would dictate and she would write. She would write down the other things I wanted him and Sam to know. Today, I couldn't make him hurt anymore than he already was.

"Baby, I'm done. Could we go back to bed now and lie down? I want you to hold me."

He crawled into bed with me and curled around me. With his arms holding me, I felt just as cherished as the first time he made love to me. I wished I could please him just one more time. But he seemed content just to lay with me in his arms.

I was hanging on to life for this. I didn't want to leave, but I knew I wouldn't be able to fight it forever. I knew I was staying until he told me it was okay to go, and I knew he was getting close to that time. I could see the pain in his eyes when he looked at me, and I knew he didn't want me to hurt anymore.

I went to sleep in his arms.

*****

Hours later, I woke in pain. He was instantly awake.

"What do you need, baby? Do you need your medicine?"

"Please?"

All my medicine was in a locked drawer in his dresser. Even though Sam hadn't tried to come into our room alone for weeks, we couldn't be too cautious. The medications, even in a tiny dose, would be lethal to him.

Ben brought the syringe of morphine to me. I hated taking it, but it helped me breathe better. He also brought the Decadron for the bone pain.

"Do you want the Ativan, so you can sleep again?"

"No, not now, it makes me too sleepy." Actually, I was afraid if I went into a deep sleep, I would let down my guard and wouldn't wake up again. I had to stay until Ben was ready to let me go.

"Are you hungry? Your mom made some good potato soup today. How about if I go get some for you? It would make her happy if you would eat some of it."

I wasn't hungry, but told him I would take some. Within minutes he was back. He rolled the head of my hospital bed up and sat on the edge of it. But I didn't have the energy to eat. He knew it.

"Here, let me help you."

I let him, only because I knew he felt so helpless and this was one thing he could do for me. The soup was good, but after three bites I'd had enough.

"Sip of water? You need to drink more. It will help wash all the poisons out of your body." I knew it wasn't true, but I took a couple sips to make him happy.

"Why don't I get a basin of water and give you a little bath? It always helps you rest so much better."

"Whatever you think is best, Ben. But you don't have to. The hospice nurse can do it tomorrow."

"I know, but I want to. It'll make you feel better."

"Ben?"

"What, Darlin'?"

"Your love changed my life."

"And your love changed mine."

I was asleep before he was done. I was just so tired.

Chapter 51

"Ben?"

"I'm here, baby."

I had wakened in the middle of the night. I know I should have let him sleep. But I had so much to tell him.

"Soon after we met, you told me we don't choose love, it chooses us."

"Gramma told me that. She also told me that once it grabs hold, it doesn't let go."

"I think love chose us."

"How can you tell?"

"After all this, it hasn't let go."

"And it won't, Darlin'."

"You also told me…difficult times can make you a better person, or a bitter one."

"Gramma told me that too."

"I expect you to be a better person after this."

"I will."

"Good." He pulled me closer to him. We sat for a long time, just appreciating the fact that we were together.

"Ben?"

"Hmmm?"

"Why did God create us?"

"You told me it was because He longed to have a relationship with us."

"Yeah…but I believe He did it for another reason."

"And what would that be?"

"So we could do something good for at least one other person." I had to stop and catch my breath. "God created us, to fulfill our purpose." I was getting so tired. It was difficult to breath…even with the oxygen.

"Ben, do you remember Mrs. Johnson?"

"Of course. How could I forget the lady who introduced me to the love of my life?"

"She fulfilled her purpose."

"She did."

"Have I?"

He pulled me even closer. "Of course you have. You've loved me, and you gave Sam to us."

"So, can I go now?"

"If you have to… but I don't want you to."

"I know, I don't want to go either. But I have to…you know that, don't you?"

"I know, Baby. But I love you so much."

"I love you too. And Sam. Do you think you could bring Sam in and lay him between us for awhile?"

"Of course."

"When he wakes up, tell him I love him, okay?"

"He knows."

"Hey, cowboy…"

"What?" He was up on his elbow, looking at me, caressing me with his eyes.

"Can you make sure he gets to see the Yankees play the Astros some time?"

"Yeah, we can do that."

"And let him decide for himself which is the better team?"

Ben grinned; he still had that dimple in his right cheek.

Epilogue

"Hey, Sam. It's time to get up, buddy. It's your fifth birthday, and we're gonna go flying today." Ben sat on the edge of his son's bed and ruffled the boy's chestnut colored hair. "Today's your first flying lesson, remember?"

The little boy opened one blue eye, then the other. "Is the weather good? Can we still go?"

"Weather's going to be perfect, and the Magic Kingdom is waiting for us."

Sam hopped out of bed, stripped off his pajamas and was dressed before Ben could move to help him. Not that he had to. Sam was becoming more independent every day, and had been saying "I can do it by myself" for two years.

Today, except for the blue eyes, he looked like his mom. And Ben knew it was from her, his son had received his sunny disposition.

"We have to eat a good breakfast before we leave. What do you want?"

"Can we have pancakes?"

"Sure. And for you, on your birthday, they'll look like Mickey Mouse. How does that sound?"

"Cool! Can we get ice cream at Disney too?"

"Well, since it's your birthday. You get to make the rules today. I guess a five year old can make his own rules about ice cream on his birthday, can't he?

"Yeah! I'm getting bigger every day. Gramma says I am."

"I can't believe you'll be going to kindergarten in a few weeks and won't be around here during the day—to help me in the grove."

"But, Dad…I can help you when I get off the school bus."

"How about if I do the work at the grove while you're at school. Then when you get home, you can help me take care of the horses? Jake is going to miss you while you're at school. He's gonna want you to spend every evening riding him."

"Wish I could ride him to school like you did in the olden days."

"Yeah, the olden days were good days. Finish those pancakes now, so we can get going."

Oh, Katy. I hope you can see him today. If you can, I know you're smiling down on your boy. He's getting so big, and he's such a good kid. Remember that day he was born? You worked so hard to bring him into our lives. If you had lived to be a hundred, it still wouldn't have been enough time for me to thank you for him. Thank you, baby, for the gift of Sam on this special day. Just wish you could be here to celebrate the day with us.

"Dad? Hey Dad! I'm done. Can we get going?"

"Not till you brush your teeth."

"But you said I get to make the rules today, and I rule that I don't have to brush my teeth."

"I did say that, but as your dad, I get to overrule some of your rules. Go brush your teeth."

*****

It took ten minutes to get to the municipal airport, and another thirty to check the plane and get it warmed up.

"Okay, Sam-the-man, we're ready to soar above the clouds. Let's get you strapped into the driver's seat here."

"Can we do a loop-de-loop?"

"Nope…that will have wait until you're thirteen. But it looks like we're going to have some big fluffy clouds to fly through."

With his son on his lap, Ben was down the runway and above the grove in no time. Every time he took the plane up he would fly over the ranch. As he looked down on it, he could almost hear Katy saying "I want to be a citrus grower."

It wasn't just a son she'd given him five years ago, she'd also given both of them a way of life that was simple, yet fulfilling.

"Hey, Dad! I can see Jake from up here. See him? He's out in the pasture. Hey Jake! I'm up here. I'll see you when I get home from Mickey Mouse land!"

*****

A trip to Disney was now a yearly birthday pilgrimage for Ben and Sam. The first time they went was with Katy on Sam's second birthday. The next year, she had to be pushed around in a wheelchair, and Sam rode on her lap. But it had been a great day. They both glowed that day, and she made Ben promise he would bring their son back every year for his birthday, for as long as he wanted to come.

"Experiences are better gifts than things, Ben. Make sure he gets lots of memorable experiences."

It had been difficult to come last year, even with Abby and her family along for the trip. Sam wanted them to come this year too, but Ben wanted this one to be about the two of them.

"Hey, Dad! Look at that cloud! It looks like the Mickey Mouse pancake I ate this morning. It looks pretty high. Can we go over it?"

"Not that one…it's time to start our descent. Are you ready, co-pilot?"

"Ready, Captain!"

*****

It was a great day. Sam was tall for his age and was big enough to do some of the bigger rides. His favorite was the Astro Orbiter.

"Hey, buddy. Before it gets too late, we have to go on the small world ride."

"That's kind of a baby ride, Dad. Do we have to go on it?"

"Yeah, I want to."

"You like that baby ride?"

"Yes, I do…it was your Mama's favorite ride. And I like to think about her when I go on it. Do you remember when we went on it with her?"

"Yeah, we have that picture of us in front of the snow people."

"She liked those snow people, didn't she?"

"She always laughed when she saw them. We need to go see them again."

I'm doing my best to make sure he doesn't forget you, Katy. But I wonder sometimes. Does he remember you just because of the pictures? Does he remember your arms around him and your sweet kisses? I do, even if he doesn't. And I always will.

"Hey dad…I remember Mama singing that small world song to me. She could sing pretty, couldn't she?"

"Yeah, Buddy. She could." *But does he really remember his mom singing it to him? Or is it just the video of her holding him, and singing to him that makes him thinks he remembers?*

*****

"You about ready to eat Sam? Do you want pizza?"

"Sure. Do we have to leave then?"

"It's almost time. Is there anything else you want to do before we go?"

"Could we send a note to mom? Like we do at home?"

"I guess we could. There are all kinds of helium balloons around here."

"Can we send her a note on a Mickey Mouse balloon this time? That way she'll have a souvenir from our trip today."

"Good idea. We'll write the notes while we're eating the pizza. Is there someplace special you want to launch it from?"

"Maybe we could go to the top of the Swiss Family Robinson tree again."

"That's a great idea. She liked that tree a lot."

"Yeah. Girls like weird stuff, don't they dad?"

"Sometimes." The pizza was ready and while they ate they wrote their notes on napkins.

"What do you want your note to say, Sam?"

"Let's see.... Hi, Mama. We're at Disney World for my birthday. I wish you were here with us cause I love you and miss you. I'm being good for Daddy. Hope you're havin' fun singing with the angels."

"That's a great note, Sam. I think she'll like it."

"Okay, now it's your turn. What are you going to say?"

"I think I'm going to tell her I had a great time on your birthday, but I missed her too. And I'll tell her I love her for giving you to me."

"That's good. I think she'll like both our notes."

While Sam ate his last piece of pizza, Ben wrote his note.

"To my beautiful Katy, We're here again...at Disney on his birthday, just like I promised you. He's a great kid. Thank you for giving him to me. He reminds me of you. I can hear your laughter every time he laughs. And he enjoys life just like you did. When he smiles, I see your smile and it lights up my world.

Today is a special birthday; he got to help me fly the plane. You told me he needed experiences, not gifts. When we flew over the grove, I thought of you, and I have to tell you...I can still smell you in the fragrance of the orange blossoms. They are blossoms you made possible for us. And just so you know, I feel you when the sun shines on me too, especially when I ride the ranch you made possible for us with your dreams. As you can tell, your spirit still saturates my very being.

But I don't feel you in my arms anymore, Darlin'. And that hurts so much. I try not to focus on the pain. Instead I focus on the reason you lived—so I could love and be love by you. And so I could have a son to treasure. I miss you and will love you forever. Ben"

They tied the notes to the string of a Mickey Mouse balloon and Sam let it go from the top of the the silly tree his mom liked. Ben and his son stood and watched it as it drifted away on a current of love.

Its destination was the other side of dawn.

Reflections of Dawn

Book Three of the Dawn Trilogy

Chapter 1

Something huge and heavy pressed down on Ben's chest. It was crushing his lungs, making it difficult to breathe. Fighting and clawing his way out of restless sleep, he bolted upright. He gasped for air, gasped again for life. He reached for Katy. Needing her, he called her name.

Through the darkness that hovered over him in the pre-dawn hours, he searched. But Katy wasn't there. Her side of the bed was empty. The darkness could not hide the reality of his life. His bed was empty. His arms ached to hold his wife, but loneliness was his only companion.

She was gone and wouldn't be back. When she left, half his soul was ripped away, leaving what remained, bleeding and damaged forever.

If it hadn't been for Sam, Ben Browning would have died with her. He knew that in every part of his being. Sam, his and Katy's son, was the reason he now lived. He had her dark hair, her joy, and her ability to see only the good in life. But Sam saw the good in the world through dark blue eyes that were a gift from his dad. Katy had said Sam's eyes were his best feature because they looked like his, but Sam was his mother's child. Sam was the miracle that came from the love he and Katy shared. Sam had been Katy's zenith, and according to her, the purpose for her life. Now he was Ben's only salvation.

Ben had waited for love and a family of his own for a long time. The day he looked into Katy's chocolate brown eyes, he knew he had come home. When she told him she was dying, he refused to believe it. Love, for him, was a forever thing.

When Katy died, Ben was sure he would die too...but he couldn't. Sam needed him.

*****

Ben looked at the clock. It wasn't necessary. He knew it was 4:23 a.m., the same time he woke every morning. It was the exact time Katy had died, two years, nine months and twelve days ago. It didn't matter what time he went to bed, he always woke up at the same time.

It was useless to even try to fall back to sleep. Sleep would not come again until he fell, exhausted, into his bed at the end of the day.

But it was okay. Early mornings had become his special time, a time to drink his coffee on the deck and think uninterrupted thoughts of Katy. Mornings had been their special time of the day when she lived. And now that he was alone, it still was for Ben.

Moving to the middle of the bed, he gave the light blue coverlet a shake and pulled it taut. Then he slipped out from under it and placed the four pillows at the top of the bed. During the night, one of them had been used to rest his head, but the other three had been lined up on her side of the bed. Several times, in the darkness of the night, he had reached over and pulled one of them close to him. He wondered at times if he'd ever stop reaching for her.

Katy had always made the bed. The best he did now was make it presentable. It probably wasn't necessary. No one would enter the room until he returned that night. It was a shrine, a sacred place where only he could come to get away from the world and relive the life he had enjoyed with his beautiful Katy.

Ben pulled his jeans on while he went to to his dresser. From the top drawer he took a small notebook. Tucking it into his back pocket, he shuffled to the kitchen where he turned on the light above the sink. He had put the coffee and water in the coffee maker the night before; all he needed to do now was turn it on.

While it brewed, he walked soundlessly to Sam's room. The Mickey Mouse nightlight put out just enough light for Ben to see the tousled, dark brown curls that covered his son's head. In the little boy's arm was the stuffed star his mother gave him four nights before she died. She told him to hold it close when he went to bed, and remember that she loved him.

She also told him to look for her among the stars in the sky when he needed to talk to her. She promised to be there, listening to him, and lighting his way. Almost three years later, Sam was still clinging to his star.

"You look just like your momma, Sam," he whispered, wanting to touch him, but fearful of wakening him. "She'd be so proud of you."

Leaving Sam's room and closing the door quietly behind him, he shuffled quietly to the bedroom next to Sam's. Six month old Molly was sound asleep, sucking on her thumb. A dribble of drool was forming on the sheet. Sweet little Molly—she had come into his and Sam's life so unexpectedly. She came, bringing with her a ray of sunlight and joy at a time when they needed her most.

Smiling, he turned away from her and closed the door as he left. Both kids would sleep for two more hours.

And Ben had two hours before he had to face his world. Two hours alone—to some it would have been a time of loneliness. To Ben, it was a gift. It was the only two hours of the day he allowed himself to think about Katy, to reminisce about the four years they had been together. He had two hours a day to focus on the only woman he had ever loved. Two hours in which he could have thanked God for the time he had with her, for the son she gave him, and for the way of life her generosity had provided for him.

But Ben didn't want to talk to God. He was still angry at God.

About the Author

After retiring from a long, rewarding career in nursing, B.J. Young continued to feel a need to nurture those who were hurting. She began to write short inspirational stories and devotionals.

Those were first published by Front Porch Publishing then by *Guideposts*, *Angels on Ear*th and the *Huffington Post*.

Her debut inspirational fiction novel, *A Portrait of Dawn* was a semi-finalist in the Genesis contest in 2012. The first edition was published in February of 2013. The second book of the trilogy, *Dawn's New Day, A Love Story* was released in June, 2013.

The Dawn Trilogy, a collection of Christian fiction novels was completed with the publication of *Reflections of Dawn* in February 2014. Mrs. Young lives in Northwest Ohio and enjoys time with her family that includes three daughters and nine grandchildren. She is a member of ACFW and Christian Writers of NWO.

She blogs regularly at:

http://www.bjyoung28.blogspot.com/

Made in the USA
Charleston, SC
24 February 2014